ACCLAIM FOR COLL

"Coble's clear-cut prose makes it easy for the reader to follow the numerous scenarios and characters. This is just the ticket for readers of romantic suspense."

—*Publishers Weekly* on *Three Missing Days*

"Colleen Coble is my go-to author for the best romantic suspense today. *Three Missing Days* is now my favorite in the series, and I adored the other two. A stay-up-all-night page-turning story!"

—Carrie Stuart Parks, bestselling and award-winning author of *Relative Silence*

"You can't go wrong with a Colleen Coble novel. She always brings readers great characters and edgy, intense story lines."

—BestInSuspense.com on *Two Reasons to Run*

"Colleen Coble's latest has it all: characters to root for, a sinister villain, and a story that just won't stop."

—Siri Mitchell, author of *State of Lies*, on *Two Reasons to Run*

"Colleen Coble's superpower is transporting her readers into beautiful settings in vivid detail. *Two Reasons to Run* is no exception. Add to that the suspense that keeps you wanting to know more, and characters that pull at your heart. These are the ingredients of a fun read!"

—Terri Blackstock, bestselling author of *If I Run*, *If I'm Found*, and *If I Live*

"This is a romantic suspense novel that will be a surprise when the last page reveals all of the secrets."

—*The Parkersburg News and Sentinel* on *One Little Lie*

"There are just enough threads left dangling at the end of this well-crafted romantic suspense to leave fans hungrily awaiting the next installment."

—*Publishers Weekly* on *One Little Lie*

"Colleen Coble once again proves she is at the pinnacle of Christian romantic suspense. Filled with characters you'll come to love, faith lost and found, and scenes that will have you holding your breath, Jane Hardy's story deftly follows the complex and tangled web that can be woven by one little lie."

—Lisa Wingate, #1 *New York Times* bestselling author of *Before We Were Yours*, on *One Little Lie*

"Colleen Coble always raises the notch on romantic suspense, and *One Little Lie* is my favorite yet! The story took me on a wild and wonderful ride."

—DiAnn Mills, bestselling author

"Coble's latest, *One Little Lie*, is a powerful read . . . one of her absolute best. I stayed up way too late finishing this book because I literally couldn't go to sleep without knowing what happened. This is a must read! Highly recommend!"

—Robin Caroll, bestselling author of the Darkwater Inn saga

"I always look forward to Colleen Coble's new releases. *One Little Lie* is One Phenomenal Read. I don't know how she does it, but she just keeps getting better. Be sure to have plenty of time to flip the pages in this one because you won't want to put it down. I devoured it! Thank you, Colleen, for more hours of edge-of-the-seat entertainment. I'm already looking forward to the next one!"

—Lynette Eason, award-winning and bestselling author of the Blue Justice series

"In *One Little Lie* the repercussions of one lie skid through the town of Pelican Harbor, creating ripples of chaos and suspense. Who will survive the questions? *One Little Lie* is the latest page-turner from Colleen Coble. Set on the Gulf Coast of Alabama, Jane Hardy is the new police chief who is fighting to clear her father. Reid Dixon has secrets of his own as he follows Jane around town for a documentary. Together they must face their secrets and decide when a secret becomes a lie. And when does it become too much to forgive?"

—Cara Putman, bestselling and award-winning author

"Coble wows with this suspense-filled inspirational . . . With startling twists and endearing characters, Coble's engrossing story explores the tragedy, betrayal, and redemption of faithful people all searching to reclaim their sense of identity."

—*Publishers Weekly* on *Strands of Truth*

"Just when I think Colleen Coble's stories can't get any better, she proves me wrong. In *Strands of Truth*, I couldn't turn the pages fast enough. The characterization of Ridge and Harper and their relationship pulled me immediately into the story. Fast-paced, with so many unexpected twists and turns, I read this book in one sitting. Coble has pushed the bar higher than I'd imagined. This book is one not to be missed. Highly recommend!"

—Robin Caroll, bestselling author of the Darkwater Inn series

"Free-dive into a romantic suspense that will leave you breathless and craving for more."

—DiAnn Mills, bestselling author, on *Strands of Truth*

"Colleen Coble's latest book, *Strands of Truth*, grips you on page one with a heart-pounding opening and doesn't let go until the last satisfying word. I love her skill in pulling the reader in with believable, likable characters, interesting locations, and a mystery just waiting to be untangled. Highly recommended."

—Carrie Stuart Parks, author of *Fragments of Fear*

"It's in her blood! Colleen Coble once again shows her suspense prowess with a thriller as intricate and beautiful as a strand of DNA. *Strands of Truth* dives into an unusual profession involving mollusks and shell beds that weaves a unique, silky thread throughout the story. So fascinating I couldn't stop reading!"

—Ronie Kendig, bestselling author of the Tox Files series

"Once again, Colleen Coble delivers an intriguing, suspenseful tale in *Strands of Truth*. The mystery and tension mount toward an explosive and satisfying finish. Well done."

—Creston Mapes, bestselling author

"*Secrets at Cedar Cabin* is filled with twists and turns that will keep readers turning the pages as they plunge into the horrific world of sex trafficking where they come face-to-face with evil. Colleen Coble delivers a fast-paced story with a strong, lovable ensemble cast and a sweet, heaping helping of romance."

—Kelly Irvin, author of *Tell Her No Lies*

"Coble . . . weaves a suspense-filled romance set during the Revolutionary War. Coble's fine historical novel introduces a strong heroine—both in faith and character—that will appeal deeply to readers."

—*Publishers Weekly* on *Freedom's Light*

"This follow-up to *The View from Rainshadow Bay* features delightful characters and an evocative, atmospheric setting. Ideal for fans of romantic suspense and authors Dani Pettrey, Dee Henderson, and Brandilyn Collins."

—*Library Journal* on *The House at Saltwater Point*

"*The View from Rainshadow Bay* opens with a heart-pounding, run-for-your-life chase. This book will stay with you for a long time, long after you flip to the last page."

—*RT Book Reviews*, 4 stars

"Set on Washington State's Olympic Peninsula, this first volume of Coble's new suspense series is a tensely plotted and harrowing tale of murder, corporate greed, and family secrets. Devotees of Dani Pettrey, Brenda Novak, and Allison Brennan will find a new favorite here."

—*Library Journal* on *The View from Rainshadow Bay*

"Coble (*Twilight at Blueberry Barrens*) keeps the tension tight and the action moving in this gripping tale, the first in her Lavender Tides series set in the Pacific Northwest."

—*Publishers Weekly* on *The View from Rainshadow Bay*

"Filled with the suspense for which Coble is known, the novel is rich in detail with a healthy dose of romance, allowing readers to bask in the beauty of Washington State's lavender fields, lush forests, and jagged coastline."

—*BookPage* on *The View from Rainshadow Bay*

"Prepare to stay up all night with Colleen Coble. Coble's beautiful, emotional prose coupled with her keen sense of pacing, escalating danger, and very real characters place her firmly at the top of the suspense genre. I could not put this book down."

—Allison Brennan, *New York Times* bestselling author of *Shattered*, on *The View from Rainshadow Bay*

"Colleen is a master storyteller."

—Karen Kingsbury, bestselling author

EDGE OF DUSK

ALSO BY COLLEEN COBLE

PELICAN HARBOR NOVELS
One Little Lie
Two Reasons to Run
Three Missing Days

LAVENDER TIDES NOVELS
The View from Rainshadow Bay
Leaving Lavender Tides Novella
The House at Saltwater Point
Secrets at Cedar Cabin

ROCK HARBOR NOVELS
Without a Trace
Beyond a Doubt
Into the Deep
Cry in the Night
Haven of Swans (formerly titled *Abomination*)
Silent Night: A Rock Harbor Christmas Novella (e-book only)
Beneath Copper Falls

YA/MIDDLE GRADE ROCK HARBOR BOOKS
Rock Harbor Search and Rescue
Rock Harbor Lost and Found

CHILDREN'S ROCK HARBOR BOOK
The Blessings Jar

SUNSET COVE NOVELS
The Inn at Ocean's Edge
Mermaid Moon
Twilight at Blueberry Barrens

HOPE BEACH NOVELS
Tidewater Inn
Rosemary Cottage
Seagrass Pier
All Is Bright: A Hope Beach Christmas Novella (e-book only)

UNDER TEXAS STARS NOVELS
Blue Moon Promise
Safe in His Arms
Bluebonnet Bride Novella (e-book only)

THE ALOHA REEF NOVELS
Distant Echoes
Black Sands
Dangerous Depths
Midnight Sea
Holy Night: An Aloha Reef Christmas Novella (e-book only)

THE MERCY FALLS SERIES
The Lightkeeper's Daughter
The Lightkeeper's Bride
The Lightkeeper's Ball

JOURNEY OF THE HEART SERIES
A Heart's Disguise
A Heart's Obsession
A Heart's Danger
A Heart's Betrayal
A Heart's Promise
A Heart's Home

LONESTAR NOVELS
Lonestar Sanctuary
Lonestar Secrets
Lonestar Homecoming
Lonestar Angel
All Is Calm: A Lonestar Christmas Novella (e-book only)

STAND-ALONE NOVELS
A Stranger's Game
Strands of Truth
Freedom's Light
Alaska Twilight
Fire Dancer
Where Shadows Meet (formerly titled *Anathema*)
Butterfly Palace
Because You're Mine

EDGE OF DUSK

AN ANNIE PEDERSON NOVEL

COLLEEN COBLE

THOMAS NELSON
Since 1798

Edge of Dusk

Published in Nashville, Tennessee, by Thomas Nelson. Thomas Nelson is a registered trademark of HarperCollins Christian Publishing, Inc.

Thomas Nelson titles may be purchased in bulk for educational, business, fundraising, or sales promotional use. For information, please e-mail SpecialMarkets@ThomasNelson.com.

Publisher's Note: This novel is a work of fiction. Names, characters, places, and incidents are either products of the author's imagination or used fictitiously. All characters are fictional, and any similarity to people living or dead is purely coincidental.

Library of Congress Cataloging-in-Publication Data

Names: Coble, Colleen, author.
Title: Edge of dusk / Colleen Coble.
Description: Nashville, Tennessee : Thomas Nelson, [2022] | Series: An Annie Pederson novel ; 1 | Summary: "USA TODAY bestselling romantic suspense author Colleen Coble launches a brand-new series set in the fan-favorite Upper Peninsula that incorporates beloved characters from her Rock Harbor series"-- Provided by publisher.
Identifiers: LCCN 2021059125 (print) | LCCN 2021059126 (ebook) | ISBN 9780785253709 (paperback) | ISBN 9780785253730 (library binding) | ISBN 9780785253716 (epub) | ISBN 9780785253723 (downloadable audio)
Subjects: LCGFT: Novels.
Classification: LCC PS3553.O2285 E34 2022 (print) | LCC PS3553.O2285 (ebook) | DDC 813/.54--dc23/eng/20211206
LC record available at https://lccn.loc.gov/2021059125
LC ebook record available at https://lccn.loc.gov/2021059126

Printed in the United States of America

22 23 24 25 26 LSC 10 9 8 7 6 5 4 3 2 1

For my beloved agent, Karen Solem. Thank you for all the ways you've poured into my life over the past twenty-two years. If not for your guidance, Rock Harbor would not exist. If not for your love and support, my life would be so barren. Thank you, my friend!

A NOTE FROM THE AUTHOR

Dear Reader,

After writing in the romance genre for several years, I wanted to follow my dream of writing romantic suspense. In 2001 I began writing *Without a Trace*. It was about a woman with a search dog who lived in an old lighthouse on Lake Superior. My agent, Karen Solem, kicked that proposal to the curb for a solid *year*, saying, "Not enough layers." *Layers*? What did she mean? Thanks to her prodding, I learned about layers, and she was finally ready to send it out. It languished on several desks, and I received a couple of rejections.

In March 2002 I went to the Mount Hermon Writer's Conference and met Ami McConnell Abston for the first time. We sat on the floor outside a workshop room, and I pitched the idea to her. She'd had it on her desk for months, but she went back to the office and bought it a few months later. As I wrote those three books, Ami and Erin Healy taught me a lot about characterization and making those layers even more compelling, and I'll be forever grateful!

Without a Trace came out in September 2003. After nearly twenty years and a total of ten Rock Harbor books later, here we are back in the U.P.! Since it first released, it's a rare day when

I don't get a request for more Rock Harbor books. I have adult novels, novellas, middle-grade books, and a children's book all set up in the frozen north where the Snow King rules.

While Bree isn't the protagonist in this new series, she and the rest of the Rock Harbor gang play huge roles in the Annie Pederson series. I have different editors now, Amanda Bostic and Julee Schwarzburg, and they are both worth their weight in gold as we set out to bring you more Rock Harbor novels! In case you want the order of the books set in Rock Harbor, here they are: *Without a Trace*, *Beyond a Doubt*, *Into the Deep*, *Haven of Swans* (formerly titled *Abomination*), *Cry in the Night*, *Silent Night*, *Rock Harbor Search and Rescue*, *Rock Harbor Lost and Found*, *The Blessings Jar*, and *Beneath Copper Falls*.

I can't wait to hear what you think about our new adventure in Rock Harbor!

Much love,
Colleen

colleen@colleencoble.com

colleencoble.com

PROLOGUE

"WAS THAT THE WINDIGO?" NINE-YEAR-OLD ANNIE Vitanen yanked her little sister's hand to pull her to a stop in the deep shadows of the pines. Chills trickled down her spine, and she stared into the darkness. "Did you hear that?"

"It was just the loons," Sarah said. "Daddy said there's no such thing as the Windigo."

Annie shuddered. "You're only five—you don't know that." While at school she'd heard the story about the fifteen-foot-tall monster who ate humans. Annie peered into the shadows, searching for sunken red eyes in a stag skull staring back at her. The Windigo particularly liked little girls to fill its hungry belly.

Sarah tugged her hand free. "Daddy said it was just an old Ojibwa legend. I want to see the loons."

She took off down the needle-strewn path toward the water. Annie's heart seized in her throat. "Sarah, wait!"

Daddy had always told Annie she was responsible for her little sister, and she didn't want to get in trouble when their parents found out they were out here in the dark. Sarah had begged to come out to see the loons, and Annie found it hard to say no to her. This was the first time they'd been to their little camp on Tremolo Island since the summer started, and it might be a long time before they had time to visit again. Daddy only brought them to get away when he had a lull at the marina. Annie loved it here, even if there wasn't any power.

Her legs pumped and her breath *whooshed* in and out of her mouth. She emerged into the moonlight glimmering over Lake Superior. Her frantic gaze whipped around, first to make sure the Windigo hadn't followed them, then to find her sister.

Sarah sat on the wooden dock with her legs dangling over the waves. Lightning flickered in the distance, and Annie smelled rain as it began to sprinkle. Clouds hung low over the water, and the darkness got thicker.

"We need to go back, Sarah." While they could still find their way in the storm.

"I want to throw bread to the loons." Sarah gave her a piece of the bread they'd gotten from the kitchen.

Annie jumped when the loon's eerie yodel sounded. The *oo-AH-ho* sound was like no other waterfowl or bird. Normally she loved trying to determine whether the loon was yodeling, wailing, or calling, but right now she wanted to get her sister back into bed before they got in big trouble. They both knew better than to come down here by themselves. Mommy had warned them about the dangers more times than Annie could count.

She touched her sister's shoulder. "Come on, Sarah."

Sarah shrugged off her hand. "Just a minute. Look, the loon has a baby on its back."

Annie had to see that. She threw in a couple of bread pieces and peered at the loons. "I've never seen that."

"Me neither."

The loons didn't eat the bread, but she giggled when a big fish gulped down a piece right under their feet.

When she first heard the splashing, she thought it signaled more loons. But wait. Wasn't that the sound of oars slapping the water? A figure in a dark hoodie sat in the canoe. Did the Windigo ride in a canoe?

The canoe bumped the dock, and a voice said, "Two to choose from. It doesn't get much better than that."

The voice was so cheerful, Annie wasn't afraid. Before she could try to identify who it was, a hard hand grabbed her and dragged her into the canoe. "I think the younger one would be better."

The sudden, sharp pain in Annie's neck made her cry out, and she slapped her hand against her skin. Something wet and sticky clung to her fingers. In the next instant, she was in the icy water. The shock of the lake's grip made her head go under.

She came up thrashing in panic and spitting water. Her legs wouldn't kick very well, and she felt dizzy and disoriented. She tried to scream for Daddy, but her mouth wouldn't work. Her neck hurt something awful, and she'd never felt so afraid.

She'd been right—it was the Windigo, and he meant to eat her sister.

"Sarah!" Annie's voice sounded weak in her ears, and the storm was here with bigger waves churning around her. "Run!"

Her sister shrieked out her name, and Annie tried to move toward the sound, but a wave picked her up and tossed her against a piling supporting the dock. Her vision went dark, and she sank into the cold arms of the lake.

The next thing she knew, she was on her back, staring up into the rain pouring into her face. Her dad's hand was on the awful pain in her neck, and her mother was screaming for Sarah.

She never saw her sister again.

ONE

TWENTY-FOUR YEARS LATER

LAW ENFORCEMENT RANGER ANNIE PEDERSON RUBBED her eyes after staring at the computer screen for the past two hours. She'd closed the lid on an investigation into a hit-and-run in the Kitchigami Wilderness Preserve, and she'd spent the past few hours finishing paperwork. It had been a grueling case, and she was glad it was over.

"I'll be right back," she told her eight-year-old daughter, Kylie, sitting on the floor of her office playing Pokémon Go on her iPad.

Kylie's blonde head, so like Annie's own, bobbed, too intent to respond verbally.

Kade Matthews looked up when Annie entered his office. Over the past few years he'd moved up and become head ranger. Kade's six-feet-tall stocky frame and solid muscles exuded competence, and his blue eyes conveyed caring. Annie thanked the Lord every day for such a good boss. He was understanding when she needed time off with Kylie, and he let her know he valued her work and expertise. "Ready for a few days off?"

"Really? With all this work on your shoulders?"

He nodded. "I can handle it. I know this is a busy time for you."

"I do have a lot of work to do out at the marina."

Since her parents and husband died two years ago, she'd been tasked with running the Tremolo Marina and Cabin Resort. She managed with seasonal help and lots of her free time, but summer was always grueling. It was only June 3, and the season was off to a good start.

He cleared his throat, and his eyes softened. "I'm glad you stopped in. I didn't want to send this report without talking to you first."

"What report?" Her tongue felt thick in her mouth because she knew the likely topic.

"A child's remains were found down around St. Ignace."

It didn't matter that it was so far. That route could have easily been chosen by the kidnapper. It was a common way to travel from lower Michigan to the U.P. "How old?"

"Five or six, according to the forensic anthropologist. I assume you want your DNA sent over for comparison?"

"Yes, of course."

They'd been through this scenario two other times since she'd begun searching for answers, and each time she'd teetered between hope and despair. While she wanted closure on what had happened to her sister, she wasn't sure she was ready to let go of hope. Though logically she knew her sister had to be dead. People didn't take children except for nefarious purposes. Annie didn't know how she'd react when word finally came that Sarah had been found.

Relief? Depression? Maybe a combination of the two. Maybe even a tailspin that would unhinge her. All these years later, and she still couldn't think about that night without breaking into a cold sweat. Avoidance had been her modus operandi. Not many even knew about the incident. Kade did, of course. And Bree. Jon too. Probably some of the townspeople remembered and talked about it, too, but it had been long ago. Twenty-four years ago.

Nearly a quarter of a century and yet just yesterday. "How long before results are back on DNA?"

"Probably just a few days. With children they try to move quickly. I'll get it sent over. You doing okay?"

She gave a vigorous nod. "Sure, I'm fine. I'll file this report and get these pictures sent to you."

"Bree told me to ask if you wanted a puppy, one of Samson's. There's a male that looks just like him."

She smiled just thinking of her daughter's delight. "Kylie has been begging for a puppy since we lost Belle. How much are they going for?"

The little terrier had died in her sleep a month ago at age sixteen, and they both missed her. Samson was a world-renowned search-and-rescue dog, and his pups wouldn't come cheap. She ran through how much she had in savings. Maybe not enough.

"We get two free pups, and Bree told me she would give you one."

"You don't want to do that," she protested. "You'd be giving up a lot of money."

He shrugged. "We have everything we need. Head over there in the next few days, and you can take him home with you before our kids get too attached and bar the front door."

She laughed. "Hunter says he's marrying Kylie, so I think he will stick up for her."

Kade and Bree's little boy was four and adored Kylie. She was good with kids, and she loved spending time with the Matthews twins.

"You're right about that. I'll let Bree know you want him. He's a cute little pup."

"What are you doing with the other one?"

"Lauri has claimed her."

Kade's younger sister was gaining a reputation for search-and-rescue herself, and she already had a dog. "What about Zorro?"

"He's developed diabetes, and Lauri knows he needs to slow down some. She wants a new puppy to train so Zorro can help work with him."

"She might want the one that looks like Samson."

"She wants a female this time."

She glanced at her watch and rose. "I'll get out of here. Thanks again for the puppy. Kylie will be ecstatic."

She went back to her office. "Time for your doctor appointment, Bug."

Kylie made a face. "I don't want to go."

At eight, Kylie knew her own mind better than Annie knew hers most days. She was the spitting image of Annie at the same age: corn silk–colored hair and big blue eyes set in a heart-shaped face. But Annie had never been that sure of herself. Her dad's constant criticism had knocked that out of her.

She steered her daughter out the brick office building to the red Volkswagen crew-cab truck in the parking lot, then set out for town.

The old truck banged and jolted its way across the potholes left by this year's massive snowfall until Annie reached the paved road into town. She couldn't imagine living anywhere other than where the Snow King ruled nine months of the year. There was no other place on earth like Michigan's Upper Peninsula. With the Keweenaw Peninsula to the north and Ottawa National Forest to the south, there could be no more beautiful spot in the world.

Her devotion to this place had cost her dearly nine years ago, but every time she saw the cold, crystal-clear waters of the northernmost Great Lakes stretching to the horizon, she managed to convince herself it was worth it.

Part of the town's special flavor came from the setting. Surrounded by forests on three sides, it had all the natural beauty anyone could want. Old-growth forests, sparkling lakes where fish thronged, and the brilliant blue of that Big Sea Water along the east side.

They drove through town, down Negaunee to Houghton Street to the businesses that comprised Rock Harbor's downtown. The small, quaint village had been built in the 1850s when copper was king, and its Victorian-style buildings had been carefully preserved by the residents.

Dr. Ben Eckright's office was a remodeled Victorian boardinghouse on the corner of Houghton and Pepin Streets. She parked in his side lot and let Kylie out of the back.

She glanced across the street to the law office, and her breath caught at the man getting out of the car. It couldn't be. She stared at the sight of a familiar set of shoulders and closed her eyes a moment. Opening them didn't reassure her. It really was him.

Jon Dunstan stood beside a shiny red Jaguar. Luckily, he hadn't seen her yet, and she grabbed Kylie's hand and ran with her for the side door, praying he wouldn't look this way. She was still trembling when the door shut behind her.

/ / /

Where was he?

Christopher Willis struggled against the bonds binding his wrists behind his back. His legs were bound as well, and a bandana or some kind of cloth covered his eyes. Dead leaves crunched under him as he sat on the ground, squirming to try to get free, and he smelled mud and moss.

The ropes or whatever held his arms fast didn't budge. To tamp down the rising panic, he ran through the events he remembered. He'd put out his campfire in the National Kitchigami Wilderness tract before he entered his tent and crawled into his sleeping bag. He'd fallen asleep to the roar of Agate Falls, a terraced waterfall in the middle branch of the Ontonagon River in the western Upper Peninsula.

A sound had awakened him, and he listened to a soft rustling before he unzipped his sleeping bag to investigate. The minute he poked his head out of the tent, something crashed down on it. The next thing he knew, he'd opened his eyes and was sitting on the cold ground.

There was no sound of the falls, so he'd been moved from his previous location. Who had knocked him out—and why? No one knew where he was either. He'd spent the past month hiking from Minnesota and through Wisconsin. Maybe someone would see his abandoned campsite and report it. Otherwise, he could disappear here and no one would know.

Panic threatened to choke him again, and he fought it back. A clear head would be the only thing that might get him out of this alive.

A rustle sounded to his left, and he turned his head even though he couldn't see. "Help! I need help." The male chuckle that answered him raised gooseflesh on the back of his neck. "Who are you? What do you want?"

The next sound came from the other direction. There was more than one person out there hiding in the thick pines. His mouth was almost too dry to speak, but he wet his lips and tried again. "Look, I won't say anything. Just let me go."

Something cold touched his wrists, and his bonds fell away. A knife? He pulled his arms forward and rubbed his wrists a second before he ripped the cloth off his eyes. He blinked in the bright sunshine and reached down to untie his ankles. Were they really turning him loose?

A voice came from his right. "If you can get away, you're free. We'll give you a head start of fifteen minutes . . . starting now."

Christopher leaped to his feet and ran forward toward the glimmer of water. He was sure there was a man to his left and to his right. He'd learned how to track as a kid from his grandpa, so he might escape these men. And what kind of game was this anyway?

Maybe a cave would hide him from them, and he spotted pine trees ahead. He paused to get his bearings and swept his gaze around, searching for a place to hide. If he could wait it out until they left, he might have a chance.

There. A small cave beckoned to his left in the side of a rocky hillside. Maybe he could pile rocks in the mouth and hunker down inside. It was his best hope since he didn't know where he was.

He darted to the cave and backed into it, then began to pile rocks in front of the opening as silently as possible. How long had it been since his escape? He patted his pockets, but of course his captors had taken his phone. Slowing his breathing to a quiet whisper, he waited.

It seemed forever since he'd crawled in here, and he could see the light through a crack at the top of the cave opening. He'd caught a glimpse of water, but it was too expansive to be the Ontonagon River. He had to be on the banks of Lake Superior.

Did he wait here and make them think he'd escaped long ago or try to make a break for it? A cramp seized his left leg, and he bit back a groan as he massaged it. Everything in him wanted to wait out the hunters, but it would feel so good to walk out the aches and pains manifesting all over his body.

As quietly as he could, he moved the rocks again until he was able to crawl out and stand. He was limping when he sidled along the face of the hillside toward the water. The sun oriented him, and he tried to think of his topography map. If he was anywhere near the Porcupine Mountains, Ontonagon would be to his right, but his captors might have taken him farther afield, maybe even up to the Keweenaw.

He turned to his left and walked along the water. If only he had a boat. When the gun's echo came, he ducked but it was too late. As he plunged into the waves, his last thought was of his parents, who would never know what happened to him.

TWO

A VISIT TO ROCK HARBOR HAD ALWAYS SEEMED LIKE stepping back in time. This little town on the banks of Lake Superior hadn't changed a bit in the almost nine years Jon Dunstan had been gone. The same Victorian buildings turned their gaily painted faces to the narrow streets, and the scent of *pannukakkua* and *pulla* wafted from the Suomi Café. He'd have to stop for breakfast after his appointment.

He couldn't help but steal a glance up and down Houghton Street on the off chance he might spot Annie, but early June was a busy time as she got the marina and resort up to full capacity during her time off from the National Park Service. He wasn't even sure he wanted to see her. Her rejection was still painful, and he didn't want to reopen the wound.

His plan was to get in and out of town as quickly as possible.

Attorney Ursula Sawyer greeted Jon at the door of her office. "Sorry about your dad, Jon."

He shook her hand and took a seat in the tufted leather chair she indicated in front of her desk. "Thank you. He's improving some, but his speech is still a little off, and he needs help to bathe."

His dad's stroke had occurred a month ago. Watching the man he'd admired all his life needing help with the simplest tasks broke his heart. He'd been a well-known and powerful attorney, and even after retirement, Dad had kept his finger on the pulse of the law world.

Ursula slid some papers across the gleaming surface of her walnut desk. "I received the power of attorney papers you sent, and I've drawn up the documents so you can sell the lake house. I will warn you that real estate up here is a little depressed, so it might take some time. There is some maintenance that needs to be done on the place too. No one has been to the cottage in years, and the roof is in bad shape."

"I see. I haven't been there yet."

This news wasn't what he wanted to hear. His patient schedule in Chicago was packed, and he'd told his partners he'd only be gone a couple of days. He could shift the load to the new doctor, but it wasn't ideal.

He signed the paperwork and slid it back to her. "Any recommendations on a contractor?"

"We have several good ones." She jotted down several names and phone numbers.

He pocketed the list she gave him. "Thanks, I'll get some estimates. I suppose I'd better get out there and take a look."

"Did you bring your dad with you?"

He nodded. "He wanted to come, but even though I wasn't sure he was up to the trip, he talked me into it. I left him at the bed-and-breakfast." Jon rose. "Thanks for your help. The Suomi Café is calling my name."

Ursula smiled. "I had *pannukakkua* myself this morning."

He couldn't have that dish any longer, but there would be plenty of great food at the café. He stepped out onto the sidewalk and squinted in the bright sunshine. The red Volkswagen truck across the street drew his attention. Annie had driven one like it.

That 1969 crew-cab red-and-white pickup was the only one he'd ever seen like it. Could she still own it?

He walked down the street to the little hillside that housed the Suomi Café. The delicious aromas took him back to every summer during his teenage years. He and his dad had breakfast here nearly every morning. Scanning the clientele in the small café yielded a familiar mop of curly red hair. Bree Nicholls was walking toward the checkout register with her search dog at her heels. Samson was a German shepherd / chow mix with a curly tail that wagged when he saw Jon.

Bree's green eyes widened when she saw him, and she smiled up at him when she reached his side. Though five three, she was a powerhouse in the search-and-rescue world. "My, my . . . Jon Dunstan in the flesh. I haven't seen you in forever. Are you here for the summer with your dad?"

"Bree Nicholls, I didn't expect to see you right off." He rubbed Samson's head.

She smiled. "It's Bree Matthews now."

"You married Kade?" He vaguely recalled hearing her first husband had died in a plane crash.

"Sure did. We have a lot to catch up on. How's your dad?"

"He had a stroke, and I came to sell the cottage. He's staying at Martha's place out by your lighthouse."

"I'm sorry to hear about his stroke, but it will be good to see him. You too." She snapped her fingers, and Samson came to heel. Her smile widened. "I have three kids now. Davy has his hands full with his younger twin siblings. Life has changed a bit since you were here last."

"The town looks the same."

"It never changes." She moved toward the door. "I'd love to stay and catch up, but we were just called out on a search for a missing man. Another hiker found his wrecked campsite last night, so I have to get to the sheriff's office."

"That doesn't sound good."

"No, it doesn't."

As she exited, he caught the headline on the town's morning newspaper lying on the counter. *Man Missing in the U.P. Authorities Suspect Foul Play.*

An ominous headline.

This area had always drawn him. Even now, he could smell the fresh water and the hint of fish. He could feel a cane pole in his hands and the cold clasp of Superior's waves. He hadn't expected such a strong reaction to being back here.

This place had nearly snared him once, and it still might pull him into its web if he wasn't careful. The sooner he could arrange for repairs on the cottage, the better.

/ / /

Pictures of Dr. Eckright's boating adventures on Superior decorated the waiting room, but Annie's gaze kept wandering to the window overlooking Houghton Street. When Jon exited the attorney's office, she had drunk in the sight of him. His square jaw was flexed, and he was biting his bottom lip the way he always did when he was distressed. His brown hair was shorter than when she'd seen him last, and even from across the street, she could see his clothing and shoes were expensive.

He wasn't the same guy running around in cutoffs and swim trunks with a fishing pole over his shoulder. At twenty-two he'd been a beach bum with hair curling over his ears and a penchant for taking any challenge, though she knew he was no slouch in the career department. He'd finished high school at sixteen and had gone straight into college, then med school with a steadfast goal to become an orthopedic surgeon. He'd completed college in three years, then med school in three years as well. He was heading to his residency at the end of that long-ago summer.

Now at thirty-four he looked every bit the professional doctor. Did he still love cherry Popsicles and Snickers ice cream bars? Did he still eat his hamburger with a smear of peanut butter and swill down iced tea by the gallon?

The nurse appeared and beckoned for Annie and Kylie to follow her to an exam room down the narrow hall to what used to be a bedroom when the place housed copper miners. The uneven floorboards made it feel like she was walking on an old ship. The nurse took Kylie's weight and height and checked her vitals before she disappeared through the door.

Dr. Ben Eckright entered after another couple of minutes. Annie didn't think she'd ever seen him without a smile on his florid face. His red hair was mostly gone except for tufts above his ears that still had a ginger hue. He always wore hiking boots and denim. She couldn't imagine him dressed to the nines like Jon.

He winked at Annie's little girl and produced a Werther's butterscotch that he slipped into her palm. "Kylie, my girl, I know this is why you came."

Kylie's face brightened. "It's not the *only* reason." She stared at it a moment but didn't unwrap it. That was the doctor's unwritten rule. No candy eating until she was outside.

Dr. Ben opened Kylie's chart and perused it. His expression went somber. "Hmm."

Worry gnawed at Annie. "I know she's lost weight. I swear I'm feeding her."

The doctor leaned toward her daughter. "How have you been feeling, Kylie?"

Kylie stared down at her sneakers. "Fine."

"Have you been tired?"

Kylie shrugged, then glanced at Annie before she gave a slight nod.

"I think we should run some tests," Dr. Ben said. "Just a little blood work at first. Maybe a stool test. I'll get you the orders."

Annie's gut clenched. A blood test meant needles, and Kylie had never had blood drawn before. "You're sure it's necessary?" Annie's own history included way too many tests and needles after the knife wound when she was a child.

"She's in the bottom percentile in weight and height. I'd like to rule out a few things. You're tall yourself. What about her father?"

"Six two."

"Then I would be a very poor doctor not to investigate further. Kylie's a big girl, aren't you, Kylie? She can handle a tiny little needle."

Kylie's lower lip quivered, but she tipped up her chin and nodded. "My best friend at school has to stick herself every day to test her blood sugar. She said it only stings a little."

"She's very brave, and I know you are too. We can draw the blood right here, and you can take the stool test home with you. Easy peasy. And for being so brave, you get another butterscotch." He slipped another wrapped candy into her hand. "Let me get Bonnie."

Annie held Kylie's hand in a tight grip while his phlebotomist,

Bonnie, drew several vials of blood. Kylie only inhaled and held her mother's gaze when the needle poked through the skin. It was over in a minute or two.

Bonnie pressed a cotton ball to the spot and covered the puncture with a dolphin Band-Aid. "You were so brave." She glanced at Annie. "We should have the results in a couple of days. Dr. Ben will call you."

"Thanks." Annie couldn't wait to get out of this place and away from the smell of antiseptic. It reminded her too much of her own trauma.

She escaped into the sunshine scented with pine and open water. Her gaze went immediately across the street, and she tensed at the sight of the red sports car. He must still be in town.

Kylie stopped before they reached the truck. "Mommy, can we go to the Suomi? I can smell the *pulla*. We could just take it home."

Annie glanced down the street toward the hillside where the Suomi squatted. "Okay, it's a deal. You earned a treat. But we just have to pop in and grab some things to take home. I've got some new campers checking in shortly, and I need to be around."

And maybe she could fatten up Kylie with some Finnish bread and fruit preserves. The thimbleberry preserves from the Jampot were made by monks up at the abbey, and Kylie loved it.

Annie left her truck in the lot, and they walked over to the Suomi. She planned to move fast. In and out at the Suomi. With any luck she'd get back to the marina without running into him. Unless he was here for a while, but she'd take one step at a time.

THREE

BREE MATTHEWS STOOD OUTSIDE THE SUOMI CAFÉ. Annie stopped and smiled. "No kids today?"

Bree had three kids: Davy, almost twelve, and twins Hannah and Hunter, who were four.

Bree hugged Annie. "Not for long. The twins are with Naomi, and I have to pick them up in a bit." She glanced down at Kylie, then lowered her voice. "You'll never guess who I just saw in the café."

Annie's smile slipped and she pinned it back in place. "Jon Dunstan is inside?"

Bree's green eyes widened. "You know he's in town?"

"I caught a glimpse of him when I got to town." Did her voice quiver as much as her insides? No one could know how his presence had rocked her.

Annie handed Kylie ten dollars. "Run inside and get some *pulla*, Bug. I'll wait here for you." Jon had never seen Kylie, so her presence wouldn't tip him off to Annie being outside. Desperate to change the subject, she avoided Bree's sympathetic gaze and fiddled with the strap on her purse.

While she grappled with something to say, a shadow fell on her face and she turned to see a woman standing with her hands together. About Annie's height of five feet six, she appeared to be around thirty. Her red hair gleamed in the sunshine.

"You're Annie Pederson, aren't you? You own Tremolo Marina and Cabin Resort?"

"That's right. Have we met?"

The woman shook her head. "I'm Taylor Moore, and I wondered if you had any job openings? I can cook and clean. I'm good with kids. I'll do anything. I've been working at the nursing home for the past month, but it's hard to lose a resident, especially after taking care of my mom while she was dying. I'd love to do something different."

Annie studied the woman's hopeful expression. "The head nurse out there is a friend of mine." Her bookings for the month were double last year's, and she'd been worrying how she was going to keep up with work being so busy.

Annie slid her gaze over to Bree, who had the same interest on her face that Annie was feeling. "I could use some help. How about you come out to the resort and we can talk?"

Taylor bit her lip. "I-I don't have a car. I've been renting a room here in town. I guess that might be a problem getting to work out of town."

"Maybe not. I can provide lodging."

The door to the café banged, and Kylie ran out with a bag of *pulla*. The breeze wafted the warm, yeasty scent Annie's way.

She couldn't go inside and face Jon, so she turned back to Taylor with a bright smile. "Let's get some coffee. Talk to you later, Bree."

Annie led the way along Houghton Street past flower-lined tree lawns. The town already teemed with tourists focused on exploring the Porcupine Mountains, Lake Superior, and the Keweenaw Peninsula. The bell on the door jingled as she pushed open the door to Metro Espresso and inhaled the scents of espresso and pastries.

An old Victorian storefront with high tin ceilings painted blush housed the coffee shop. Debris was easy to sweep up from the wooden floor, and the bright windows added to the airy feel. Several tables were taken by people Annie didn't recognize—probably tourists. She directed Kylie to save them a table while she and Taylor ordered.

"What would you like?" Annie asked.

Taylor's gaze swept the glass display of Finnish pastries and other delicacies. "A mocha sounds good."

The woman seemed hungry, and Annie gestured to a donut-like pastry. "Have you ever had breakfast meat pie? It's filled with minced meat and rice." Without waiting for a response, she ordered two of them for Taylor. "I'll have a caramel latte and a mocha." Annie paid for the order, then joined Taylor and Kylie at a round iron table in the corner.

Kylie had already broken off a piece of *pulla*, and the thimbleberry jam inside the bread was all over her face.

Annie settled in the chair and laced her hands together. "So, tell me about your work history."

Taylor handed over a résumé. "My mother was ill for a lot of years, and I took care of her until she died six months ago. Since then, I've worked odd jobs like waitressing and cleaning hotel rooms. The folks at the nursing home like me, and I have good references you can call."

Annie looked over Taylor's work history. "How'd you hear about Tremolo Marina?"

"One of the other aides at the nursing home found me crying in the bathroom after I found a resident gone. She knew I'd been struggling with grief and mentioned you might need help with the summer season starting."

Annie didn't reply as their coffee and pastries arrived. What should she do? Her parents had always taught her to help those less fortunate. Lately, she hadn't felt all that fortunate as she'd struggled to make ends meet, but at least she and Kylie had a roof over their heads and food to eat. They might not have the newest electronics and a mansion, but they were doing okay. They'd be fine if she could turn things around at the marina and actually make a profit instead of it being a drain on her regular salary.

"I can offer you room and board plus a small salary." Annie named a modest weekly stipend. "I could use some help with general chores around the place. Cleaning boats and cabins, cooking, and yard maintenance. It's hard work and long days though. I'll need to check your references first. I might need some help with Kylie on occasion. Maybe taking her fishing or swimming when I'm tied up."

"Of course." Eyes shining, Taylor looked up from the last bite of her second meat pie. She gulped down her mouthful of food as she gave a vigorous nod. "Kylie and I will get along just fine, right, Kylie?"

Kylie licked jam from her fingers and nodded. "I like her, Mommy."

"I'm a hard worker. You won't be sorry."

It would be a help to have another pair of hands. Annie's gaze went to her daughter, who looked pale in the morning sun streaming through the window. The worry she'd shoved aside earlier came surging back, and she prayed the tests found nothing seriously wrong with her baby girl.

The overgrown lane back to the cottage was Jon's first clue of just how bad he was going to find the property. Overgrown thimbleberry and blackberry shrubs clawed at the sides of his car, and he tried not to imagine the havoc they were wreaking on the glossy red paint. Maybe he should have parked on the road and walked to the property.

His dad clutched the armrest for dear life but said nothing as the vehicle broke free from the restraining vegetation into a wide expanse of tangled, knee-high grass surrounding the cottage. The gray and weathered boards of the structure showed the power of Superior's gales, and when Jon cut the engine and stepped out of the car, he heard the waves rolling to shore. Moss grew on the roof and creepers were beginning to overtake one side of the house. Nature hadn't waited long to begin to take back what was hers.

He helped his dad out of the car, and they walked toward the house.

"Rough shape," his dad mumbled.

Jon exhaled and bit his lip. "Yeah, it is. Wait here."

The porch still seemed sturdy, and Jon mounted the steps to the front door to insert the key. When he stepped inside, he winced. The odor of mold and damp struck him in the face. A storm had broken a window, and the wooden floorboards beneath the shattered glass had warped. Could that be repaired, or would he have to replace the whole floor?

He went back outside to help his dad up the steps and into the house. His father wandered around the space while Jon took out his phone and made notes of what needed immediate attention: window replacement, roof, exterior painting, floor repair, kitchen and bathroom remodels, as well as inside paint and staging in order to prepare it for selling.

A huge job. Too big to leave totally in the hands of a contractor. He would need to either make frequent trips back to check the progress or stay here until the job was finished.

Would it be so bad to take some time off? He hadn't had a real vacation in years, and this place brought back so many memories. Annie, her blonde hair flying in the wind and her blue eyes alight with mischief and fun. Right off the shore here, they'd swung out from the limb of a big tree to drop into the freezing water before cuddling on the shore to warm up. He'd learned to surf out on those cold waves, and sometimes he and Dad had come up here for cross-country skiing.

Best not to think of Annie. Those memories led to the final breakup, a painful moment that still made his chest ache.

He scanned the paper with the contractor names Ursula had given him. The second name held a vague familiarity. Hadn't they gone to summer camp together? Sean lived in the area, while Jon was a frequent visitor. He punched in the number and a male voice answered on the first ring.

"Sean Johnson."

"Hi, Sean, this is Jon Dunstan."

"Dunstan! The troll returns. You still surfing, man? The waves are rockin' out there today." Yoopers called anyone who lived below the Mackinac Bridge a troll, but Jon had been in the U.P. often enough, he usually bristled at the term.

Jon smiled at the enthusiasm in Sean's voice. He'd been a good guy back in the day, though they hadn't run in the same circles much. "It's been way too long since I did much of anything except work. I hear you followed in your uncle's footsteps and are a contractor now?"

"You heard right. You planning to fix up the old place, eh?"

"I am. Could you come by and see what you think?"

"I can stop by right now. I was on my way out to Tremolo to go surfing, and I'm nearly to your drive."

"The drive is overgrown. If you value the paint on your truck, you might park on the road and walk back. I'll take care of that drive first thing."

"My old truck will laugh at the bushes. Be there shortly."

While he was waiting, Jon checked on his dad and found him asleep in a wooden rocker on the back porch. Hopefully it would hold him. The lake was usually visible from back here, but vegetation had blocked the view. He'd have to tend to that when he cleaned up the drive.

He went back inside and glanced out the fly-speckled windows at the sound of an engine. A battered blue pickup was squeezing through the lane opening. He pocketed his phone and went out to meet Sean.

Sean unfolded from the pickup. At six feet four, he towered over Jon's six-foot-one height, and his bulky muscles strained the arms of his tee. He still wore his curly dark hair short, and his hazel eyes took in the condition of the cottage.

Jon shook his hand, noticing the calluses. "Hard worker."

He grinned. "More like a hard player. I've gotten into mountain climbing. Have a remote cabin up near Freda with killer climbing."

"You go alone? That doesn't sound safe."

Sean shrugged. "What can I say? I'm good at it, eh? And I like to be alone sometimes. No one goes up there, not even my uncle. He's in a nursing home with dementia." He examined the place and whistled.

"Looks bad, doesn't it?"

"It's gnarly, man. Superior likes to claim her own. Need a new roof for sure. And paint."

"Water damage inside too. Let me show you." He led Sean inside.

The contractor grunted when he saw the water damage. "Common oak boards. I've got some in my storage barn so I should be able to repair the floor instead of replacing the whole thing."

He trailed after Jon through the kitchen, bathroom, and three bedrooms. "Last updated in the fifties."

"I want to sell the place, so the kitchen and bath need to be modernized, right?" After being around the Yooper, Jon nearly added *eh* to the end of his question.

"It would be easier to sell if you did. Properties aren't going very fast, but this one has a primo location on the water. So, it would be worth the effort." Sean put away his notepad. "I'll work up some numbers for you."

"How long will it take?"

"I have a good crew, so about a month."

"What about the windows?"

Sean stepped over to look at the living room window. "Most people will use this place as a summer camp, not a year-round place, but the frames are rotting, eh? You could put in single pane, though, if you want. Cheaper, especially when you don't have AC and will have them open most of the time."

Made sense to Jon. "Okay, let's do that. I can handle painting the walls and the exterior."

And just like that, he realized he'd been searching for an excuse to stay. To unwind here in this place that had meant so much to him growing up.

Sean arched a brow. "You're gonna become a Yooper, eh? Think you can handle it, city boy?"

Jon grinned at the word that meant a troll who moved to the U.P. "What, you looking to scare me off because I'll ride the waves better than you?"

"You challenging me, eh? You're on." Sean stuck his pencil behind his ear and turned for the door.

Jon walked him out. It felt good to sense he might still fit in here, that this place might welcome him back like a prodigal son. He might fall back into the rhythms and customs he'd grown up with.

FOUR

THE TINY CABIN WASN'T MUCH. ANNIE SELDOM RENTED it out because it was such a disappointment to guests. A minuscule bathroom with a shower barely wide enough to turn around in was attached to a bedroom only big enough for a twin. She'd tried to make it homier by putting in a daybed instead of a twin bed, but the cheery red quilt didn't make up for the lack of size and amenities.

On the way home she'd called the nursing home and had gotten a rave recommendation for Taylor from her friend who managed the nursing staff. That glowing endorsement had quieted any misgivings she'd had initially.

"I know it's not very big," she told Taylor. "But the communal building has lots of seating and nooks where you can relax and read or whatever you like. And there's a nice pavilion outside."

Taylor's gaze swept the room. "It's nice. More than I've had. And you said the days are long so I'll only be in here to sleep." She dropped her backpack onto the daybed. "I can get started now if you like."

"Wouldn't you like to stroll around and get used to the place before you start work?"

Taylor's bright-red hair swayed in a shake of her head. "I like to keep busy. What do you need me to do first?"

Annie glanced out the window at Kylie swinging from the tire attached to the tree branch of a big oak. "How about you keep Kylie occupied for the day? I want to get started painting and she'll want to help. If she's underfoot, I won't get anything done."

Taylor's smile came, a timid expression. "Fishing?"

"There's a little lake a bit east of here. We have a golf cart you can take. Kylie will show you."

"That sounds fun. Thanks again for the job." Taylor slipped back through the door and went to Kylie.

The little girl's smile bloomed, and she hopped out of the tire swing to lead Taylor to the shed where they kept the sports gear. Annie waved at them and went to the dock to meet an incoming boater.

She got them settled in their slip and turned to lead the family of four to their cabin when she saw something bobbing in the heavy Superior surf. What was it? A dead fish? A cormorant maybe? She grabbed a pole to try to retrieve whatever it was and was huffing by the time she maneuvered it close to the dock.

When she knelt, she bit back a scream, and her heart pounded at the sight of the back of a person's partially submerged head. The rest of the body became more visible as it bobbed nearer to where she crouched.

Her mouth dry, she stared at the poor soul. It appeared to be a man. Thinking the victim might still be alive, she tried to pull him in, then saw the hole in the back of his head. She scrambled back on her haunches and dug her phone out to call the sheriff's department. This wasn't government land so it was his jurisdiction, not hers.

She gave the details about the discovery to the dispatcher, who promised to send out Sheriff Kaleva or one of the deputies. After hanging up the phone, she sat staring at the body in the lake. She couldn't let the waves carry him back to Superior's depths, so she retrieved a strap from her nearby boat before she pulled him closer with the pole again so she could lash him to the pier.

An eagle soared overhead and peered down with interest on the body floating off the pier. She settled in to protect the man from any predators while she waited for help to arrive. The cold waves beat at the victim, but the strap held him close to the pier. It seemed like forever, but it was only twenty minutes before she spotted the flashing red light atop a sedan pulling into her resort.

She rose and turned to meet the two figures who got out of the sheriff's car. Sheriff Mason Kaleva himself, easily recognizable from his stocky bulk, strode toward her. In his forties, his light-brown hair was starting to gray, and the older he got the more his Finnish heritage showed. His blond deputy, Doug Montgomery, towered over him by several inches, but Doug's mild manner always caused him to lag back whenever the sheriff was around. His jowly cheeks and slow drawl had most of Rock Harbor residents calling him Deputy Dawg.

Sheriff Kaleva stepped onto the pier, and his gaze went to the body bobbing in the waves. "Good job securing him. Did you recognize him?"

"No, I didn't touch him other than lashing the strap around his waist to make sure Superior didn't claim him."

Even that had been hard. Her usual duties consisted of search and rescue, wildfire investigation, protecting piracy of timber, protecting archaeological artifacts, dealing with drug movement, and handling vehicle accident investigations. Murder wasn't a usual occurrence on national park lands.

Mason nodded and crouched beside the body. "I called for

a state forensic tech since you reported the man had been shot. Clearly a homicide, so I'm not going to touch the body other than to see if there is an ID on him."

He drew on a pair of Nitrile gloves and leaned over to gingerly probe the man's jeans. "There's a wallet. Doug, put on some gloves and hold the body still so I can get it."

Doug did as ordered and lowered his three hundred pounds down to the pier with difficulty. "Got him, Sheriff."

Mason didn't reply as he focused on retrieving the wallet. It took some finesse to get it out of the wet jeans, but he finally had it in hand.

When he opened it, he inhaled and stood. "It's the hiker reported missing last night." He held out the driver's license for the deputy to see.

Annie had been following the story about the missing hiker, and she put her hand to her mouth. "Christopher Willis?"

Mason spared her a glance. "Don't repeat that, Annie."

"I won't."

Murder. She stared at the forest pressing in from the north. There was a cold-blooded killer out there.

/ / /

With sunset came more tension. After supper Annie kept glancing out the window as twilight deepened. Was whoever killed the young hiker lurking out there somewhere? According to the sheriff, Christopher's tent and belongings had been worn and old. He'd been hiking awhile. Not much was known about him yet, but Mason suspected he was a transient hiking through the area.

She jumped when the knocker *thumped* on her door and

automatically reached to hold back Kylie who liked to answer the door. "I'll get it."

Kylie frowned but sat back on the yellow sofa with her book while Annie peeked out the pane at the top of the door. Anu Nicholls, owner of Nicholls Finnish Emporium, stood outside with a smile. She was the mother of Bree's first husband and still was very involved with Bree and her family. Her daughter was married to Mason. She was in her sixties with short blonde hair and a kind manner. Since she was dressed in slacks and a blue top, she had probably come straight from the shop.

Annie opened the door. "Well, this is a nice surprise. I was going to bring you the rugs tomorrow."

Anu stepped inside and shut the door behind her. "I had to go to Houghton to meet a buyer for dinner and thought I would stop on the way back to save you a trip. Besides, I had something else I wanted to talk to you about." She gave the air a sniff. "You made *kalakukko* for dinner?"

"I did." The Finnish meat pie with fish and bacon was Kylie's favorite dinner.

"Smells wonderful." Anu glanced over to Kylie. "Did you enjoy your dinner, *pupu*?"

"I helped Mommy make it. I'm writing a story, Miss Anu. Want to see?"

Anu went to the sofa to take a look at the picture book Kylie was working on, and Annie followed. The bears in the pictures were a little misshapen, and the people were stick figures, but Kylie had worked hard on it.

"If this is for school, you'll get an A-plus," Anu said.

Kylie beamed. "I'm going to put it on Mommy's refrigerator."

Annie squeezed her daughter's shoulder. "Good job, Bug." She gestured to Anu. "My rug room is this way." Annie led the way to the spare room where she had her wooden floor loom set up.

Shelves along one side wall held stacks of completed rag rugs in various shades of blue. Her specialty rugs mimicked the colors of Lake Superior. Her Finnish grandmother had taught her how to use the loom, and the craft soothed her. The room held the aroma of the pumpkin candles she often burned while working in the evening.

Annie picked up a stack of rugs. "How many do you want? You said you'd sold out already?"

Anu nodded and produced a check from her purse. "I brought payment for all of them."

Annie glanced at the check as she took it. Over two thousand dollars. The money would help with paint for the buildings and other needed repairs. "This is a lot."

"I increased the price when they began to fly off the shelves. Tourists did not blink at the cost. Of course, they are worth it. I advertised them as Shades of Superior as we talked about. That seemed to draw attention." She looked around the room. "I would take thirty if you have them."

"I do." The check in Annie's jean pocket was for only ten. If Anu's shop sold all thirty in short order, it would be a much-needed windfall.

Anu's blue eyes crinkled in a smile. "Wonderful. I do not think it will take long to move them. We have the summer festival coming up, and they will sell quickly."

The good news lightened Annie's spirits, which had been on the floor since finding the body this morning. "Is that what you wanted to talk to me about? Getting more rugs?"

"It is something else. Do you ever sell any of your cottages?"

"No, they're just for rent."

Anu ran her hand over the rug still attached to the loom. "I love my shop, but I have been thinking about going to part time. I love it out here, and I thought it would be a wonderful place to retire among the pine trees where I can listen to the birds and the wildlife."

"I'm shocked. I never imagined you might retire."

"Neither did I. But I am getting older. I have started having someone else do the travel to Finland for me, which is helpful, but sometimes I long for a retreat where I can imagine I am back in Finland. Never would I move there because Bree and the children are here, but I should love to have a cabin with a sauna outside by the lake where I can go for a dip."

Annie wanted to accommodate her longtime friend, and her mind raced. "I do have a dilapidated cabin on the far side of the property. The area is overgrown, and the place needs a lot of work. I've never bothered to fix it up because it's so far from the rest of the cabins. I'd be willing to sell it to you for a small price if you want to fix it up. You'd need to put in a driveway and everything."

Anu's eyes widened. "I am not afraid of a reno. It sounds like something I would like. Square footage?"

"Two bedrooms in just under a thousand square feet. At least I think that's it. It's been ages since I've been out there."

A loon called a warbling tremolo, and a shudder ran down Annie's back. She curled her fingers into her palms and worked on keeping her breathing slow and easy. It was early for them to be sounding off.

"It sounds wonderful," Anu said. "Can I come back out tomorrow afternoon in the daylight and take a look?"

"Of course. I'll be happy to have someone love it."

And she'd be overjoyed to never have to think about the place where her life changed forever.

FIVE

JON SET DOWN THE CHAIN SAW FOR A MINUTE TO WIPE the moisture from his brow. The mercury hovered close to ninety, and the humidity was nearly as high. But his car could maneuver the driveway without risking its paint now. He took a sip of iced tea, then grabbed his saw again and went to the path to Lake Superior to chop back the vegetation.

A few minutes later, he stood on the sand with the waves rolling to shore and the scent of the water in his face. No one had tracked through this sand in years, and he set down his saw again, took off his sneakers, and stepped into the cold water of his childhood. The waves washed against his ankles and he waded out in his shorts. He stared out over the blue water. All the stories he'd heard growing up of the Big Sea Water came flooding back. About the Windigo and Michibeichu the lake dragon.

He'd forgotten how much he loved this place. He gazed to his right, toward the Tremelo Marina. Was Annie still there? She'd said she would never leave there, but time could change things. He shaded his eyes with his hand and stared at the pier and the boats rocking in the waves. A few people moved around, but he was too far away to make out any features.

If he hung around, he was likely to run into Annie, so why not do it on purpose when he was prepared to see her?

"Thinking about Annie?"

Jon turned at his dad's words. "Caught me."

Jon looked a lot like his dad when he was younger—same brown hair and green eyes, same height of six feet one. But Dad had lost twenty pounds since his stroke, and Jon didn't like the pale skin and frail muscles he now saw. He'd grown up thinking his dad was the most powerful man in the country—and his oratory in front of a judge and jury were legendary. Now he'd be hard to understand.

His dad walked to his side and looked down at the water's edge. "Never did understand how you let her get away."

"She wouldn't leave here. You know all that. I couldn't see making a living here. It's not large enough to support an orthopedic surgeon. It wouldn't be a lucrative career here."

"There was always Madison. It's close enough to drive."

True enough. But what had grated on Jon was how easily Annie was able to walk away from a life with him, especially when he was hurting over losing his mother. And the worst thing was, she hadn't immediately defended him when he was a suspect in the disappearance of the two girls he'd met in the Porcupine Mountains nine years ago. Didn't she know him well enough to be sure he was no killer? She was no Ruth like in the Bible. She didn't love him enough to leave here and strike out for a new life. He'd no sooner left town than she'd married his best friend too. He'd never understood it. But it wasn't worth arguing about with his dad.

"I'm thinking about going to see her so I can control how that all happens. Want to go along?"

If his dad was along, Annie would watch her tongue. Maybe that made him a coward, but he called it being smart.

His dad stared at him for a long minute. "You gotta do this yourself, boy. 'Sides, it's time for a nap."

"Want me to run you back to the Blue Bonnet?"

His dad shook his head. "Snoozing on the back deck sounds better."

Jon picked up the saw and headed toward the cabin. "I'll shower and get it over with."

"And I'll pray for you. Whatcha going to do if she's remarried since Nate died?"

The question stopped Jon in his tracks. That would be a hard pill to swallow for some reason. "You hear something about it?"

His dad meandered back to the house with Jon beside him. "She's a beauty. Stands to reason she moved on."

"I didn't move on." He wished he could call the words back. His dad would think he was pathetic. "I mean, no time. I have a busy life."

"I call it a lonely life."

That too. Jon often worked nights because of trauma cases, and the few times he'd tried to date, he'd been called out before the night was over. Few women were willing to put up with that kind of irregular schedule. He was beginning to dislike it himself. He came home to an empty house at night and watched TV until he fell asleep. He'd thought about getting a dog, but that didn't seem fair either. The animal would be alone too often without regular potty breaks.

But it was the life he'd chosen. He'd walked away voluntarily, and he had a good career. His reputation had grown to the point where he had to turn new patients over to one of his partners. It was everything he'd worked and prayed for.

Wasn't it?

/ / /

Annie stepped back to admire her work. The forest-green paint on the cabin blended with the color of the pine needles and the birch leaves fluttering in the wind. The moist air from the lake blew away the smell of paint fumes. She could hear Kylie talking with Taylor as they came this way from their fishing excursion.

Kylie burst through the hemlock trees holding a stringer of bluegill. "Look, Mommy! I caught two fish. Taylor caught the others, but they're all big enough to keep. Can we have fish for dinner?"

"Good job. Those are big ones. Take them to the fish shack, and I'll be along to help you clean them. Unless Taylor knows how to do it?" She lifted a brow in Taylor's direction.

Taylor was smiling and windblown with a flush on her cheeks from excitement. "It's been a while, but I think I can remember how to filet them. Kylie, you have to help descale them."

Kylie bounced on the toes of her sneakers. "That's my favorite part."

Annie dunked her paintbrush in a bucket of water. "And you usually come in covered in scales, so you'll need to hop in the shower."

"Maybe a swim first?"

The thought of her daughter in the same water as the body she'd found yesterday made her shudder. But she couldn't keep her out of the lake forever. She had to let go of her fears no matter how hard it was. What happened when Annie was nine was an isolated incident. This was a safe area.

"Okay, a swim first." Annie gave her daughter a quick hug. "Put the fish in the fridge when you're done."

"Okay, Mommy." Kylie trailed after Taylor to the fish shack down the path.

Annie finished washing out the paintbrush and hammered the top of the paint bucket. She turned toward the drive when she heard tires *pop* on the gravel. A red car rolled toward the parking lot, and it took a second for recognition to hit. Jon's sports car. Here at her place. He had to have come to see her on purpose, and her traitorous heart leaped.

Could he have come back here to find her? But no, that wasn't likely. She'd already heard he'd returned to get the family cottage ready to sell.

She turned toward his Jaguar as his tall form unfolded from under the wheel. The outer corners of his green eyes crinkled with his smile, and it was all she could do to hold her stern expression.

He looked good—too good. The years had been kind to him. She'd almost forgotten how handsome he was with his square jaw and sinewy muscles. His muscular legs and arms showed he still worked out. Did he still love cold sports, like surfing on Lake Superior and cross-country skiing? Maybe he went to a gym now instead of using logs and rocks to work out in the yard. The fancy car would indicate more civilized ways to keep fit.

And even in shorts, he somehow looked more polished than the teenager she'd fallen for so many years ago.

His smile wavered but didn't leave his tanned face. "Hello, Annie." He held out a cherry Popsicle. "I bring a peace offering."

Without thinking she took it. He nearly always had one in hand through the summer months. "Jon," she said in an even voice she hoped warned him not to get too friendly. "What are you doing here?"

She shot a glance toward the fishing shack and prayed Kylie and Taylor wouldn't come out while he was here. She wasn't prepared to explain a past relationship to her daughter. Kylie adored her father and wouldn't want to learn Annie had once loved another man.

This man.

He moved closer and shuffled from one foot to the other. "I thought it was the neighborly thing to do to let you know I was back in town. Dad's here too. He had a stroke."

"I was sorry to hear about it. Your dad's always been good to me."

Jon's mother had died in a hit-and-run the day before they broke up, and she pushed away the internal reel that played of that night. They'd both cried a lot that day.

"I'm sorry about your parents—and Nate. How'd it happen?"

"Their boat engine exploded, and they were too far from shore to make it. You know how cold and deep the water is out there. Their bodies were never recovered."

"And Nathan's body?"

"We didn't find him either." She didn't want to talk about her husband to his best friend.

"Superior never gives up her dead," he murmured. "And you're running things here all by yourself?"

She folded her arms across her chest. "For two years now."

"How's it going?"

"It's not easy. The economy has been down lately, and people are more apt to visit Sault Ste Marie or Mackinac Island than my little corner of the U.P."

He glanced around the parking lot at the vehicles there. "Looks like you have a full house right now."

"Pretty full."

As long as he stuck to small talk, she might get through

this. She unwrapped the cherry Popsicle and took a bite before it melted all over her hands.

Leave, leave, she silently urged him. It was so difficult to hold on to her composure around him. Did he still wear Eternity cologne? Once upon a time she'd thought his scent meant eternity together for them.

How wrong she'd been.

Kylie and Taylor came from the fishing shack with the cleaned fish.

Jon smiled at Kylie. "Nice plate of fish you have there. Looks like you missed a few scales. I'll have to show you my trick for getting them all."

Kylie's smile faded. "Daddy showed me how to get the scales off. He was the best at it."

Jon's smile vanished, and he nodded. "I'm sure he was."

Her back rigid, Kylie stalked past him and vanished into the house with Taylor.

Annie shrugged. "She's a daddy's girl and can get offended easily if she thinks someone is implying her dad wasn't the best at everything."

"I'll try to be careful."

Annie shifted her gaze to his car. "Looks like you're exactly where you wanted to be."

"It's a busier life than I'd expected. Not much time for a social life. Or even to see my dad. I'm taking off a few weeks to renovate the cottage, so you'll probably see me around. I thought I might rent a boat from you so I could go fishing."

"I have a few available. Rowboat or motor?"

"Motor. I want to be able to get into some of my favorite inlets without getting blisters from the oars."

His continued presence wore on her nerves. If this exchange today had proven one thing, it was that her heart hadn't fully healed from his defection, even though she'd thought it had. She'd have to be on her guard constantly around him.

"I'll deliver it to your cottage."

"I appreciate it."

He could get in his car and go away. But when he said his good-byes and got into the vehicle, she would have given anything to call him back.

SIX

BLUE JAYS SCOLDED ANNIE FROM THE CANOPY OF trees as she led Anu along the overgrown path to the dilapidated cabin in the woods. The forest smelled of pine and dead leaves. Annie had last been here with Jon that last night, so she hadn't been here in almost nine years.

The lock resisted the key at first, but she managed to wiggle it in and open the door. "No one has been in here for ages." Stale air rushed at her when she stepped in.

Memories pummeled her like a tsunami, and bile burned the back of her throat. That last night here had ruined everything—her purity, her self-respect, her relationship with Jon and with her parents.

Anu followed her into the main room, a space of about twenty by fifteen. The kitchen on the far end was comprised of an old wood cookstove and a few cabinets made of plywood. The floor was pine and looked flat and undamaged. The walls were pine, too, and so was the ceiling.

"Good space." Anu wandered to the kitchen. "I will gut this and put in white cabinets. Perhaps a quartz countertop. I love that the wood floors are all over. I will paint the walls white and leave the ceiling natural wood. The windows and doors will need to be replaced, and I noticed moss on the roof as we got close, so it will need to be redone."

Annie could see her vision. The pine contrasting with white would be light and airy. Modern yet a bit rustic. "I'm glad you aren't put off by the amount of work. I warned you it was rough." Annie pointed to a door to their left. "There's the main bedroom. The bath is here."

She opened another door beside the kitchen and winced at the state of the bathroom. A broken toilet and stained tub matched the dilapidated shower. The whole thing would need to be gutted.

Anu peeked in behind her. "Good size. I can make this cute. I do not need a tub so a tiled shower will suit me well." She backed out of the bathroom and turned to the bedroom. "If the bedroom is large enough, I will take it."

She twisted the knob and stepped into the space. Annie trailed her into the bedroom. An old iron twin bedstead and a table with an old lamp were the only furnishings, but the room could easily hold a king bed and more dressers.

"Oh, it is a wonderful size. I will not have to get a different bedroom set. Mine will fit in here nicely."

"And if I remember, there's a very large closet." Annie crossed the room and opened the closet door.

There was an odd smell she couldn't quite put her finger on. Maybe like something had died in here and left the faint trace of decay. She reached up to yank on the string to turn on the light. The walk-in closet had been empty the last time she'd been in here, and she blinked at the heap of clothing in the back corner.

Wait. That was more than clothing. She caught a glimpse

of hair. A body. No, two bodies. All piled in a heap as though someone had dropped them there.

"Oh dear Lord," Anu whispered behind her.

Annie reeled back and slammed the door. "I need to call Mason. I don't want to disturb any evidence."

Anu was pale and nodded. "I think they were women. The tops they wore." She shuddered. "And I saw a necklace."

Annie had seen lace and ruffles, too, but not the necklace. "It's hard to say how long they've been here since I haven't stepped foot inside in so long."

Mason answered on the first ring. "Sheriff Kaleva."

"Mason, I've just found what appears to be two female bodies in the closet of an empty cabin I own. Anu is here with me." Anu was his mother-in-law, and he might want to bring his wife to calm her down, though Annie thought the older woman was handling it well.

"In the cabin she was interested in buying?" Mason asked.

"Yes. It's the isolated one on the north edge of my property."

"I know where it is. I'll call forensics and we'll be there shortly. Don't touch anything."

"I closed the closet door and we'll leave the premises. We'll wait for you in the parking lot."

"Good."

The call ended, and Annie gestured for Anu to follow her back outside. "I'm sorry you had to see that."

"Do not worry, *kulta*. I am an old woman and have seen much in my life."

Back out on the walk toward the cabin, Anu looked back at the house. "I wish to buy this place."

Annie blinked. "Are you sure?"

"Death is a constant companion in our world. Those poor women did not likely die here. I saw no blood and nothing to dissuade me from settling here. I can even see the lake through the trees. It's very peaceful. We can discuss it later, but I do wish to buy it."

Annie had come to the same conclusion. The bodies had been dumped here, not murdered here. And she had no doubt it was murder. Two women wouldn't crowd into the back of a closet and die. This was something sinister.

They retraced their steps to the parking lot, and Annie's tension eased when she heard children laughing and splashing in the pool. The murmur of their parents' voices and the distant sound of a lawnmower brought back a sense of normalcy. She looked around for Kylie and waved when she saw her on the pier fishing with Taylor.

All was well here, but there was horrific news to be told once the identity of the women was determined. She hadn't been able to tell how they'd died. Or even when. But the lack of a strong scent of decay meant they'd been in that closet awhile. Maybe years. Mason would have to go back through missing persons data to find them.

She recalled the mental snapshot she'd stored away of the scene. At least one had been blonde. The only blondes she knew that were missing were the teenagers Penelope Day and Sophie Smith. But they'd disappeared in the Porcupine Mountains, not here.

A terrible thought shook her. Jon knew about this cabin. They'd been in it together a few days before they'd broken up. And when he'd left Rock Harbor, it had been under a cloud of suspicion related to the girls' disappearance. They'd had no proof, so he'd been allowed to go off to school, but some people still thought he had something to do with it. And now he was back.

/ / /

Annie never used to be so on guard around him, and seeing her on edge like that this morning had torn Jon up. She'd dropped off the boat and left without a word, though if she'd known Dad was inside, she might have stopped to say hello to him.

The room reeked of paint. Jon stepped back and studied the color on the living room's test wall. The light gray added a modern touch to the old place that buyers should like, though he would miss the old rustic feel that was about to vanish.

This place wouldn't be theirs any longer. It would be an ending he wasn't sure he was ready to face. Especially now that he'd seen Annie again. No matter how often he reminded himself she'd quickly married his best friend, seeing her again had stirred embers he thought went out long ago.

The front door banged, and he turned to see his dad stumble into the room. "Got tired of watching the lake, or was the sun too hot?" he asked his father.

"Neither. Something going on down at Annie's. Sheriff's car came screaming onto the property with the bubble light going. We should go see what's wrong—make sure she and the little girl are all right."

Jon's heart kicked in his chest, and he threw down the paintbrush. "You feel up to the ride?"

"Sure do." His dad hustled after him as fast as his awkward gait would allow.

Jon assisted him down the steps and into the Jag, then helped him with the seat belt before Jon slung himself under the steering wheel and peeled down the rutted dirt driveway. What could have happened at Annie's? A drowning? Another missing hiker? He prayed Annie and her daughter were all right.

He didn't try to baby the car over the bumps in the road as he zoomed down to Annie's marina. The sheriff's car was in the lot, and he saw Mason and Annie heading for the woods with one of the deputies in tow. Where was Kylie? A quick look around didn't reveal her location, but maybe she was with her nanny somewhere.

"Go on, catch up with her," his dad said. "I'll hang out on the dock with Anu. I can't walk over that rough ground anyway."

He hadn't noticed Anu on the dock until his dad mentioned her. "You sure?"

"Go!"

Jon's long legs ate up the yards between Annie and him, and she turned when she heard him crashing through the dry leaves.

She stopped, and Mason continued on with the deputy. "You shouldn't be here."

"Dad heard the siren and saw the commotion. I had to make sure you and Kylie were all right."

Her disapproving frown eased from between her eyes. "We're fine. This is a crime scene, though, and Mason won't want you here."

"Another missing camper?"

"No." Her lips clamped shut, and her gaze narrowed as if she was thinking about telling him something.

"What is it?"

"You remember the old cabin we never use?" Color swept up her neck, and she didn't hold his gaze.

The memories of that place hadn't let him be in all these years. "Of course."

She quit looking at the wildflowers and stared at him again. "Anu wants to buy it so I was showing her around. We found two bodies in the bedroom closet. They appear to be two women."

He gasped and took a step back. "Murdered?"

"I'm sure they were. But not recently. The coroner will have to tell us their identities and time of death. I don't know much more than that." Her gaze sharpened. "You ever go back there after that night, Jon?"

He frowned and shook his head in confusion. "I left a couple of days later, remember? I never went back. Why would you ask that? Did I leave something behind?"

There was something she wasn't saying that would explain the question in her blue eyes, but asking her wouldn't get him any answers. This was an investigation, and she wouldn't reveal any secrets or information about what had happened.

"Well, I can collect Dad and get out of your hair. He was very worried about you."

She glanced toward where his dad sat on a bench by Anu. "I'll go say hello. Mason won't want me messing in his investigation anyway."

She fell into step beside him, and they went out toward the older couple. His dad was smiling and relaxed, and Jon eyed him for a long moment. He hadn't dated since Mom died, and Jon hadn't seen him so comfortable in a woman's presence before. But then he'd known Anu a long time. She often joined them for a cookout in the old days. She'd been good friends with his mother.

His dad spotted them. "Beautiful Annie. You haven't changed."

They reached the bench, and she smiled down at him.

"Neither have you, Mr. Dunstan. When I heard you'd had a stroke, I thought I'd find you infirm and older, but you look great."

He gave her a wry grin. "Nice way to soothe th' old man. Anu here told me 'bout your gruesome discovery. Glad it wasn't anything to do with you or your little girl. Where is she, by the way? I'd like to meet her."

"She went to town with an employee to get ice cream. I'll bring her over sometime though." She glanced back toward the woods. "I'd better go, but I wanted to say hello."

Jon watched her hurry off, then glanced back at Anu. He might learn more from her.

SEVEN

FROM WHERE HE STOOD ON THE DOCK, JON STRAINED to hear anything from the cabin, but it was too far away. The only sound was seagulls cawing and waves lapping on the shore.

He settled onto the pier and hung his legs over the side while he waited for a lull in the conversation between his dad and Anu. When Dad took a swig from his water bottle, Jon saw his chance.

"So you're still going to buy the cabin?" he asked.

Anu smiled and nodded. "Oh, yes. It will be very charming. Just what I need."

"Big job? The last time I was in there, it was very rough."

"It will need to be completely gutted and redone. A new roof, kitchen, bathroom. But it has good bones, and I can see the lake from the porch. The seclusion will be most welcome."

"Which might be why someone had dumped two bodies."

His dad choked on his water, and Anu patted his back. "Are you all right, Daniel?"

"Fine, fine."

Since the stroke his dad sometimes had trouble swallowing. It worried Jon, but the doctor had said it wasn't uncommon.

Dad's choking spell had derailed Jon's question, and he wasn't sure how to bring it up again, but Anu folded her hands in her lap and answered without him having to prod her. "Death stalks us all, my dear Jon. The cabin is not to blame, nor does it hold on to any evil done in its walls."

"Neither of you could tell who the women were?"

Anu shook her head. "I saw a bit of blonde hair, but nothing distinguishable. And only a faint scent of decay remained, so they have been dead for quite some time. No blood either. Someone placed the poor souls there."

Blonde hair. His mind jumped to the teenage girls who went missing nine years ago. Could it possibly be them? He gave a slight shake to his head. They'd disappeared in the Porkies. Why bring their bodies all the way down here? That made no sense.

But Annie's reaction made perfect sense. She knew Mason had suspected him. He'd always wondered if she believed him when he said they were alive and well when he left them at the Lake of the Clouds. He shouldn't have been hurt, but the pain in his chest told him he still cared what she thought about him.

A movement caught his eye, and he looked back toward the woods where Mason and Deputy Montgomery appeared. Annie walked beside Mason and was listening intently to whatever he was saying. He wanted to join them and hear what they'd found, but didn't all the TV shows indicate a murderer hung around the scene? His being here could implicate him even more. Maybe the whole town thought he was involved.

Don't overreact. It could be some other blonde women. Even now, Mason might know the identities.

Mason stopped and looked out at the pier where they all congregated. He said something to Annie, and they walked toward the dock while Doug went to meet a van pulling into the parking lot. Probably the forensic team.

Jon tore his gaze from the forensic members as they exited the van and smiled at Mason. "Sheriff."

"I heard you were back in town," Mason said. "I'd like to have a chat if you don't mind."

That didn't sound good. "Of course. Here?"

Mason glanced at Anu and shook his head. "Let's sit on Annie's porch. You can tag along, Annie."

She had her head down and wasn't looking at Jon. Another bad sign. He followed them across the parking lot and through the yard to Annie's cottage. The scent of beef wafted through the screen door. She hadn't been in there, so either the nanny was cooking or she had something in the Crock-Pot.

Mason gestured to one of the rockers on the porch. "Have a seat." He settled on one of the chairs, and Annie went to the swing.

She still hadn't said anything to Jon, and he glanced at her expression before he sat in the chair. Shock? Fear? He couldn't read her with her head bent and her blonde hair falling across her face. Maybe she wanted it that way.

Mason took out a pen and pad. "You already know Annie and Anu found two bodies in the old cabin."

"I heard that, yes. Did you identify them?"

He shouldn't have asked. Better to wait for Mason's questions and answer only his queries. Stupid, stupid.

"Not conclusively, but they appear to be two blonde females. The clothing appears to be something younger women would wear. We all know two blondes went missing nine years ago, and you were the last to see them."

This was bad, very bad. He stared directly into Mason's gaze. "That you know of. I didn't hurt those girls, Mason."

"You knew about the abandoned cabin?"

"I'm sure Annie told you I did."

Her head came up when he spoke her name, and tears shimmered in her blue eyes. Fear. That was what she was feeling. Fear he might have done this or fear for his freedom?

Mason fixed him with a steely stare. "It would go better for you if you are honest here. I'm not saying you hurt them intentionally, but there are cliffs and dangerous areas in the Porkies. If they fell, you might have thought you had to hide them."

Hands on his knees, Jon leaned forward. "Sheriff, those girls were alive and well when I left the park. I didn't do this. I wouldn't hurt anyone. I'm a doctor, for Pete's sake! I have dedicated my life to helping others. Don't waste your time looking at me when you should be finding the real killer."

He rose and went toward the steps. "I'm taking my dad home. I've said all there is to say."

As he walked away, he heard Annie say, "What would have been his motive?"

"Could have been anything," Mason said. "An accident he tried to hide. Rape. Or just because he wanted to."

"I believe him, Mason."

"You would," was all Mason answered.

It was a small comfort to hear her stand up for him, even now. Shoulders stiff, he stalked toward the dock. For all his protests, he realized he might be in big trouble here.

Legs dangling over the side, Taylor sat on the dock by the beach and watched the little girl splash around in the water. Her mother had always said Taylor had to have goals, but she wasn't sure if Mother would approve of having achieved this goal. She'd roll over in her grave if she realized Taylor was here at this place. In fact, she'd likely take a hairbrush to her.

Taylor suppressed a smile at the thought of defying her dead mother in such a significant way. She'd been unable to stand against the whirlwind called Mother all her life. What did that make her? Smart, gutless, or something in between?

Annie had been welcoming and friendly so far, but that didn't mean much. Most people could turn kindness on and off like a faucet when it suited them. Taylor liked Kylie though.

"Taylor, look at me!" The little girl dove under the cold waves until her feet disappeared.

Taylor watched for what seemed like too long. She was about to hop into the water herself when Kylie's head bobbed up by her feet, and the little girl's cold hand clamped around her ankle.

She bit back a scream. "You're freezing!"

Kylie's slicked-back hair made her blue eyes and smile seem bigger. "You should get in. It's great."

"I think I'll wait until the water warms up."

"That doesn't ever happen. You get used to the cold."

"Is that why your lips are blue and quivering?"

When Kylie started to splash her, Taylor pulled up her legs and scooted back. "Oh no you don't." She glanced at her watch, a relic that used to be her mother's. "We should go help your mom with dinner."

"Okay." Kylie swam toward the shore, then stood to walk the rest of the way out of the water. She grabbed a towel draped over a chair and pulled it around her shoulders. "That feels good. I was colder than I thought. Can I have some hot chocolate?"

"If it's okay with your mom. We can make chocolate chip cookies, too, if she doesn't mind."

With only a day on the job, Taylor was still feeling her way through what she was allowed to do.

"She won't care. Mommy always has so much to do. I'm glad you're here to help her. She's been so sad."

Taylor pressed her lips together. What did Little Miss Perfect have to be sad about? "That seems odd. She lives in this gorgeous place, and she has you."

"Well, my grandma and grandpa died, and so did Daddy. And we don't have a lot of money. Mommy says Grandpa had lots of debt, and Daddy was self-employed. He worked on boats, and his life insurance wasn't there." Her forehead wrinkled as she sought for the word. "Left?"

"Lapsed?"

The little girl brightened. "That's it. He forgot to pay it or something. But Mommy rented the island and fixed things up. She works really hard. She said the resort belongs to me, and she wants it to be here for me when I am old." Kylie rubbed the towel over her wet face. "She cries sometimes at night. So do I. I miss them too. How far away is heaven?"

Taylor blinked. "I-I have no idea. A long way away." She figured saying she didn't believe in heaven would be a sure way to get her fired.

"Do you think Daddy can see how well I've learned to swim? Can Grandma hear when I tell her I miss her?"

"Sheesh, kid, you ask a lot of hard questions. You need to talk to your mom about that kind of stuff."

"I do. She says no one knows for sure, but she thinks they know we're okay and they're looking forward to seeing us again.

She said when we get to heaven when we're old, it will feel like a blink of an eye to them. That seems weird."

The whole conversation was weird and uncomfortable. Taylor struggled to find a way to change the topic. "Did you just learn to swim? You're really good at it."

They fell into step to walk to the main cabin where Annie and Kylie lived. Taylor hadn't been inside yet.

"Mommy had me take lessons last summer, but the coach said I was a natural."

The little girl took Taylor's hand in a gesture that warmed her. Kylie was so caring and accepting of who Taylor was. She had never even mentioned her garish red hair or the tattoo of an elephant on her arm other than to say she liked them.

Taylor would never be as beautiful as other women she saw, so she'd settled for something that made her stand out, something *she* liked, even if no one else did. And her expectations had mostly been proven right over the years. Don't assume anyone will like you. Don't look for approval from anyone but yourself. Please yourself because what other people think doesn't matter.

The problem with that was she realized she wanted approval on some level. Living for herself had proven lonely these past few months. Even though Mom had never given her anything but slaps and tight lips of distaste, it had been better than the same reaction from strangers.

Taylor gave a slight shake of her head and followed Kylie to the porch of the cottage. From here she could hear music playing. Tim McGraw was crooning out "Live Like You Were Dying," a maudlin song if she'd ever heard one. She'd been dying and not living most of her life, and the song was a reminder of that.

The scent of something chocolaty like brownies hung in the

air, so Annie hadn't started the corn yet, and Taylor felt a wash of relief. She hadn't wanted to appear to be shirking her duties of helping with the cooking too.

The only thing that could derail her plans was to get fired—something she was determined couldn't happen. She slipped her hand into her pocket and found the necklace that brought her luck. She'd need it.

EIGHT

THE WAIL OF THE LOONS.

Annie woke with a start, and the sound of the loons brought panic surging to her throat. The scent of pine wafted in through her screened window. The room was totally black.

You're okay and safely in your bed.

The loon's call came again, and she reached over to flip on her sound machine. Nothing. The power was out.

She sat up and reached for her phone to turn on the flashlight. The illumination pushed back her fear a bit. The lump in her throat refused to go down, and her pulse jittered along her veins. It was only on nights like this that she thought about moving away. As long as she didn't have to listen to the loons, life was good. But the second she was forced to hear their eerie call, she plunged right back into the nightmare when she was nine.

A *creak* caught her attention, and she swung her feet out of bed to rest her soles on the cool wood floors. Was Kylie awake? She hurried out the door in her pajamas and down the hall to her daughter's room. The flashlight on her phone illuminated Kylie's form sleeping on her side in the bed.

The noise came again, and Annie turned toward the kitchen. She made her way through the dark house. The light from her phone didn't push back the shadows much. She reached the kitchen and shone the flashlight around the space. Nothing but her neat counters and appliances. The noise came from her left, and she turned to shine the light that way.

The door to the attached garage stood open and swayed in some kind of breeze, which shouldn't be happening. If not for needing to protect Kylie, she would have run to get her gun, but her daughter was sleeping down the hall, and Annie couldn't leave the door open with her back turned.

She approached the opening and focused the light out into the garage. Her truck loomed in the darkness. Beyond it she could see the open main garage door.

The hair rose on the back of her neck. The door was operated by an opener. Someone would have had to have been inside to open it. She slammed the connecting kitchen door shut and locked it, then ran back the way she'd come. She snatched her gun from the safe in her bedroom closet, then ran into Kylie's room. She shut the door behind her and locked it, then checked to make sure her daughter was safe.

Kylie's chest rose and fell in easy movements. She hadn't noticed anything wrong.

Annie went into Kylie's closet and pulled the door shut behind her before calling 911.

"Nine one one, what is your emergency?" the male dispatcher asked.

"I may have an intruder. I'm locked in the bedroom with my daughter." Annie told him about the open garage doors.

"I have a deputy out that way. He should be there in five minutes. Stay on the line until he comes."

"I need to guard my daughter. I'll watch for him. Thank you." She ended the call. She'd spent too many years in law enforcement to allow her attention to be diverted when she needed to be on guard.

The closet door squeaked as she opened it. She shone the flashlight around the room. Empty except for her sleeping daughter. Should she scoop up Kylie and take her with her to flag down the deputy? Leaving her here alone wasn't an option.

She shook her head. Better to awaken Kylie. It seemed an eternity before Annie saw the sweep of headlights on the drive and the red strobe atop the deputy's car as it rolled to a stop in front of her cottage. She stuck her gun in the waistband of her pajamas, then unlocked the bedroom door and lifted Kylie in her arms. The little girl mumbled but nestled against her chest and didn't awaken.

Annie rushed for the front door and leaned Kylie's weight against the wall as she fumbled with the lock. It clicked, and she stepped back to get it open. When she stepped out onto the porch, Deputy Montgomery was hefting his bulk out of the car to lumber toward her.

The beam of his flashlight touched her face. "You okay, Annie?"

"Yes, we're fine. Can you search the house and make sure no one is inside?"

He nodded and turned back to his car to open the passenger side. "You and Kylie can wait in my car. Lock it up. I'll be right back."

She sank into the seat with Kylie in her arms. Her bare feet touched crumpled food sacks and napkins. He shut the door behind her, and she locked it.

His light bobbed around the house before disappearing into the garage. It reappeared as he went to the front and inside the house before the lights came on. Maybe the power was back.

It seemed an eternity before Doug returned. She unlocked the door and opened it. "Anything?"

His broad face was somber. "Someone shut off your main breaker, Annie. The garage door to the backyard had a busted lock so I think he went in that way, opened the main garage door, and turned off your breaker."

"But why?"

"Maybe a prank by some teenagers? You say the door to the kitchen was open too?"

Her pulse fluttered in her neck, and she nodded. "Can I go in now?"

"I'd like you to see if anything looks disturbed."

She nodded again and carried Kylie back inside. The little girl didn't stir when Annie put her into bed and backed out of the room.

Annie walked around the house from room to room but found nothing out of place. Maybe whoever had done this hadn't come inside. Or had he come in and stared at her while she was sleeping? Could it have been the same man who dumped the bodies in the old cabin?

She suppressed a shudder and vowed to get some outside cameras. This couldn't happen again.

/ / /

After the shock the night before, Annie relished the warmth of the sun on her arms and face as she painted one of the cabins. Moving her muscles and staying busy helped her forget that someone had tried to scare—or even harm—her. Kylie swung lazily in the tire swing, and Taylor sat on a blanket nearby sunning herself.

The roar of a boat motor rose above the sound of Lake Superior's wind and waves. Annie shaded her eyes from the bright June sun, and her pulse skipped when she recognized the huge boat approaching the dock of Tremolo Marina and Cabin Resort.

Max Reardon's megawatt smile focused on her, and she waved. One of his crew hands hopped off the boat and wound a rope around a piling, then steadied the rocking craft while Max stepped onto the dock. A sudden wave nearly pitched him into the water, and he yelled at the young man.

"It's not his fault," Annie said. "The waves are brutal today."

Max frowned but didn't argue with her.

No one would mistake Max for anything but what he was—someone used to the best in life. His slacks held an impeccable crease, and his shoes screamed Italian leather. Those brown eyes were hard to resist, and Annie had been in awe of him ever since he'd leased Tremolo Island after her parents died. That lease had been a lifeline for her. He'd paid handsomely for the life lease, which gave him the rights to make improvements and use the property for his lifetime. Plus, he paid a yearly stipend. The lump sum he'd given her up front had paid for much needed improvements to the dock and pier. Without it she would have had to close the resort.

He was easily pushing sixty-five to her thirty-three, and she'd never been around anyone so wealthy. It was interesting to see how the other half lived. She didn't care for his temper though. It reminded her too much of her dad's constant yelling.

"Good morning," she said.

His gaze swept over her. "You made the trip out here worth every bit of seasickness."

Oh sure. Like faded denim shorts and a Finlandia University

tee did anything to highlight her figure. She was certain she had paint on her face too. "Seasick? I would have guessed you could handle bigger waves than the Big Sea Water could throw your way."

A dimple flashed in his left cheek. "I managed to persevere."

Kylie sidled up beside Annie and edged toward Max. "Did you bring me a sucker?"

"Would I come out here without a lollipop?" He produced a grape one from his shirt pocket and handed it to Kylie.

She grinned and unwrapped it, then stuck it in her mouth and sat on the dock with her legs dangling over the choppy Lake Superior waves. Taylor stared from the blanket too. Max's looks and charm served as a magnet to women of all ages.

"Don't let the waves grab you," Annie told her daughter.

"I won't, Mommy."

She turned back to Max. "It's not time for your lease payment, so what can I do for you this morning?"

"I stopped by to invite you to a dinner party I'm having at the lodge next week. Saturday, not this coming Saturday but the next one. I wanted to give you plenty of time."

Her smile tried to slip away, but she held it in place. "I-I wish I could, but I don't like the island."

"I wanted to show you what I've done with the place. I've cleared some of the brush and have spruced up the lodge. Wait until you see the additions I've made."

If it was different, maybe it would dispel the nightmares she'd had about the place. But since she hadn't stepped foot on the island in all these years, the thought of seeing those towering pines again made her hand stray to the scar on her neck. The scar on her heart from that night went much deeper than the one the knife wound had left.

"I'll think about it, but that's all I can promise for now. What time is it?"

"Six o'clock. I can send the boat for you so you don't have to navigate in the dark on the way home."

He was always so thoughtful, which added to his charm. She hated to disappoint him. "I'd need to find someone to watch Kylie."

"You can bring her."

She was shaking her head before he stopped talking. "I don't want Kylie there."

He gave her a quizzical glance and shrugged before he handed her a thick embossed card. "Stick this on your bulletin board and think about it."

"I will."

He glanced toward the buildings lining the water. "Looks like all your buildings could use some paint. It'll take you a long time by yourself. Want me to send a crew over? I'd be glad to help out."

"I took some time off from work. I can manage, but thanks." She didn't want to be beholden to anyone, even though she had no idea how she was going to get it done with the day-to-day duties of cleaning cabins and cleaning up the grounds. And that didn't even take into account keeping the boats in good shape and managing the marina.

Not enough hours in the day. But she couldn't afford to hire a professional painter. And Taylor could help as well. Annie would try to get done all she could on her vacation.

She walked him back to his boat and waved him off before returning to her daughter, who was still savoring her sweet treat.

"Why don't you like the island, Mommy? I'd like to see it sometime. It looks really pretty from the boat."

Annie had never told her about Sarah because she didn't want to scare her, but maybe it would reinforce her warnings about strangers. Kylie was old enough to hear at least a bit of the story. "I had a sister named Sarah. A stranger snatched her away one night out on the island. That's why we always use the code word so you know not to go with anyone who doesn't have it. What's our code?"

"Tremolo," Kylie said.

"Very good. What do you do if a stranger tries to get you in a car or boat?"

"Scream and fight. Don't go along with him."

She hugged her daughter. "You're so smart. Want to help me paint?"

Kylie's blue eyes widened. "Can I?"

"I could use the help." She gave her little girl a small container of paint and a trim brush, then set her to work around the door of the cabin.

Annie touched the scar on her neck. Whoever took Sarah was long gone after twenty-four years, so why did her fear for her daughter never go away?

Her phone rang, and she saw it was Kade. "Hey, boss, what's up?"

"Sorry to bother you on your vacation, but we've had a call from a distressed mother. Her son was camping out near Sleeping Bay, not far from you, and is overdue checking in via satellite phone. Would you have time to see if he's stranded on the beach there?"

"Any excuse to stop painting would be welcome. I'll run out and take a look." She ended the call and handed off her paint roller to Taylor.

She'd find the camper and be back in a jiffy.

NINE

JON SHOULD BE WORKING AND NOT OUT HERE ON Superior, but the blue water had called to him this morning. Two hours, that was all. But it would be enough to recharge. The motor's thrum blended with wind and waves out in Sleeping Bay. Jon, hand on the throttle, veered toward the tip where he'd always found good fishing. He started to bypass a campsite near where the sand disappeared into the pine and deciduous forest, then paused as his gaze took in the destruction around the campfire.

He lifted his voice over the motor's sound and aimed for the shore. "Hello?"

Clothing lay strewn about, and the tent was partially collapsed. The wood in the firepit had been scattered, and the cooler was open, its contents dumped out.

Was that a cry?

Black bears roamed up here, but predation against humans was rare. And wolves had plenty of food so they'd be unlikely to attack a camper. Mountain lions had begun to repopulate up here, too, but they were aloof, and he didn't think it likely one of them had attacked a campsite.

The boat's hull bumped sand, and Jon tossed the anchor overboard before he stepped over the side. He sucked in his breath at the cold water, then waded through thigh-high waves to the shore. "Anyone here? You need help?"

Gulls squawked, but he could swear he'd heard a faint call for help. He peered inside the damaged tent. Empty. "Anyone here?" A kayak was partially hidden in the bushes by the forest's edge.

Should he call the Coast Guard for help? He took out his phone. No bars. He was on his own here since the small boat had no marine phone. He walked farther from the water and stepped into the shade of the forest. The scent of pine and last year's dead leaves rushed over him. A faint trail led away from the shore and back toward a lane out of the woods. There were no vehicles as far as he could see.

"Anyone here?" He listened but heard nothing this time. Maybe it had been a gull or an eagle.

He retraced his steps back toward the campsite, but a movement in the bushes stopped him. A white shoe appeared, and he rushed to push back the foliage.

A young man clad only in gym shorts lay on his side under the shrubs. He looked fresh out of high school. Scratches marred his face, and mud caked his hands and legs. Mosquito bites reddened his skin in many places. He blinked bleary blue eyes and licked his lips before trying to sit up.

"Steady." Jon supported his back. "Follow my finger."

The young man's eyes tracked his finger as it moved. "I don't think you have a concussion. Are you hurt anywhere?" Jon ran his hands over the man's arms and legs. No broken bones, just cuts and contusions from what Jon could tell. He wished he had his stethoscope to check out his heart and lungs.

The man shook his head. "Sore. Two dudes attacked me, but

I got away. I don't have anything valuable, so I don't know what they wanted."

Jon helped the man to his feet and steadied him as they went back to the campsite. "Did you recognize anyone?"

"Never seen them before. I'm not from here though."

When they reached the campsite, Jon snagged a beach towel from the ground and draped it around the young man's shoulders. "What's your name?"

"Eddie. Eddie Poole." He dropped onto a log and put his face in his hands. "Got any water?"

"Sure." Jon saw a bottle of water in the sand and grabbed it instead of going back to the boat. He uncapped it and handed Eddie the bottle.

The camper took a long swig. "Thanks. I don't think I want to stay out here any longer. Can you help me get back to town? I don't think I can paddle my kayak."

"You bet. I'd call for help but there are no cell towers out here. Did the guys who attacked you say anything?"

"Nothing that made sense. The big dude said something about me being a fast runner, which would make the game more fun."

Game? Jon shook his head. Nothing made sense.

His best bet was to head for Annie's place. It wasn't far, and he could call for help from there. The sheriff needed to investigate the assault, and Eddie would need help getting all his stuff gathered up.

"Let's go in my boat. We can come back later for your things. I'd like to get you to a hospital for X-rays and neuroimaging tests of your head to make sure you don't have a concussion." He omitted his worry about a TBI. A traumatic brain injury would be much more serious—and obvious.

"What do you remember after you got away from the men?"

"Nothing much. Just bits and pieces."

Uh-oh. Retrograde amnesia was a poor sign. Jon wanted an MRI or CT scan pronto.

Eddie wobbled when he rose. "I'm pretty woozy."

Jon held on to his elbow and helped him manage the choppy waves to the motorboat. Eddie practically fell inside it before managing to crawl to a seat and get settled. Jon pulled up the anchor and started the engine.

They'd barely gotten out of Sleeping Bay when Eddie started throwing up over the side. The nausea increased the likelihood of a brain injury, and Jon didn't like the look of him. He needed to test his reflexes and his cranial nerve function. He throttled up the motor and headed for Annie's as fast as the old motor could go.

/ / /

The lake breeze cooled her hot face, and Annie slowed the motor on her boat as she scanned the sandy shore. The young man had a satellite radio and hadn't missed checking in during his month-long trek across the U.P. until now. With the discovery of the bodies yesterday and the camper two days ago, she was on high alert at a report like that.

The sun glared off the water and practically blinded her, and she shaded her eyes with her hand. Was that another motor she heard? She cut the engine and the sound grew closer. She recognized the boat as one of hers before she placed the man piloting it.

Jon had picked up more of a tan since yesterday, and the windblown look of his hair was more like the young man she first fell in love with. Her gaze went to the other man with him lying across the bench, his head resting on the boat's railing.

"Ahoy! You need help?" she called.

Jon waved and the engine cut off in time for the boat to slew close enough for her to grab hold and tie the two crafts together. "I was on my way to the marina in hopes you were there. I found this guy injured near a campsite. He's suffering mostly from hypothermia, I think. He was in his underwear when I found him, and I got him dressed in clothing I found strewn around the site. He's dehydrated too."

Annie assessed the young man's pale skin. "Are you Eddie Poole?"

His blue eyes widened, and he nodded. "My parents called you?"

"They did. I was out here looking for you. You missed a check-in with them."

"They're on the protective side, which is why I wanted to do this by myself before I started college." His smile was more like a grimace on his muddy face. "I clearly made a mistake with that idea."

"He was throwing up, but his pupils looked good. I checked," Jon said.

"I get seasick, and it's really choppy today," Eddie said. "My head doesn't hurt."

She handed over a bottle of water. "More water. And I have some beef sticks that are pretty good. Food will help your strength."

"I am hungry," he admitted.

She gave him a beef stick, then glanced at Jon. "Let's take him to the marina and warm him up. I can run him to the hospital in Houghton faster in my truck."

Jon released the rope between the two boats. "Glad you happened along. I'll see you there."

Once his boat roared off, she pushed her engine hard and

reached the dock before the smaller craft Jon had rented from her. How had he stumbled upon the guy? She didn't want to think about the two missing girls again, but her mind wouldn't leave it alone. Jon had left the area right after the girls went missing, and while she'd never believed he was involved, wasn't it at least a little strange the hikers vanished as soon as he returned?

On the surface he appeared to be in Rock Harbor only to get the cottage ready to sell, but was there more to it? She tied off at the dock and stepped ashore to wait on Jon's boat. Letting her emotions rule her investigation wouldn't be wise, but it might be difficult to think objectively around him. Talking to Kade about this would be necessary.

He would expect her to look objectively at Jon's whereabouts and motives for being here. If she couldn't investigate with honesty, she had no business being part of the law enforcement team on the forest property. A law enforcement officer had to be ready to follow the trail no matter where it led.

But she didn't have to like it.

When they arrived, she tied up Jon's boat and took Eddie's arm as he disembarked. He seemed a little weak and shaky so she kept a grip on him as they headed for the shore.

Jon hurried to take Eddie's other elbow. "I've got him. Easy. Let me know if you feel like you might vomit."

She kept her hand on Eddie too. This was her job, not Jon's. Owing him anything might make keeping control of the investigation even trickier. When they reached the grassy area, she got Eddie settled on a bench before checking his pulse and breathing again. He seemed stronger and less rattled.

"Let's run over to the hospital," she said.

Eddie shook his head. "I feel much better. There's nothing

seriously wrong—just cuts and bruises. Jon said I didn't have a concussion, and I know nothing is broken. I don't have insurance, so there's no need to rack up a high bill in the ER."

"Let me check your reflexes and pupils again," Jon said.

After a few minutes Jon stood and stepped back. "Pupils and reflexes are all right. Watch for any vision disturbances, a headache, or numbness or tingling in your extremities. If any of those occur, have someone call an ambulance."

"I'm fine," Eddie said with a trace of impatience.

They couldn't force him to go, and he seemed coherent and in charge. "Can you tell me what happened?"

He launched into a tale of being chased while she jotted it down on a notepad. "One guy talked about a game? Any idea what he meant?"

"Not a clue." Eddie rubbed his forehead and looked out over the water. "I want to get my kayak and go back. I don't think I want to run the risk of seeing those guys again. I've had all I want of hiking by myself for now."

Jon glanced at her. "You're the law here. Your call, Annie. I can run out and grab his kayak."

"I'll take him out to get it. I want to check the site for any evidence."

She could have done it later, but to her shame, she wanted to be around Jon a little while longer. She should know better. He'd hurt her once, and she might be setting herself up for more.

TEN

JON STEERED THE BOAT BACK OUT THE WAY THEY'D come. Waves slapped the boat's metal hull as he eyed Annie's silhouette outlined in the bow by the glaring sun.

Eddie sat in the middle of the boat and watched her with an appreciative expression Jon didn't like. Coming back here had been a mistake, but he was in too far to leave now. His dad would want him to see the remodel and sale of the cabin through to the finish.

He raised his voice and pointed. "There's the beach." He slowed the motor and guided the craft in to just offshore.

Annie jumped overboard in her khaki shorts and pulled the boat closer to the sandy shore before Jon tossed the anchor overboard.

Eddie swung his legs over the side. "I'll get my kayak. Thanks for the help today."

"We can tow your kayak behind the boat," Annie said. "No need for you to paddle all that way back after your ordeal."

"I'd rather paddle. It will feel good to move my muscles."

She nodded and splashed through the two-foot-deep water to the shore. She took out her phone to take pictures of the disarray at the campsite. He shut off the engine and watched her wander down the shoreline a bit before he went to join her.

She jumped when he spoke behind her, and he put his hand on her shoulder. "I found him over this way."

"I think his attackers came ashore here." She moved away from his touch and pointed out drag marks in the sand. He felt a pang for the way things used to be. He said nothing and led her to the crushed vegetation and shrubs where he'd found the young man. She snapped more pictures before retracing her steps to the campsite.

Eddie had already packed up his tent and was stuffing his strewn belongings into a backpack. Jon was satisfied with his color, and Eddie didn't look like he might keel over now, though he kept shooting anxious glances into the forest's shadowy recesses.

"Anything else you remember about the attack?" Annie asked.

Eddie shook his head. "It all happened so fast. I told you everything."

"Okay. I'm going to take a look around."

Jon didn't like the idea of her going off on her own. "I'll come with you."

She lifted a brow. "I can handle any attack, Jon. I'm trained law enforcement, and I'm usually on my own."

He didn't like it, but he nodded. She'd been living life without him for years and had done well for herself. Her safety wasn't his job, but he couldn't help tracking her with his gaze until she vanished into the forest.

Eddie zipped the tent bag. "I don't think she should be in there by herself."

"You heard her. She won't welcome either of us implying she's incapable of handling the situation."

Eddie pulled on his lower lip. "I hope she doesn't take long. I want to get out of here."

Jon hefted the bag with the tent and stuffed it into a dry bag before he stowed it in the bow of the kayak. "Your eyes are bright, and you have color in your cheeks. I think you'll be okay. You can go ahead and get started, and we'll catch up with you."

Eddie nodded and put his belongings in the other dry bag and stashed it in the kayak. He shoved the kayak to the edge of the water and climbed in, then picked up the paddle. "See you there."

Jon listened to the *slap* of the paddle on the water for a moment before sidling to the forest's edge. Where was she? Were those men out there watching and waiting for a chance to grab her, or was he letting his imagination run wild? Eddie's attack had been over for hours, and the men would have hightailed it out of here before law enforcement showed up.

At least that was the logical thing to do. No one ever said criminals were logical though.

He heard something and tilted his head to listen. A bird or a cry from Annie? He didn't wait to find out but plunged into the cooler understory of the woods. His sneakers crunched through last year's fallen leaves and dead pine needles, and he paused a minute to see if the sound came again. Nothing but the noise of birds twittering in the branches overhead.

He was no frontiersman, so following her trail wasn't in his list of talents. Which way would she have gone? A few rocks poked above the moss and vegetation in the small clearing, and several caves in the hillside stood on the other end of the open area. He'd never explored this section of the U.P. before. Annie might know it like her favorite snowmobile trail.

"Looking for me? I told you I'd be fine."

He turned at her voice, and she emerged from a small cave. "Find anything?"

She brushed dust from her hands and nodded. "Looks like they holed up in this cave. There was a fire in the mouth of it, and the embers were still warm. No real clues except for the sneaker tread in the dirt. I took pictures and will run it through analysis when I get to the office and see if I can identify what brand of shoes they were wearing."

"Eddie was eager to leave, so I told him we'd catch up with him."

She nodded. "Let's get going. I don't think there's anything else helpful here."

That hadn't gone well. He followed her and realized he'd been useless.

/ / /

The scent of fresh paint lingered on the breeze as Jon parked in the drive and exited his Jaguar. He wanted to check out the progress before he joined his dad at the Blue Bonnet Bed-and-Breakfast. Martha Heinonen would keep his father well cared for until he got there. She'd been happy to see him again.

He frowned as he neared the porch. The front door swung open in the wind and slammed back against the siding. He bounded up the steps and grabbed it before it could smash again. When he closed it, a slash of red paint scarred the exterior of the door.

Justice for Penelope.

Penelope Day was one of the two girls who had gone missing nine years ago. Not a day went by that he didn't wonder what had happened to her and Sophie Smith. If he'd acted differently, would they still be around? His behavior wasn't something he was proud of. And what if the killer had dumped the bodies at Annie's? It would put him in the bull's-eye of suspicion again.

Was there any more damage? He yanked open the door and stepped into the living room. Sean had already repaired the wood floor and removed the kitchen cabinets. Jon wandered through the space and saw no more graffiti, so he went back outside and walked around the house. More red paint marred the back door.

Leave now or face the town's wrath.

People in town hadn't forgotten the incident, and maybe they never would. Small towns had long memories, and he was sure the discovery of the bodies yesterday had spread through the grapevine quickly. What had he been thinking to come back here? He'd been comfortable in his practice in Rochester.

But not happy. Not content. Maybe he never would be.

He touched the paint. Still damp. Whoever had done this hadn't been gone more than an hour. It would be a good idea to put up some security cameras. He pulled out his phone and dialed the sheriff's office. When the dispatcher answered, he told her about the vandalism, but her bored tone told him little would be done about it.

This was hardly life or death. It would be up to him to discover who hated him and what he should do about it.

He got back in his car and drove through Rock Harbor, down Whisper Pike to Houghton Street and past the businesses that comprised the downtown. Tourists gaped at his sports car, and he gave a little wave. The Jag attracted attention everywhere he went, and it was beginning to wear on him. Maybe he should get an SUV.

The Blue Bonnet had been built by a famous captain from

the area so his wife could watch for his return, and it was the last house on Houghton Street before it curved into Negaunee. Bree's lighthouse home was next door.

Gravel popped under his tires, and he parked in a spot to the left of the bed-and-breakfast. The scent of lemon wax and some kind of pine cleaner greeted him when he stepped into the foyer and went past the gleaming wood reception desk into the parlor with its Victorian furniture. The pink cabbage-rose furniture was more comfortable than it looked. Here in the parlor, he caught an appetizing whiff of something beefy cooking.

Martha Heinonen sat with his father at a game table with a Scrabble board spread out between them. Though in her sixties, Martha's skin glowed a healthy hue of pink and was infused with fresh air and hard work. Strands of silver were just beginning to highlight her hair, and her exuberance made her even more attractive. Dressed in a pink-flowered dress with a soft skirt that swirled around her still-shapely calves, she looked every inch the lady. Someone had once told her she resembled the monarch Queen Elizabeth, and since then she'd played up any likeness to the hilt, a fact Jon's father found fascinating.

"There you are, dear boy," Martha said. "I wondered if you'd be home in time for dinner. I have homemade pasties baking."

"They smell delicious," Jon said.

Martha sent a flirtatious smile his dad's direction. "It's all I can do to keep your father out of them until dinner."

"It's been a long time since I've had such good food," his dad said. "Not since my wife died."

There was definitely something brewing between the two, even though they'd only been here two days. And while Jon didn't begrudge his dad some happiness, he didn't want him to rush into anything. And he didn't want someone to think he'd make a good husband because of his wealth.

Not that Martha was that kind of woman. But still, did Jon need to warn his dad to slow down a little? He glanced at Martha and pursed his lips. She was the type who would know everything about everyone. Maybe she'd know who could have vandalized the property, but he didn't want to worry his dad.

As if on cue, his dad hefted himself up out of the chair. "I think I'll lie down awhile before dinner."

"Take the elevator," Martha said.

"The stairs are good exercise for my heart." The older man went to the sweeping staircase in the entry and began to climb them.

Barely breathing himself, Jon watched his father haul himself up the steps until he stood panting and victorious at the top. After a short rest, he went on down the hall to the bedroom.

Jon glanced at Martha. "Someone doesn't want me here." He told her about the graffiti painted on the door. "Have you heard anyone complaining about me being here?"

Martha's blue eyes grew shadowed. "Oh dear, Jon, I don't like to hear about this. There has been some grumbling about that old case. I've tried to squelch it, but suspicion runs deep here. And with those bodies found yesterday, everyone is abuzz with interest in that old case."

"I didn't hurt those girls. I only gave them a ride."

And was the last to see them. That said a lot, and there was no way to prove his innocence.

ELEVEN

ANNIE'S HAND HOVERED OVER THE ENTER KEY. SHE hadn't looked at that old case in years—mostly because she didn't want to consider Jon's role in it all. She *knew* in her heart he'd never physically hurt anyone. But she owed it to the community to be aware of any danger he might pose now that he was back. If those bodies proved to be the remains of those teenage girls, she wanted the old details to be fresh.

She took a sip of black coffee and grimaced. Bitter. Why did he have to come back and upset her peace of mind?

She hit the key, and the screen filled with text. Her gaze lingered on the faces of Penelope Day and Sophie Smith. Both seventeen, blonde, and best friends. In the photo they stood shoulder to shoulder with bright smiles. Dressed in hiking shorts and boots, they both wore backpacks over their tanks. Penelope's hair was in a ponytail, and Sophie had hers up under a Dodgers cap. Her heart broke for the families still grieving and yearning for truth and resolution. She knew that heartache all too well.

She leaned forward and read through the notes. The girls had hitchhiked along M107, where they'd gotten out of the back of a farm truck. They'd been picked up by Jon on the west side of Silver City, and he'd taken them to Lake of the Clouds, where he said they'd parted company. A security camera in Silver City caught him stopping his pickup to give them a ride, but no proof existed of his claim to leaving them at the lake. She'd seen him at the lake with them herself.

The deputy who'd interviewed him had remarked he seemed nervous and cagey. Jon hadn't offered any extraneous information and only answered what he was directly asked. That didn't mean he'd killed them, but it could indicate he was hiding something.

She took the papers she'd printed and went down the hall to Kade's office where she dropped into the chair in front of his desk. "There was an attack on a hiker."

He listened while she went through what she'd learned about Eddie's ordeal. "Where is Mr. Poole now?"

"I rented him a campsite close to the grub hall. Given his scare, he would like to have gotten a cabin, but they're all full so I gave him a spot surrounded by other campers. If anyone comes too close, he just has to call out for help."

Kade pursed his lips. "Any idea who did it or why?"

She handed him her phone. "I'll send these pictures to you, but here's what I saw. He didn't have a good description of the men."

Kade flicked through the pictures, then handed the phone back to her. "A game. Did he have any idea what the men meant about that? Some kind of scavenger hunt or what?"

"No idea. He was spooked, and he might have a concussion, but he started recovering once he got some food and water in him. I think his vomiting was due to dehydration."

"I'll kick the report up to headquarters and see if there are any other attacks." He twirled a pencil in his fingers. "I heard Jon Dunstan is back in town."

The joys of living in a small town. Everyone knew everyone

else's business, though in this case Bree had probably mentioned it to him. "He found Eddie Poole and brought him to me."

Kade rocked back in his chair. "I heard two bodies were found in a cabin at your place."

"Two blonde women. Mason said it would be a few days before we get the autopsy reports and DNA."

They exchanged a long look, and Annie knew he shared her concern about the incident nine years ago. Everything in her wanted to believe in Jon, but she couldn't discount the evidence. If she truly believed in him, she needed to find out who killed those girls before suspicion turned into a juggernaut that landed him in jail.

Reviewing the evidence again might be the thing to do now that he was back in town.

"I'm going to go pick up the puppy now," she told Kade. "Is that okay?"

"Bree is home. I'll text her and let her know you're coming."

She thanked him and went to her car. She drove down Houghton Street past the bed-and-breakfast, then turned in the curve onto Negaunee. The lighthouse on the lonely cliff overlooking Superior glowed in the fading light. Bree had restored the Fresnel lens, and the light would be turned on as darkness fell.

Annie parked and got out. The smell of boat exhaust hung heavy in the moist air blowing in from the lake. A ship's horn bellowed a lonely note in the middle of the bay.

Bree opened the door almost immediately when Annie pressed the doorbell. Annie's gaze went to the wriggling, fat puppy in Bree's arms. "Oh, he's darling."

Samson pressed past Bree's legs with his curly tail wagging, and Annie took a moment to pet him. "You have a cute puppy, Samson."

She wound her fingers in his wavy coat. He seemed a breed all his own. Part German Shepherd, part chow, and all love.

Bree deposited the puppy in her arms. "He's eight weeks old, and I've got his food and bowls all ready to go with you. I sent the twins out back to play so they didn't see him leave." With two bowls and a bag of puppy food in her hands, she stepped through the door onto the porch with Annie. "You okay? You seem a little distracted."

Bree always seemed to sense her thoughts, and Annie could always rely on her to give good advice.

"I was thinking about those girls who went missing the week Jon left. Jon's involvement was never fully vetted."

Bree's green eyes narrowed. "I never believed he had anything to do with it. You suspect him?"

"Knowing him, I don't believe he would do anything like that. But I saw him with the girls." Annie sat on a rocker with the puppy in her lap. "The date was July second, the day we broke up. I threw my engagement ring at him." She rubbed her head. "It had all started when he stopped to tell me he'd landed a residency spot at Mayo. He assumed I would move to Rochester, but I'd just graduated from law enforcement academy. I'd been offered a job with the park service. Maybe it was my fault because I didn't take his mother's death into how emotional he became."

Bree settled into the other rocker. "I remember."

"He expected me to give up my dream without even talking about it. I can't remember everything we yelled at each other. It was ugly though. We'd both accused the other of being selfish."

All this time later, she still didn't know who was right and who was wrong. Maybe it was both. If he'd loved her, they would have figured out a way to make it work. If she'd truly loved him, maybe she would have packed her bags and found a park service job near Rochester.

"Do you know why you reacted so strongly?" Bree asked. "Was it about Sarah?"

Annie stared at her. "How did you know? It felt like I was abandoning her, and I didn't understand how he could ask that of me. But it was more than that." She rubbed her forehead. Some of it was too personal to talk about.

Bree reached over and squeezed her hand. "Sarah went missing twenty-four years ago. There's nothing you can do to change that. You can't bring her back."

"Kade told me they'd found a child's remains down at St. Ignace," Annie said. "I keep hoping we'll find her, lay her to rest."

"That can happen no matter where you are. Kade would keep you informed of any new developments."

Annie's gaze went out to the water where a freighter plowed through the waves. "I've never wanted to live anywhere but here."

"I've always felt you wrapped yourself in your responsibilities to everyone but yourself, Annie. Sometimes you have to figure out what you want without assuming you have to sacrifice yourself because of the past. I think you punish yourself for failing Sarah. You were a child. You couldn't have stopped that man."

"She was my baby sister. I should have screamed or something. It was like my throat was frozen. I couldn't make a sound."

"You have to get past it somehow. Sarah wouldn't want you to lop off all joy and happiness because of something you couldn't stop."

Bree's head came up at the sound of children inside. "Uh-oh. You'd better vamoose before the twins try to take back the puppy. We'll talk more later."

Annie raced for her truck with the puppy in one arm and the food in the other. Right now, she'd focus on Kylie's reaction to a new puppy. Later, when she could think, she'd ponder what Bree said.

/ / /

What was he doing here?

Jon parked his car and got out near Tremolo Marina's cabins. The scent of freshly mown grass lingered in the air along with a hint of brats cooking on a grill somewhere. The laughter and murmur of campers over the way in the clearing around the pavilion wafted toward him on the wind.

"Was there another attack? Is Eddie okay?"

He spun at Annie's voice behind him. She was getting out of her old Volkswagen pickup with a puppy in her arms. The orange and gold light of the setting sun turned her blonde hair a reddish hue, and her gaze darted toward the campers parked in the RV resort area.

"I haven't seen Eddie. I came to talk to you about something else."

Her blue eyes went cautious. "Is it your dad?"

Jon approached her and rubbed the head of the black-and-brown puppy. "Fat little thing. I like its curly tail."

"It's one of Samson's pups. You didn't answer my question."

Did she care about his dad, or was she being polite? "Dad's fine, but I need your help. The cabin was vandalized. It appears to be someone who thinks I had something to do with those girls who went missing. This has probably resurged because of the bodies found in the cabin. Even if the victims don't turn out to be the girls, I need to clear my name, but I don't know how to even begin. I thought maybe you could solve the mystery of what happened to them. That's your expertise, right? Investigating crimes."

"My jurisdiction is national park lands. The girls went missing on state land so this isn't my baby."

"But you could still look into it."

She nodded. "I reviewed the records today. They vanished without a trace, and the case has gone cold. There have been no new leads in years."

The puppy licked his fingers, then its sharp little teeth nipped him. "Ouch!" He pulled back his hand. "Do you suspect me, Annie? What aren't you telling me?"

"I've never believed you could hurt anyone." She held his gaze for a long moment. "I saw you, Jon. You sent me that text about going to Lake of the Clouds, so I went to talk to you. I found your truck parked there. I walked up to the boardwalk and saw your arm around the taller one, Penelope. She kissed you, and you kissed her back. I know that doesn't mean you hurt her, but you did more than just give them a ride."

His face went hot, and his fingers curled into his palms. Perspiration broke out on his forehead. "My behavior that day wasn't the best, and I've regretted it, Annie. You'd thrown your engagement ring in my face. Plus, my mom had just died, and I was hurting. After we got to the Porkies, the girls brought out some beers."

"You hate alcohol."

He nodded. "But I was hurting enough to force down two bottles. I know it sounds like I'm making excuses, but I'm just trying to explain what happened. There's no excuse for it, and I know that. Did you see me push her away and walk back toward my truck?"

A sheen of moisture crept into her eyes. "No. I saw you kiss her, then I ran back to my truck. I couldn't stand to watch."

"Nothing else happened. I left the girls up there on the viewing platform and drove straight out of the park and back to our cottage. Dad was there. I had no idea something happened to the girls until I saw the missing persons report on television. I knew I needed to call and report what I knew, but before I could look up the number, the deputy showed up asking questions. He'd found the video of me picking up the girls in Silver City and had a lot of questions."

"Then you ran away. That made you appear guilty."

"I didn't run away. Summer vacation was over, and I had to get my things packed in Chicago to prepare for the move to Rochester. I left when I'd planned to all along." He saw the doubt in her eyes. "Ask my dad if you don't believe me."

She shifted the squirming puppy. "Were there any other people up on the viewing platform when you left?"

"It was summer—of course there were other people. Several families, a group of men on a fishing trip, some older women on a girls' trip. They didn't seem to be paying any attention to Penelope or Sophie."

"Did you hear any names or see anything that might help identify other people there that day?"

Trying to remember, he rubbed his head. "There was a white van with lettering on the side. I parked beside it. Something about fishing. Let me think." He paused and tried to remember. "Bunyan Fisheries. You ever heard of it?"

A spark of excitement shimmered in her eyes. "No, but it's a new lead. There's nothing about it in the notes."

"They didn't ask me about identifying any of the people."

"I'll see what I can find out. Anything else?"

He looked out at the beautiful sunset. A memory hung just out of reach, but he couldn't quite catch hold of it. "That's it for now, but I'll think about it some more."

She rubbed the puppy's head. "Kylie doesn't know about the puppy yet. She's going to be so excited." The puppy whimpered and squirmed again. "You have to potty, little guy?"

She set him on the grass at the edge of the gravel parking lot, and the puppy immediately squatted and did his business before sniffing the ground.

"Mommy?"

They both turned at Kylie's voice. The porch light shone down on the little girl as she stepped away from the screen door.

"Taylor and I fried fish for dinner. It's ready."

"Come here a minute, Bug. I have a surprise for you."

"Did you get more *pulla*?" The little girl's bare feet whispered along the grass as she approached.

Her gaze stayed fixed on her mother, and she didn't notice the puppy until he let out a little bark. Kylie gasped and stopped at the edge of the parking lot. The puppy cowered as she rushed toward him, but she scooped him into her arms, and he licked her chin.

"A puppy? You got me a puppy?"

Annie's smiled widened. "He's one of Samson's. You're going to be responsible for training him. He has big shoes to fill in the search-and-rescue world."

"I will. Thank you! Thank you!" She hugged her mother with one hand before frowning at Jon. "Why is he here again?"

"Kylie, mind your manners."

"Hello, Kylie." Jon saw the dislike in the little girl's face but wasn't sure what he'd done to trigger it. Could his remark about showing her how to clean fish offend her that much? "I'll head for home. I'll let you know if I think of anything else."

He could feel Kylie's gaze bore into his back as he went to his Jag. Her animosity was a wrinkle he hadn't expected.

TWELVE

ANNIE WALLOPED HER PILLOW INTO A BETTER SHAPE and buried one ear in it. She'd spent an hour weaving rugs before bed, which usually relaxed her, but sleep was elusive tonight. The puppy had cried for hours until she put him in a crate with a hot water bottle and a ticking clock. He'd finally settled down around one o'clock.

Her eyes were heavy, but she was wide awake. Jon coming to her for help had surprised her. The way he'd kissed Penelope was seared into her consciousness, but at least now she knew what had happened. He'd never been a drinker, and their fight had been catastrophic.

Was she making excuses for him because she wanted to or because there was evidence?

She swung her legs out of bed and reached for her MacBook tipped on its side against the bedside table. She opened it on her lap and typed in *Bunyan Fisheries*. There were lots of hits, and she went to the business's webpage.

It was located on Paul Bunyan Road, not far from Ontonagon. There were multiple pools and tanks, and the place advertised all types of bass, bluegill, catfish, and crappies. She studied the pictures of the men working there. They were mostly in their twenties, maybe transients. She'd pay them a visit in the morning.

If she was ever able to get some sleep.

"Mommy?"

Annie jumped when Kylie spoke from the door. "Did you have a bad dream?" She set her MacBook on the floor and threw back the covers. "Come climb in bed with me."

Kylie scampered across the wood floor in her Moana pajamas and snuggled into Annie's bed. Annie drew her close, then pulled the covers over them. She relished the coconut scent in Kylie's hair and the clean little girl smell of her.

Kylie threw her arms around Annie's neck. "Are you dating that guy?"

"What guy?"

"The guy in the red car. I don't like him."

"You don't know him, sweetheart."

"I don't like the way he looks at you. He's scary. You should marry Max instead. He brings me suckers."

Annie smoothed her daughter's hair back. "Max is old enough to be my dad."

"But he's nice."

That was true enough, but Annie didn't want to go there. "I'm not planning to marry anyone. I'm going to be your mommy, and we'll live here at the resort where you can swim and fish all you like. Okay?"

"Okay." Kylie brushed her lips across Annie's cheek before she flipped over to her other side. "Night, Mommy." Her voice was muffled and sleepy.

"Good night. Sweet dreams." Annie settled deeper under the sheet and lightweight comforter. The sound of the noise machine should have made her drift off, but her thoughts squirreled around too much. How did Jon look at her? She hadn't noticed anything special. There was too much distance and distrust between them now. Kylie was misreading things.

A scratching sound caught her attention, and she sat up again. The puppy lay quietly in his crate, and he didn't appear to have budged. The noise came again, and she thought it came from the window. Was Eddie in trouble?

She slipped out of bed and tiptoed to the window. Her hand hovered on the blinds, but she dropped her hand back down. Maybe she should peek out another window and surprise whoever it was. This window was securely locked so no one could get inside. Kylie would be safe.

She went noiselessly across the floor to her closet and grabbed her gun from the safe before she slipped to Kylie's bedroom. She sidled across the room until she was at the window overlooking the garden. Kylie's window was only about five feet from the one in Annie's bedroom.

She couldn't hear the scratching sound in here, but she pulled back the blind just a bit and peered outside into the moonlit yard. Shadows shrouded the figure standing outside her window, and she couldn't tell if it was a man or woman.

It could be Eddie trying to see if she was awake. Should she go check on him?

No. Leaving Kylie in here alone was out of the question. She headed back to her bedroom and approached the window again. The best thing to do was to see who it was and handle it. After taking a deep breath, she yanked back the blinds—nothing. No figure leering in, nothing but flowers gilded with moonlight and a lone raccoon scampering up a tree.

Where had the person gone? Had it been Eddie? Or maybe the person who had been after him or some weirdo Peeping Tom?

The guy couldn't see in through the plantation blinds, so a peeper seemed unlikely.

She peered through the moonlight toward the tent campsites. No figures moved around, and Eddie's tent appeared to be zipped.

She let the blinds fall back into place and went to double-check the doors. It was a long time before she slept.

/ / /

The sun peeked over the horizon in the early morning sky when Jon headed to his car to get the pole rod from the trunk. He'd tossed and turned all night after asking Annie to help clear his name. The knowledge that she'd seen him with the girls shamed him. He regretted so much from that summer.

As he neared his car in the Blue Bonnet parking lot, the alarm on his Jag went off, and he saw two figures running away. "Hey!" He gave chase and managed to tackle one into the dew-drenched lawn.

He pinned him, then rolled him over. A teenage boy not even old enough to shave glared up at him through the floppy blond hair hanging in his eyes. "What were you doing with my car?"

"Just looking at it, mister. It's dime."

"Dime?"

"A ten. Super nice."

The kid struggled, and Jon let him up. "Where's your friend? He didn't care to stay and help you?"

"You scared us."

Jon grabbed his forearm and marched him over to the car to check it out. "Did you scratch it?"

"No. I told you—we were just checking it out."

There didn't seem to be any damage so Jon let go of his arm. The boy bolted away, then turned to yell back at him. "You're going to jail, mister! When your car is up for auction, I'll buy it." Still laughing, he vanished around the corner of the building.

Jon didn't bother chasing him down again. Was that what the whole town thought? That he was guilty? He grabbed his fishing gear and walked down the old metal steps to the lake. No one was down here, which surprised him, but he could use a little peace and quiet.

He settled on a rock and put his cane pole together, then tossed the bobber into the water. It wasn't the best place for that kind of fishing, but there was something mesmerizing about watching that bobber go up and down in the waves. Even if he caught nothing, it helped him think, and the beauty of God's creation soothed his soul.

He spotted a figure approaching along the rocks and recognized Eddie. "How'd you get out here, buddy?"

Eddie looked pale in the light of the sunrise. "I went out to the road and hitchhiked. My parents are picking me up today, and the woods freaked me out. I keep thinking those guys are going to come get me. I remembered something one of them said." He shuddered and gooseflesh popped up on his arms. "One of them said, 'Bet he can run faster than Chris Willis.'"

Jon gasped. "The camper that washed up at Annie's place."

Eddie nodded. "Knowing that, I wanted to get out of there."

"It sounds sinister. You'd better tell the sheriff."

"I will. I needed a little time by the water. This whole thing has spooked me."

"Did you say good-bye to Annie?"

Eddie shook his head. "She wasn't up yet, but could you thank her for me? And tell her I saw someone standing outside her window last night."

That got Jon's attention. "A Peeping Tom?"

"He wouldn't be able to see in because her blinds are tight. But someone stood in the garden outside her bedroom, and it looked like whoever it was touched the window. I didn't like it and I hollered out. The guy ran off."

Jon didn't like the mental picture. Who would want to frighten her—and why? "I'll tell her. Did you recognize the guy?"

"Too dark. Not tall though. Maybe my height. Not as tall as you."

"What about your kayak and gear? Does it need to be brought to town?" Not that he had a truck to do it, but he might be able to rent one to help the guy out.

"I rented it all from the outfitters. I've arranged for it to be picked up." Eddie stuck out his hand. "Thanks for everything."

"You're welcome. Glad it all turned out okay."

Jon watched the younger man climb the rickety iron stairs to the street level. He'd have to make sure Annie knew someone had been outside the cottage last night.

THIRTEEN

THE MINUTE KYLIE WAS OUT THE DOOR WITH THE puppy and Taylor to play, Annie headed for the tent encampment. As she neared, she saw Eddie's tent was dismantled and packed in its bag with his sleeping bag neatly rolled up and stowed beside it. She looked around at the other tents. The scent of frying bacon from an iron skillet drifted her way, and she went over to talk to the couple seated on logs around the campfire.

"Good morning," she said with a smile. "Gretchen and Henry, right?"

The couple was in their forties. Hiking was their passion, and they were usually gone most of the day.

Gretchen tucked a strand of red hair behind her ear. "You have a good memory. Want some breakfast?"

"I already ate, but thank you." Annie gestured toward Eddie's tent. "Have you seen Eddie Poole this morning?"

Henry, a slim guy with an erect posture, shook his head. "He was gone when we got up. Tent was packed up and everything. I never heard a peep out of him all night."

"Did you see anyone prowling around in the wee hours? Like around one?" Annie asked.

"I put on my eye mask and took a sleeping pill. A heavy-metal group couldn't have awakened me." Henry glanced at his wife. "You hear anything, Gretch?"

"Not a peep. Didn't he say he was going to hitchhike to town today? He probably got up early to do it."

Eddie must have recovered his courage. And better not to tell them she'd had someone at her window in the night. They might pack up and move out, and Annie needed all the spaces rented. "Thanks. Have a great day hiking. Where you headed today?"

Gretchen flipped the bacon. "We're going to the Porkies today to hike."

"Have fun." Annie walked to the playground to see how Kylie was doing with the puppy. "Figured out a name for him yet, Bug?"

Kylie gave a final tug on the rope toy, then let the puppy have it. "Nothing seems right yet. I have to get to know him better."

Annie knelt and rolled the puppy onto his back to rub his fat tummy. His pink tongue came out, and he squeaked with joy. "He's a cute little guy. Listen, I have to go to work for a while. I'll be home in time to cook dinner though."

"I thought you were on vacation."

"I'd planned to be, but I'll have to work some." She glanced at Taylor. "Call me if you need me."

"Sure," Taylor said.

The young woman seemed happier here. The stress lines around her eyes and mouth were more relaxed, and her muddy-brown eyes were serene. This place was a haven that eased the tension away from people.

Annie walked toward her vehicle, but before she could get behind the wheel, Jon's red Jag pulled up beside her.

His window ran down, and he smiled at her. "I was hoping I could catch you. I ran into Eddie in town this morning. He spotted someone standing outside your bedroom window last night. He chased him off but couldn't identify him."

She nodded. "I wondered if it was Eddie trying to get the courage to come to the door. It's disconcerting that it wasn't him."

"Yeah, I don't like it. Eddie is leaving town, by the way. His parents are coming to get him, and the outfitters will stop by to pick up his stuff. He said to tell you good-bye."

So that answered her questions about Eddie.

"He also mentioned he remembered something about the encounter with his attackers. One of them said something about him running faster than Chris Willis."

She gasped. "That sounds like the men who killed the Willis man."

"I told him to tell Mason before he left town, and Eddie said he would."

"Let me check and make sure that happened." She tapped out a text and sent it off to Mason. Moments later he responded. "Eddie showed up and told him." She looked over at Jon. "I'm heading to the fishery this morning."

"I'd like to go with you."

She started to tell him no, then caught herself. "You might recognize someone."

"I hope to. It might help us."

Us.

When had this become a joint investigation? While she believed in his innocence, she didn't want to be naive either. If life had taught her one thing, it was that people could do things you never believed possible. She'd once trusted Jon with her future, and it had fractured into glass shards. With Jon, she'd allowed herself to forget the dark edges, the black holes threatening to shred her. Sarah's fate should have seared that fact in her memory—and it had for a time. Until Jon came along with his winning smile and eyes green as sea glass.

He'd made her hope for the first time, but the trust she had in him had proven false. She needed to be on her guard in case he failed her again.

"You want to ride with me?" he asked.

She stared at his sports car. His desire for the finer things of life had been part of what had stolen him away from her. "No thanks. We might be on rough roads out to the fishery. My Volkswagen can take the beating."

He nodded and ran his window up, then got out and slid into the passenger seat. "Where's Kylie today?"

"With Taylor."

Making small talk with him set her teeth on edge, so she turned up the radio. Garth Brooks belted out "The Thunder Rolls," and she smothered a smile. Very apt. She shot a glance his way before staring at the road ahead. His head was down, and his hands were clenched in his lap. He got the point.

She took pity on him and turned the music down a bit. "When are you going back to Rochester?"

"I don't know yet. When the house is done. I arranged for three weeks off, but it might not be enough. You remember Sean Johnson? He's doing the work and said he could get it done quickly."

"I see him around."

He turned his head and stared at her. "If you were so broken up about seeing me with Penelope, why'd you marry Nate the minute I was out of town?"

The abrupt question made her gulp, but she tipped up her chin. "It wasn't the minute you left."

"A month later. A *month*, Annie. Your ring finger barely had time to get tanned again. I knew Nate was crazy about you, but I never thought you'd flip and marry him like that."

Why should he expect an explanation? "You were the one who ran off, Jon. You didn't care that my parents were practically bankrupt or that my heart was shattered. You don't know how my dad—"

She looked at her hands and didn't answer his question. "Nate was there for me. He picked up the pieces. I knew I'd never be happy again, but at least I could make him happy."

She gripped the steering wheel harder. "And to my surprise, Nate made me happy. You know how he was—always thinking of other people. If he hadn't been worried about Mom that day, he'd have stayed home. But she had to go for chemo treatments, and he insisted he could pilot the boat while Dad tended to Mom on the way back. She liked going to Houghton by boat instead of by car. It was faster, and the water soothed her after her treatment. If she needed to throw up, she could lean over the side of the boat."

He turned his head and stared out the window. "I miss him."

"So do I." She clamped her mouth shut and resolved to say nothing more.

/ / /

Jon had stepped into that one.

He stared at the sign for the fishery up ahead. The last thing he'd wanted to do was discuss Nate. Good old Nate. His best friend. And robber. He'd robbed Jon of the chance of getting back with Annie. Before Jon had been able to process what had happened and what to do about it, Nate had a ring on Annie's finger.

It had happened so fast. There was no room in Annie's life for Jon after that. And he wasn't the type to try to break up a happy marriage. His father had danced around the news for the longest time before breaking it to him that his best friend had married the only woman Jon had ever loved.

Was it any wonder he'd never managed to make a relationship work again? Broken trust would do that.

Annie drove into the potholed parking lot and stopped the vehicle. "Let's see what we can find out."

Her door squealed when she opened it, and Jon glanced her way. "Needs some grease."

"Along with a half dozen other maintenance chores. There's never enough time."

He could do that for her. It wouldn't take long. All he had to do was watch for the right opportunity to snag her truck and do a few things. He got out and followed her to the main building, a low-slung wooden structure with weathered boards and a metal roof. The door was locked, so they followed the sound of voices to a pond structure a hundred yards away.

As soon as Jon spotted the tall guy with brown hair under the brim of a John Deere hat, he recognized seeing him at Lake of the Clouds. He looked to be in his thirties with a rangy build and reddened hands from hard work.

"I saw that guy," he hissed to Annie. "The one in the green hat."

She nodded but didn't reply as she stepped forward with a smile. "I'm LEO Pederson. Who's in charge here?"

"LEO?"

"Law enforcement officer. A ranger," Annie said. "And you are?"

"Glenn Hussert. I own the fishery. What can I do for you, Ranger Pederson?"

Jon noted a wedding ring on the guy's left hand, but that didn't mean much. It had been nine years, and besides, even married guys attacked young women. He studied Hussert with a hard stare. The guy appeared innocent enough, but Jon desperately wanted to find something, anything, to track a lead to what happened to Penelope and Sophie.

"I'm investigating a cold case, and an eyewitness report put you at Lake of the Clouds at the time the young women went missing."

Hussert glanced at his workers listening with avid attention. "Let's go to my office. This way."

They followed him across the weedy lawn to the building. He unlocked the door, and they stepped into a dark interior that smelled of mud and fish.

Hussert gestured to a broken-down sofa. "Have a seat. Coffee?"

Annie glanced at the grungy sofa before she perched on the edge. "No coffee, thanks."

Jon settled beside her and grimaced at the rank odor of sweat and fish guts wafting from the cushion.

Hussert poured himself a mug of sludge and went to stand near them. "So, what's this cold case? It's not unusual for me to be at Lake of the Clouds. It's one of my favorite spots in the area. Great fishing. Me and the guys go there every chance we get. A cold case, you say? When was this?"

"Nine years ago on July second. Two young women went missing. Seventeen, blonde, and beautiful. Penelope Day and Sophie Smith." Annie took out her phone and handed it to him with a picture of the young women showing.

He studied it before he handed it back to her. "Never saw them before."

Jon bit down on his tongue to keep from bellowing at the man. He was lying. The guy had watched Penelope especially. And just like that, Jon remembered what he couldn't grasp last night.

He tried to signal his feelings to Annie, but she kept her attention glued on Hussert, so Jon slumped back on the sofa and let her do her job. She'd be furious if he interfered. She had authority to ask questions—he didn't.

Annie held out the phone again. "Take another look. It's been a long time. Their parents are still left wondering what happened to them all this time."

"So they've never been found? I thought maybe you were investigating a murder when you said cold case."

"Their disappearance is the cold case." When he didn't take the phone again, Annie pulled her hand back. "Who would have been with you that day?"

Hussert shrugged. "A lot of my workers are transients who work for a few weeks before moving on. I doubt I have anyone working here now who went fishing with me nine years ago. And I don't remember who those workers were."

"I'd appreciate it if you checked your records to see who worked for you back then." She rose and handed him a card. "My email is on the card. Please email me what you find, or I'll get a court order and check it out for myself."

Hussert grimaced and palmed the card. "You're barking up the wrong tree, Ranger. This has nothing to do with me or my fishing buddies."

"If I don't hear from you in two days, I'll be back." Annie turned for the door, and Jon followed her.

He took a deep breath of clean air that washed away the fishy, rancid odor. "He's lying, Annie. I remembered something when you were talking to him. He asked the girls if they wanted to join them for beer and brats. Penelope laughed it off, but he might have put more pressure on them after I left."

"I wish you'd spoken up."

"I didn't want to interfere in your investigation."

Her blue eyes went thoughtful. "He looked familiar to me, but I can't think of where I've seen him." She shrugged and headed to her vehicle. "At least it's a lead. That's more than I had this time last week."

FOURTEEN

THE SUOMI CAFÉ BUSTLED WITH MIDMORNING ACTIVITY, and the scent of the cardamom in the *pannukakkua* wafted in the space. Even though she'd had breakfast, Annie wasn't about to miss out on the Finnish oven pancakes that always came served with thimbleberry jam here.

She sat in a booth with Jon across the table from her and didn't look at the menu. "Only *pannukakkua* will do."

Jon studied the menu before he set it down. "I wish I could have it."

"Why can't you?"

"About a year ago I found out I have celiac disease. I can't eat anything with gluten. It's a pain to figure out what to eat, but in this case, an omelet should be safe. No toast."

"No nisu toast, no *pulla*. That's terrible."

"Tell me about it." He took a sip of his coffee. "It's agony to smell it and not be able to have it. So, what's next with figuring out what happened to Penelope and Sophie?"

"I'm hoping Hussert sends me his employee list, but we'll see. I might have to get a warrant."

Her phone dinged, and she glanced at it. Dr. Eckright had Kylie's results and wanted to see her. She frowned at the lack of detail. Why didn't he tell her upfront what was wrong? Was it something serious?"

"You seem troubled. Everything okay?"

"I need to see Kylie's doctor. Just routine."

"Now?"

"He has time right now, so I think I'll run across the street and talk to him. It shouldn't take long. Go ahead and order for us, and I'll be right back." She slid out of the booth and headed for the door. There was no traffic so she darted across the street to the doctor's office. His nurse took her right back to the room, and Dr. Eckright joined her in minutes.

He shut the door behind him. "I have the results of Kylie's blood work."

His somber tone made her gut clench. "Is she all right?"

"It's not what I was expecting, but it makes sense with her problems with gaining weight and height. It appears she has celiac disease. A biopsy is the only real way to confirm it, but I don't think we need to put her through that with such overwhelming evidence in the blood and stool tests. All of her antibodies I tested for it are elevated. And the stool sample showed she carries the gene for celiac disease, so that's pretty definitive."

Her thoughts zoomed to Jon. He had celiac disease. "What causes it?"

"It's often hereditary. Are you feeling all right? Did Nathan have celiac disease?"

"I'm fine, just processing it all. Nate was always very healthy. He loved bread and pancakes. And he didn't have problems with weight loss or anything like that."

He'd always been healthy as a horse. He was a marine mechanic and worked hard to support them. She couldn't remember any time he'd stayed home sick. She tried to think of anyone else in her family who might have had celiac disease. *Hereditary.*

The pressure in her chest grew until she couldn't breathe. "What do we do about it?"

"You change her diet. Gluten is found in wheat, barley, and rye. That means you need to read every package. Things you don't expect to have gluten are full of it, like soups, flavoring packages, even flavored potato chips. The gluten helps the flavoring stick to things like chips. I know it's going to be a big change and a lot of work for you, but she'll see improvement within a couple of weeks."

"That's good. How long does she have to do it?"

"It's lifelong, Annie. This isn't something that goes away. It's an autoimmune disease, so you want to address it right away to make sure she doesn't develop another one. Things like type 1 diabetes often go hand in hand with celiac disease. It's not something to take lightly."

Annie's eyes filled at the thought of Kylie having to deal with this for her entire life. "She's going to hate this. Her favorite breakfast is *pannukakkua*. And she loves *pulla*."

"There are many good gluten-free flours out there now. Play around with them and see if you can make her favorite foods with some of them. There are good gluten free breads too. Canyon Bakehouse is a good brand. Sami's millet sourdough. There are others too. See what she likes."

Annie blinked back the moisture in her eyes. While she was grateful Kylie wasn't facing something like cancer, this news would rock their worlds. How did Annie keep her safe once school started? And what about birthday parties with cake and ice cream? Kylie's life would never be the same.

Hereditary.

Her thoughts kept swinging back that way, and she had to

face some truths she might not want to examine. For nearly nine years she hadn't let herself think about what might have been. She had been determined to force life into the pattern she expected. Placid and known, not unsettled and secret.

But it couldn't be, could it? Jon had believed he was sterile after a bad cycling accident when he was sixteen. What exactly had he said? She couldn't quite remember.

She licked her lips. "How is a paternity test done?" Her hand flew to her mouth, and she gulped. Her secret had seemed safe all these years, but now it was bubbling to the surface.

The doctor's face betrayed no surprise. "It's a fairly simple procedure. The father swabs his cheek, and you send it off for analysis. In less than a week, you usually have results."

"I-I see." She swallowed hard. "You must think I'm a terrible person."

The doctor's brown eyes softened. "Of course not, Annie. You haven't had an easy road of it, especially lately. I'm not going to sit in judgment over your mistakes. We all make them. That's between you and God."

And she'd asked God many times to forgive her. She knew he had. The problem was she hadn't been able to forgive herself, and this new wrinkle brought all her sins out into the light to be examined.

"Is it possible to secure the DNA without a cheek swab? I mean, could I get DNA off a coffee cup or something?"

"It's not legal for paternity tests. The possible father must be notified of the test."

Her cheeks burned at the thought of talking about it. "It probably doesn't matter anyway. How Kylie got it doesn't change the fact we have to adjust her diet."

"There might be other genetic issues you'll want to know about in the future."

Annie chewed on her lip and looked down at her hands. She had no idea what to do, but she didn't have to decide right now.

/ / /

Jon took the last bite of his omelet and glanced at his watch. Annie had been gone an hour. He'd thought she would be back by now. He waved at the server and held up his coffee mug, and she brought over the pot.

"Molly, isn't it?"

The skinny, fortysomething woman nodded. "If you're watching for Annie, I saw her head into the ladies' room. You might be prepared with a shoulder to cry on. I'll bring her *pannukakkua* out as soon as she's at the table."

His chest squeezed. Bad news about Kylie?

When Molly walked away to tend to another customer, Jon watched for Annie. She wasn't a crier. He'd only ever seen her cry the night his mother had died. Even when they broke up the next day, she hadn't cried. She'd been angry, but tears weren't a weapon in her arsenal.

When she emerged from the restroom, her red eyes told the story. She managed a smile, but he wasn't fooled.

He waited until she slid into the booth and took a sip of her water. "Molly is bringing your food in a minute. What's wrong?"

Her eyes filled again. "Kylie has celiac disease."

He exhaled. "It's not the end of the world, Annie. She'll learn to deal with it. There are lots of options these days. I'll help her."

He remembered the little girl's hostility and inwardly winced.

Getting past that prickly reserve might prove a challenge, but he'd give it a try.

"It feels overwhelming right now. The things she likes will be off-limits. And birthday parties and other events at school will be challenging."

He hadn't thought about the problems kids faced. As an adult he understood the specifics of his condition, but it would be harder for an eight-year-old to grasp. "I'll get her some of my favorite things."

"Not even a pastie. Cooking for her will be overwhelming. We won't be able to eat out much."

"Sure you will." He gestured down at his plate. "You quickly learn all it takes is real, whole foods. Processed stuff is mostly out, but meat, vegetables, and fruit all work fine."

A frown crouched between her eyes. "This is a big deal for a kid, Jon. You don't get how hard this will be for her, and I don't want to see her suffer. She's already gone through so much with losing her grandparents and dad."

"I get that." He pulled out his phone and quickly placed an order from Sami's for gluten-free bread, chips, and cookies. "Some stuff for her will be here in two days. I've gotten to be a decent cook myself. I'll whip her up some gluten-free brownies tonight to show her she doesn't have to feel deprived."

Molly brought the *pannukakkua* and put it in front of Annie. "Here you go, love."

Annie stared at the food with an expression of loathing. "Thanks, Molly." She picked up her fork. "I should enjoy it while I can. I couldn't possibly eat it in front of Kylie. Same with pasties and *pulla*. My diet will have to change too."

A little girl couldn't be asked to eat something else when her mother scarfed down what she really wanted. Jon hadn't had to deal with that. He could handle it when someone else at the table ate a treat he couldn't have. An eight-year-old wouldn't be so sanguine about it.

He reached across the table and took her hand. "I'm sorry." There was nothing else to say.

She gulped and pulled her hand away. "Thanks."

He sipped his coffee and watched her play around with the custardy pancake. The thimbleberry jam oozed over the sides, and she mopped it up with a piece of *pannukakkua*. He could almost taste it himself even though it had been years since he'd had any.

He'd gotten used to the deprivation, but this new journey was still stretching in front of Kylie and her. There wasn't any way he could circumvent it for them.

She looked up with reddened eyes. "You'd make a good dad."

He gave a wry twist to his lips. "I can't have kids, remember?"

"Why are you so certain?"

"The doc said scar tissue from the biking accident made it impossible."

"Maybe he was wrong. You were sixteen at the time. And maybe something could be done about it even if it is true."

"Why are we talking about this? I don't have plans for marriage. I haven't had much time to date other than casually." There'd been one woman he thought might stick around, but when he mentioned he couldn't have kids, she ghosted him.

Annie looked back down. "I just wondered."

Her diffident manner made him wonder what was going on behind those beautiful blue eyes. She'd always been upfront, no secrets. What you saw was what you got. Now she seemed more mysterious, someone unknown. But a woman he wanted to get to know all over again. Coming back to Rock Harbor had upended everything, and he wasn't sure how to deal with it.

Did he dare think about pursuing a relationship with her again? There was Kylie to consider. She clearly didn't like him for some reason. He could work on that, but what if she never got over her dislike? Annie's daughter's happiness would be her primary goal.

And even if he got past Kylie's dislike, he'd burned his bridges with Annie, and she'd run straight into Nate's arms. He wasn't sure he could get past that betrayal. That news had rocked him on his heels nine years ago.

Even knowing all those reasons for *why not*, he found himself staring at her bent blonde head and wondering what she'd do if he told her how he was feeling.

FIFTEEN

TAYLOR PAWED THROUGH THE PASTEL PAJAMAS NEATLY folded in the bedroom drawer. Annie had nice things. She didn't care if Annie realized someone had been in here—it might scare her, which was a good thing. She hadn't said anything about the other night, and Taylor didn't think she'd even seen her outside the window. Only that troublemaker who'd yelled at her.

Taylor wanted Annie uneasy and frightened. She wanted Annie to know how fear made your heart race and your mouth bone dry. She wanted Annie to hear a roaring in her ears as she waited for the next blow to fall. She wanted her to eventually experience the metallic taste of blood in her mouth.

The thought left Taylor giddy.

She'd left Kylie playing with camper kids on the playground, and their squeals and laughter assured Taylor all was well, and she had a few minutes to snoop.

She wandered to the closet and examined the clothes hanging there. Nothing sexy or interesting. Just slacks, jeans, and modest tops. Annie was a beauty, but Taylor had never seen her in anything that showed off her figure. It was like she wasn't interested in attracting a guy's attention, which made no sense.

Taylor would have loved to find a man's admiring gaze on her. Her mother hadn't allowed her to date. She believed all men were evil and after only one thing, but Taylor had met a few decent men since her mom had died. The problem was they were all taken.

But once she'd evened the playing field with Annie, maybe she'd join a dating site and see if she could meet someone good and kind. Kindness was important. It was something Taylor had longed for all her life. She'd seen other mothers at school comforting their children and had wondered what it might feel like to experience it again.

Taylor left the closet door open and wandered down the hall to the other bedrooms. Kylie's room was of no interest to her, but the third bedroom was the master with an attached minuscule bathroom. It had been largely untouched since the death of Annie's parents, and Taylor's pulse ratcheted up at the thought of exploring it.

She paused inside the door and examined the photo of a smiling couple. The woman looked very much like Annie. The mom's blonde hair was shorter and a little darker, but she had the same blue eyes and smile as her daughter. Wings of gray at the temples of her father's dark hair gave the man a distinguished look.

She stared at his even features. What would it have been like to grow up with a father? Did Annie realize how fortunate she was? Tayler doubted it. Annie appeared to be the type of person who took everything as her due and didn't have much empathy for people outside her little world. As long as all was well with Kylie and her, she didn't care about anything else.

At least Kylie knew what it was to be fatherless. Taylor grew more and more fond of the little girl. Maybe *she* should be Kylie's mother. Kylie would be better off than being with Annie, who was much too focused on work. Kylie's mother had been gone more than home ever since Taylor had been hired.

She let herself dream of a life with Kylie beside a beach somewhere. A real beach, not that cold, capricious one on Lake Superior. One with warm waves and sunshine. Maybe Jon would come with them, and he'd look at her with those dreamy green eyes that made her melt inside. They'd sip drinks with little umbrellas in them as they watched their daughter play in the water. He'd touch her hair and her cheek oh so tenderly.

It was such a wonderful dream it brought tears to her eyes, and she sniffled. She'd had plenty of experience with dreams when her reality was so painful. But life had to look up now, right? She could change her future by willing it into being. She'd read that somewhere.

She moved farther into the bedroom and looked around the space. A king bed sat between two long windows. Taylor touched the quilt that appeared homemade. Had Annie's mother created it or bought it? A picture of Annie and another little girl was in a frame on the right-side table. Kylie looked just like the older girl in the picture.

Taylor stared at it for a long minute. The two looked very much alike with corn silk–colored hair and blue eyes. One was several inches taller than the other, and they both proudly held up a fish on a pole.

Idyllic days that hadn't lasted. Most days like that don't. And some people never experience them at all. Without consciously planning it, Taylor grabbed the picture frame and took the photo out, then stuffed the picture in her shirt.

It was hers now.

/ / /

Kylie's hair was still damp from her swim before supper. She sat at the table and stared at the grilled chicken, fresh corn on the cob, and raw veggies. "I thought we were having spaghetti for dinner."

Annie forced a smile. "You love corn on the cob."

Her daughter hated it when plans changed, and Annie had promised spaghetti with garlic bread this morning. A meal that was clearly out of the question with the celiac disease diagnosis.

She settled beside Kylie and pulled her over onto her lap. "Honey, the doctor knows what's wrong with you—why you're losing weight. You have celiac disease. It means when you eat gluten, it hurts your intestines. So you can't eat it anymore."

Kylie looked blank. "What's gluten?"

"It's a protein found in certain grains like wheat, barley, and rye. We have to change your diet and find some things you like that don't have gluten in them. Regular pasta and bread have a lot of gluten, so I can't fix spaghetti until I find a pasta that's safe for you."

"*Pulla* is bread."

"It is, and you won't be able to eat it from Suomi Café. I'll have to find a recipe that uses other grains."

The taste felt daunting to Annie.

Tears welled in Kylie's eyes, and she slid off Annie's lap. "That's not fair!"

"I know, Bug. Life isn't always fair. But I promise I'll do my best to find substitutes for the things you like. Jon will help me. He has the same disease. He's already ordered you some bread and other things he thinks you'll like."

"I don't want anything he gives me." Kylie burst into sobs and ran from the room.

Annie exhaled. That hadn't gone well. She forced her shoulders to relax. Her mind had worried through every possible explanation for the celiac disease diagnosis. She pulled out her phone. Nate's parents would know about his health. Maybe someone else in his family had it. That should be her first assumption—not jumping to an impossible conclusion.

Annie didn't speak to them often, and Kylie had only been around them three times in her life. Nate's dad was CEO of a big corporation, and they traveled to Asia often. They hadn't shown much interest in being grandparents, and Nate had made her promise she'd never let them make Kylie feel unloved.

She called up the number, and Nate's mother answered on the second ring. "Annie, what a nice surprise. We just got in from a fund-raiser. How's our perfect granddaughter?"

"Growing like a weed. Listen, Maryanne. Kylie was diagnosed today with celiac disease. Was Nate ever tested?"

"Nate never gave us a bit of trouble and hardly ever even went to the doctor. I can count on one hand how often he had a cold. Is this hereditary?"

"It can be but not always. I thought I'd see if it ran in the family."

"That's the trendy disease where you can't have bread, right? I've never believed it's a real thing. I don't know anyone in our family with it." A man's voice rumbled in the background. "Give my love to Kylie. I have to go get cocktails prepared. Talk soon. Kisses."

Kisses. All platitudes. Maryanne had no idea how to show love to anyone. Nate had been scarred by his parents' neglect.

So, no celiac disease in the family. That meant nothing though. The doctor said it wasn't always passed from a parent. Maryanne wouldn't know everyone's medical history. It could have come from a great-great-grandfather or someone more distant.

Jon had mentioned his inability to have children again today. He couldn't possibly be Kylie's father.

Please, God, don't let me have to deal with something like that.

Dealing with Kylie's new diagnosis would be hard enough without adding a paternity issue into the mix. How could she even explain something like that to her daughter? Or anyone else for that matter?

When she yanked open the drawer to pull her pajamas from the dresser, she frowned at the disarray. Nothing was neatly folded as usual. Had Kylie been in here searching for something?

It would be very unlike her daughter to rummage through her things, especially in this top drawer of a tall dresser. She was small for her age. Annie found her favorite blue pajamas and tossed them onto the bed before she shut the drawer and checked the one underneath it. She bit her lip when she discovered the same mess inside that one. And the one after that. The bottom drawer was scrambled too.

Someone had been in her house. In her bedroom.

She crossed the room to her bedside table and pulled open the drawer. Usually her Bible was in the front with neatly coiled charging cables to the back for her phone and e-reader, but the cables were strewn out and trailed across the top of her Bible. In her closet she found hanging clothes pushed to one side and a shoebox of pictures on the floor with the lid off.

Why would someone rummage through her things? They hadn't even tried to hide their intrusion. It was almost like they wanted her to know her security had been violated. What was the person looking for? With the discovery of the bodies on her property, she had to worry that someone wished her harm.

Should she call it in? Having a deputy tromping through

would upset Kylie, who was already sulking in her bedroom, and Annie doubted they'd find anything. Still, Mason should know about this.

She called his number, and he answered immediately. "No word on the bodies yet, Annie."

"That's not why I'm calling. Someone seems to have gone through my things." She explained what she'd found in her bedroom.

"What about the rest of the house? Kylie's room?"

"I haven't looked there. I didn't want to alarm her yet."

"We might be able to lift fingerprints, though this guy is bold. I'd guess he used gloves."

"That's what I thought too. Just wanted you to know."

"I'll send someone out to dust for prints in the morning, just to check. Any idea how the guy got in? Was the door unlocked?"

"I don't lock it during the day. Kylie and Taylor are in and out constantly. And you know how it is here—we usually don't worry much about that kind of thing. I guess I need to start."

"Sounds like it. Do you have a security system?"

"No."

"I think you'd better get one."

"I'll check into it tomorrow before I head out on the water." She planned to take Kylie fishing.

She didn't want to change her lifestyle and be constantly looking over her shoulder. But she had Kylie to think about. She would check her daughter's room tomorrow. In the meantime, it wouldn't hurt to check the kitchen and living room.

She ended the call with Mason and, phone in hand, padded quietly through the house to check the drawers. Nothing seemed amiss. The locks on the doors and windows appeared secure, and the pole light outside shone down on a quiet landscape.

She unlocked the front door and stepped out onto the porch. The faint chords of a banjo twanged from a firepit in the camper section, and she heard the low murmur of voices. Dusk had nearly given way to nighttime, and stars had begun to twinkle in the sky. The place felt peaceful and serene. The intruder might have entered much earlier and was long gone.

At least that's what she wanted to believe.

SIXTEEN

PERFECT. ANNIE'S TRUCK WAS PARKED IN THE LOT. JON glanced around to make sure he didn't spy her beautiful blonde head, but she must be out on the water since her boat was missing.

He got out of his car and checked the truck door. Unlocked. In Rochester you didn't dare leave anything unlocked for a minute, but in this beautiful place it was hard to remember danger still hid behind trees on occasion. The missing girls had found that out.

He'd wanted to call Mason this morning to see if there'd been an ID on the bodies, but he didn't dare draw attention to himself. Better to skate under the radar and glean what information he could. Martha would know the minute news came down.

He popped the trunk of his car, then retrieved oil and tools. He'd come prepared with every possible part replacement. The sun shone down with glaring heat even at ten in the morning, and he had to pause several times to wipe the perspiration from his brow. He changed the oil and air filter, checked the tire inflation, filled the water reservoir for the wipers, and replaced them as well. The spark plugs looked bad so he replaced them too. He greased the squeaky door hinges, then stood back and examined it.

Would she notice any difference? He wasn't going to tell her what he'd done.

"Hey!"

He turned at the female voice and saw Taylor heading toward him. Her brown eyes narrowed and her mouth went tight.

"Everything okay?"

She gave a timid smile. "You're working on Annie's truck?"

"Just some routine maintenance for her." He thought about asking her to keep it quiet, but that would raise her suspicions. Better to act like it was something Annie had asked him to do. "Annie told me what was wrong with it."

"I see. She didn't mention it to me, but that's very nice of you."

"Just helping out a friend."

Taylor nodded. "She left me in charge of the resort, so I wanted to make sure nothing fell through the cracks. I made brownies this morning. Would you like one?"

"I thought I smelled something baking. I can't eat gluten."

"Neither can Kylie, so I found a recipe for gluten-free ones made from black beans. I think they're pretty good."

He'd fielded enough female attention to notice the flirtatious sweep of her lashes and the inviting smile she sent his way. He'd better steer clear of her as best he could.

He thanked Taylor again as he said good-bye, then glanced toward the woods. Did he dare take a look at where they'd found the bodies? Not smart. But maybe some of the campers would have heard more information than he'd gleaned.

He crisscrossed the lot and stepped into the cool shadows of the trees. Campers and RVs filled most of the spots, and on the far side of the resort, the cabins all appeared to be rented. Annie was having a booming summer from the look of things.

He spotted a couple sitting on an old log in front of a smoldering firepit. The man poked at it with a long stick.

"Good morning," Jon said.

The man's head swirled toward him, and he straightened. "Good morning."

Jon introduced himself.

"Gretchen and Henry," the man said. "You staying here too?"

"I have a cottage down the way. Enjoying your stay?"

"Love it here. We just got back from a hike."

"I hear there was some excitement here on Tuesday."

"Sure was," Gretchen said. "I saw them carry two bodies out in bags. Sad. One of the forensic people said she thought they were teenagers. If they hadn't been dead such a long time, I would suspect they had been killed by the guys who chased Eddie."

"Forensics said they'd been dead a long time?"

The man nodded. "Years she said. Mostly just bone and hair."

This was sounding more and more like Penelope and Sophie. But why bring them here? Was the killer someone who knew Annie? He didn't like to consider the possibility, but the guy would have had to be familiar with the resort and that remote cabin. No stranger would likely know about this place.

He chatted a few more minutes with the couple before heading back toward his car. As he neared the lake, he saw Annie and Kylie docking. Annie's head turned his way, and he waved. He'd hoped to get out of here before being seen.

He went to help her tie up the boat and steadied it as she stepped onto the dock. Kylie, puppy in her arms, hopped ashore without taking his hand.

"Cute puppy. Does he have a name yet?"

"Not yet," Kylie said in a stiff voice.

"He looks like a Milo to me."

Annie tightened the rope's knots to the dock. "What brings you over? Your dad here too?"

"No, just me. I wondered if the bodies were identified yet."

"Not yet." There was a tension in her voice, and she glanced back toward her house.

"Something wrong?"

She watched Kylie run off with the puppy before she answered. "Someone was in my house yesterday, in my bedroom."

He listened to her run through what she'd found. It lined up with what he'd been thinking around the firepit with Gretchen and Henry. "I don't like it, Annie. It sounds too personal, and we can't discount the fact someone dumped the bodies on your property. You have an empty cottage I could rent?"

She lifted a brow. "I can protect myself, Jon. I've been doing it for years."

It was a jab at his desertion, but he deserved it. "I don't doubt that, but an extra pair of eyes never hurt."

"We're booked up." She stalked off toward the shore after her daughter.

And that ended that.

/ / /

Over the weekend Annie's heightened awareness of danger seemed to mellow. Church helped settle her fears, and spending time with the campers and her daughter gave her back a sense of normalcy. On Monday morning she climbed into her truck for the first time since Thursday and turned the key.

The engine sprang to life and purred almost like it was new.

She pulled the door shut, and it didn't squeal like a frightened piglet. What had happened to her truck?

Maybe it was her imagination, but she thought it didn't bottom out on the rutted gravel road as easily either. Could Max have had someone stop by to work on it? It seemed like something kind the wealthy man might do. He'd noticed the maintenance needed on the buildings, so maybe he'd heard her truck's engine missing.

She'd have to ask him and thank him.

With the truck purring along, she reached Rock Harbor in short order. Mason's SUV was in front of the sheriff's office, so she parked beside it and went inside where she was waved back to his office.

He looked up from the papers he was studying. "I was about to call you."

"ID?"

"Yeah. Penelope Day and Sophie Smith."

The air went out of her lungs, and she sat hard into the chair across from his desk. "I'm glad they've been found, but why in one of my cabins? I don't like it."

"I don't either. It feels personal. Just to keep you in the loop, we're taking a hard look at Jon Dunstan."

"I found out a few things from him." She told Mason about the trip to the fishery and the other things Jon had remembered.

"Why are you just now telling me this? Did you inform the sheriff in Ontonagon County?"

"Not yet. Sorry. I was focused on the victims' identities and then my break-in."

"You talked to the owner of the fishery and he claims he didn't see or speak to Penelope, but Jon said he did?"

"Exactly. The fact Glenn Hussert lied about it is troubling. There would be no reason to lie if it had been an innocent and brief meeting."

"Unless he forgot. It's been nine years."

"I can't imagine anyone forgetting speaking to one of the girls. Their faces have been plastered on the front page of every paper in the country, since Penelope was the daughter of a federal judge. Hussert would have seen her picture in the days right after her disappearance and recognized her."

Mason studied her face. "True enough. You ever stop to think Dunstan's lying? He could be trying to divert attention from his own guilt."

Her face heated. "I don't believe he killed the girls."

His expression remained impassive. "What did you make of this Hussert?"

"Cagey. He didn't make good eye contact. I felt he was hiding something even before Jon told me what he remembered."

"I'll get in touch with a judge to issue a court order for the employment records." Mason leaned back in his chair. "You really don't believe Jon is guilty?"

"I don't. But I'm smart enough to know my feelings are involved."

"At least you're honest about it." He fell silent and laced his thick fingers together. "To tell you the truth, I don't want to believe it either. I've always liked him. But we can't let our personal feelings get in the way of the investigation."

"I agree. That's why I'm telling you everything I know. Jon asked for my help in clearing his name. Did you know his cabin was vandalized?"

Mason frowned. "No, that news hasn't made its way to my office. Minor infractions usually don't."

"Someone painted graffiti on his doors and warned him to get out of town. Finding the bodies in the cabin resurrected all the old suspicions."

His phone rang, and he picked it up and listened. "Send him in." He leaned back and sighed after he hung up. "Penelope's dad is here."

"Judge Day?"

"Yep. I called him as soon as we got back the DNA. Because it was his daughter, we got a quick turnaround on the results." Mason rose as the door opened.

Frank Day wasn't the kind of man to attract attention until he spoke. Slightly built and only five seven or so, his light-brown hair and eyes blended with his skin so well he seemed colorless. But when he spoke, that deep, commanding voice made everyone in the room sit up taller or stand at attention. He'd sent some of the most powerful people in the state to jail and was known for being fair but stern.

This morning the sadness in his eyes covered over any other expression. His gaze went from Annie to Mason. She'd never met him, but he didn't ask her to leave.

Mason came out from behind his desk with his hand extended. "I was sorry to have to give you such sad news, Your Honor."

"Her mother and I are relieved we can lay her to rest. That we finally have closure." His gaze flickered to Annie. "And you are?"

"This is LEO Annie Pederson. A law enforcement ranger. Your daughter and her friend were found on Annie's property. She called me as soon as she discovered the bodies."

He gave a quick nod. "Thank you for that. When can I see Penelope?"

"Are you sure you want to? There isn't much left, Your Honor."

The judge didn't wince. "I have to make sure. I'll recognize her hair and her clothing."

Mason moved toward the door. "I'll take you there now."

Annie followed them out but didn't call attention to her presence. The judge would need this time by himself. She couldn't imagine anything worse than losing Kylie. How had her parents coped with Sarah's loss? It wasn't something Annie wanted to dwell on.

SEVENTEEN

REMODELING THIS HOUSE WAS GOING TO TAKE FOREVER. Jon stood back and inspected the wall he'd finished painting. Sunshine bounced off the light color and made the space look bigger, but he had lots more surface to cover with the pale gray.

He grabbed a cold bottle of water, then went out to the back deck and dropped down to dangle his legs over the side. He took a gulp from his bottle and watched the blue shimmer of Lake Superior. He inhaled the aroma of grass and lake to clear out the paint fumes from his lungs. A big boat, radio blaring, roared past with four teenage boys laughing and cutting up as it zoomed away.

Tires popped on gravel, and he glanced at his watch. Just before noon. His dad was at the bed-and-breakfast, but it might be Sean here to start the roof. Jon jogged around the side of the house and nearly stepped on a chipmunk. He caught a flash of red through the foliage before he spotted Annie's pickup.

In uniform, she got out and stood looking at the house with her hands on her hips. She spotted him when he was a few feet away. "That roof is really bad."

"Sean is replacing it next. I don't want to do much inside in case we get a cloud buster and the water does more damage. What brings you out?" He bit back his question about the bodies found in her cabin.

"We have ID on the bodies. As we suspected, the remains are Sophie Smith and Penelope Day."

He winced. "This is bad, Annie. I don't like it that the killer brought them to your place. It's very weird, and it honestly scares me for your sake. I think you should leave, stay somewhere in town around people."

Her mouth twisted. "Oh, that will work. Abandon my resort and marina. My customers would crucify me on social media with bad reviews. We'd never recover. And hello? It's not like I'm out there by myself. Every one of my fifteen cabins is rented, and the RV spaces are all taken. The business from the marina is brisk. All I'd have to do is scream, and help would be there."

"I don't want anything to happen to you. Or Kylie."

"I'm taking precautions. While I was in town, I picked up a couple of security cameras and some new locks."

"That's good. Want me to install them for you? I'm pretty handy with a drill."

Her gaze bore into him. "You have always known your way around tools." She turned and looked at her truck. "You wouldn't happen to know how my truck started running better all of a sudden, would you? I mentioned the screeches in the door, too, and someone lubed it."

She'd figured it out by herself. He hadn't thought she would. "I had a few minutes."

"What all did you do?"

He ran through the list of repairs he'd made. "You should be good to go on maintenance for the rest of the year."

"Thank you. You didn't have to do it. I would have gotten around to taking it in sooner or later."

"I think it would have been later. I didn't want you breaking down somewhere. Could be dangerous. What's Mason have to say about the case?"

Would she talk to him about it? It didn't take a genius to see she still held him at arm's length—probably because she wasn't convinced of his innocence.

"If it's any consolation, he doesn't think you're guilty. That doesn't mean you're off the hook. He'll investigate the way he always does, but his gut believes you're innocent of this."

"And what's your gut say?"

The *rat-a-tat-tat* of a woodpecker drew her attention, and he couldn't read the expression in her eyes. Maybe she wouldn't even answer. She'd been less than open about how she felt about most everything. The situation was so different from the long summers they'd spent together in the past. Maybe those days couldn't be recovered. Too much pain lay like broken glass in the path between them.

She walked over to peer into the tree where the woodpecker drilled for bugs. "This tree is rotted. You need to have it taken down so it doesn't fall on your new roof."

And his question remained unanswered, just as he suspected. "I'll add that to my very long list."

Her gaze swept the cabin again before coming back to rest on his face. "What I think about your innocence doesn't matter. The truth will come out."

"It matters to me."

"I have never seen violence in you. I would have to see strong proof to believe you did this."

His knees went a little weak at her admission. "I didn't, Annie. I have my faults, but I'd never do something heinous like that."

She looked over his shoulder at his car. "Has your life been everything you hoped for, Jon? Money, fame, a burgeoning career—were they worth it?"

He hesitated before answering. That question had been haunting him for months. The what-ifs had rattled around his head in the dead of night for way too long. What if they hadn't argued that night? What if he hadn't left town? What if he'd stayed here and married her? He could have practiced in Houghton, though it hadn't seemed large enough for his ambitions nine years ago. Now he wasn't so sure.

He held her gaze and let his heart seep through. "No, Annie. It hasn't been everything I hoped for. A big city can be lonely, and working twelve-hour days doesn't leave much time for pursuing friendships. The happiest days of my life have always been in Rock Harbor. Maybe they always will be. But I picked my path. No one forced it on me, so I have no one to blame but myself."

He didn't want to see the pity in her face so he turned back toward the house. "Want something to drink?"

Once, her eyes had held so much more than pity and regret. And he couldn't change it now.

/ / /

Annie turned over the surprising admission that Jon regretted his decision to leave her.

Birds sang in the branches to her right as she stared at his back heading toward the cottage. The worrisome piece of Kylie's paternity tried to rise to the forefront of her mind, but she pushed it aside. He'd already told her he was certain he couldn't have kids. There was no way she could ask him to take a test now.

Annie hadn't thought he'd ever admit he made a mistake.

It was more than surprising—it stole her breath and the level ground under her feet. All these years she'd imagined him happy and fulfilled with his chosen path. And it touched her that he was worried about her.

She followed him into the cottage reeking of paint and sawdust and glanced around. "You gutted the kitchen and bathroom."

"I tore out everything so Sean could get to work. Saved money for me to do the demo." He opened a red metal cooler and extracted two water bottles.

She took the bottle he handed her and uncapped it. "Penelope's dad, Judge Day, is in town. Sophie's parents too. They are likely going to push Mason hard to find a suspect. We need to find more possibilities for Mason to focus on other than you. Judge Day might not have heard your name yet, but if he stays in town, someone will tell him."

"You're still going to help me?"

"I told you I would."

"So what's next?"

She hesitated. Mason wouldn't want her to reveal too much information—not when he considered Jon a person of interest. "We'll start looking for the other men with Glenn Hussert that day. Now that the bodies are found, forensics might turn up something too."

"It's been so long. I'm not sure how much evidence would have survived. Does Mason have any idea when the bodies were moved to your old cabin?"

"I hope you understand, but I can't say too much about the case."

He nodded. "I get it. I'm still a person of interest. What would be interesting to find out is if any of the people working at the fishery knew you or had stayed at your resort."

"He could have known my parents. They would have owned it back then."

"The girls were a few years younger than you. Had you ever met them?"

No one had ever asked her that. She shook her head. "Their pictures didn't look familiar. They were both from Sault Ste Marie."

"But they could have stayed here with their families when they were younger. Did your parents keep records long term? Can you go back and check names and dates?"

His suggestion made sense. "They put records on the computer some years back, and there are some paper records in the attic. I'll take a look. Couldn't hurt."

And she could ask the judge himself if he'd ever stayed at the resort or rented a boat from her parents. Maybe he knew her parents. It was a long shot, but the question might yield something.

"Want some help looking?" he asked.

It was dangerous to be around him too much. "Sure. There are a lot of boxes to go through in the physical files."

Now why had she agreed? *No* had been on the tip of her tongue. She wasn't some weak-willed female who crawled back to the one who'd tossed her aside. What was it about Jon that made her agree so easily? She hadn't even put up a good fight.

Water in hand, she headed for the door. "I'm going home to search now. You can finish your work here and come later if you want. It will take hours to go through everything."

"I'm at a good stopping point. I finished the wall I wanted to paint. And I'm hungry. I haven't had lunch yet. Have you eaten? I could run into town and get us something to eat. Pasties for you and something else for me."

She turned back. "No pasties for me. I can't eat them in front of Kylie. I'm doing my best with her diet, but I haven't gotten to the store yet to get the right replacements for things like pasta. We did get the supplies you had sent though. I need to go to Houghton for most of the specialty items."

He frowned and bit his lip. "That needs to be done right away, Annie. Maybe the doctor didn't impress on you how important it was, but she could develop another autoimmune disease if you don't follow through on her diet."

She knew he was right, but it seemed so cruel to take away Kylie's favorite foods. "Maybe I'll go to Houghton as soon as I check those records." She went down the porch to the driveway and stopped by her truck. "I can get them organized now while I wait on the list of employees from the fishery."

He touched her elbow. "I'll go with you. I know the best brands to look for."

He followed her to the marina in his car. When they arrived, she checked on Kylie, who was playing Pokémon Go while Taylor watched. Jon found the musty boxes of records while she checked the ones on the computer.

"These records are a mess for the year," she said. "We had construction going on, and Mom skipped more days than she recorded. I've done the best I can for now. Let's go to Houghton for food."

He nodded and put the lid back on the box before following her outside. "Let's take my car. It will be faster."

She frowned at the sports car. "Will groceries fit in that little thing?"

"Unless you buy out the store, they will. We're just getting staples."

She wasn't convinced, but she slid down into the leather seat that enveloped her as if it had been molded for her.

He shut her door and went around the front of the car while she snapped on her seat belt and glanced at the dash. The scent of rich leather and luxury surrounded her, and she stretched her legs out.

He climbed in and buckled up. "Ready?"

"As long as you don't scare me to death."

He grinned and started the car. "You might want one after you ride in it."

Fat chance of that. She wouldn't want the loan payment. And she didn't want to yearn for things she'd never have. Like Jon himself.

EIGHTEEN

THE KEWEENAW WATERWAY FLOWED BY WHERE THEY sat at an outdoor patio finishing up a Mexican feast. The fresh scent of water mingled with the sweet aroma of roses planted along the sidewalk. It was almost like old times.

Jon and Annie had started dating the summer after she turned sixteen and had gotten engaged when he was nineteen and had just finished college in three years. They'd planned to get married during his residency, but the big breakup had happened. During those years they often enjoyed coming to Houghton for dinner. This restaurant had been one of their special places.

Annie scooped up the last of her salsa with a chip. "Good to know Mexican food has some safe dishes for Kylie. She loves fish tacos with corn tortillas."

"My favorite too. Anytime you eat out, you'll need to impress on the server the importance of having no cross contamination. There are enzymes she can take to help with accidental exposure too."

"I have so much to learn." Her lids flickered, and she stared down her hands. He was beginning to notice she didn't like to talk about Kylie with him. Or maybe it was part of her keeping him at a distance.

His gaze wandered to the next table, and he narrowed his

eyes to look closer. "Annie, I think that guy was one of the men with Hussert. It's the blond one with the big arms."

She turned her head in a casual manner as if she was gazing at the water. The guy was about thirty with biceps that strained his black tee. His calves below his shorts bulged with muscles too. He must be a bodybuilder. The woman he was with appeared to be in her early twenties. Blonde, like Penelope and Sophie, and obviously smitten by the guy.

"You're sure?" she asked.

"Not positive. If I heard his voice, I think I'd know. His voice was high-pitched for a guy. I remember thinking how his voice didn't match his muscles."

"Let's take a stroll closer to the water." She grabbed a handful of chips as she rose from the wrought-iron chair.

He nodded and left payment with a tip for the meal on the table before falling into step beside her. When her hand slipped into his, it startled him and he nearly pulled away before he realized it was for optics. They needed to appear as a couple taking a romantic stroll along the water.

As they passed the other couple, he heard the man speak in that high-pitched tone he remembered. "It's him."

Her fingers tightened on his. "I don't want to tip him off. Let's linger and feed the ducks until they leave so I can get his license plate." She paused and began to break off bits of tortilla chips.

Quacking, the ducks swam nearer. He watched the couple through the corner of his eye as the man accepted the check and handed over his credit card. "He's paying, so they should be leaving soon. Should we go to the parking lot and watch for them to get to their car?"

"We don't know where he parked. I think it's safer to be occupied here and then follow as if we're parked near the same area."

He took a chip from her hand and fed the ducks too. "You're the boss."

The server seemed to take an excruciatingly long time to bring back the man's credit card. When she finally appeared to have him sign, Jon exhaled and tossed the last of his chip. "Be ready."

She gave a slight nod. When the couple rose, Jon took her hand again and meandered in the direction the couple walked. They went across the street to a different parking lot than where Jon had left his Jag. As he passed through his lot, he noticed several teenagers clustered around his car, and when he made a move to interrupt them, Annie jerked on his hand.

"Focus," she said.

He nodded. The car was insured, and the teenagers were probably just admiring it. The couple ahead of them paused, and the man glanced back. Jon made an impulsive decision and slipped his arm around Annie, then pulled her close for a kiss. She tensed, and her hand went to his chest.

"Relax," he whispered. "I think he's suspicious."

He felt her exhale, and her sweet breath whispered across his face. So familiar it made his heart stutter. Her lips were as soft as he remembered, and it took all his strength not to deepen the kiss.

She pulled away. "They're moving." She sounded out of breath.

He couldn't have replied if his life depended on it. Taking her hand again, they strolled after the couple as if they had all the time in the world.

"When we get there, they might be pulling away. We'll have to memorize the plate quickly," she said.

"I'll take the first digits, and you take the last few."

"Maybe we'll get lucky and he'll have a vanity plate," she said.

A black Camaro was pulling away when they reached the lot, and Jon spotted the blond in the passenger seat. "There they are."

The car turned toward the street, and he could read the plate. "We lucked out. It's BSTRONG. A Michigan specialty plate."

"I'll send it to Mason." She stopped and pulled out her phone to tap in the plate digits. "You think we can follow him?"

"We can try." He led her in a run back to his Jaguar, and they climbed into the seats.

He didn't pause to buckle up but headed down East Lakeshore Drive in the direction he'd last seen the Camaro. "See them anywhere?"

She leaned forward in her seat and looked down every side street they passed. "I think we lost them."

"But we have the plate number. Mason will get the address, and we can pay him a visit. In the meantime, let's shop for food."

He needed a distraction to keep from thinking about how she'd felt in his arms again after all this time.

/ / /

Annie wandered behind Jon in the grocery store as he filled the cart with gluten-free food. If she hadn't had this case to focus on, Annie would have struggled to keep herself from going back for another kiss. So many years had just evaporated when his lips touched hers. She felt like she was twenty-four again and all the fear and heartache had vanished.

But it wasn't really gone. That trauma couldn't be erased, and she had to remember to keep her distance. This whole charade today was her fault too. They hadn't had to pretend to be a couple. They could have been business partners talking about office problems along the river. She'd been the one who took his hand, and she'd felt his shock when she did.

Touching him again had felt electric. She'd felt the connection just like the first time. So the rawness in her heart was of her own doing. She couldn't blame Jon for this one.

He tossed in some pasta. "Tinkyáda is the best gluten-free pasta. She won't be able to tell the difference."

He'd loaded her up with granola, various gluten-free cereals for her to try, Kind bars, gluten-free graham crackers, even gluten-free pretzels and cheese snack crackers.

She looked over the haul. "I had no idea there were so many replacements."

"We need some flours to replace those in cooking too. There are gluten-free blends to make cupcakes and muffins, or you can buy bags of different flours and combine them."

"Let's do what's easiest for now."

"We have to be able to make pancakes. I'm going to work on perfecting a gluten-free *pannukakkua*. I'd like to find one for myself as well as her." He paused to do a search on his phone. "This recipe looks good. I just need Pamela's baking mix." He led her down another aisle and selected the gluten-free flour blend. "Nuts make good snacks too."

She grabbed some bulk containers of mixed nuts, then stopped in the frozen food aisle and stared at the frozen breads. "Gosh, this stuff is expensive too."

"Yeah, it's not cheap. Rudi's is good and so is Canyon Bakehouse, but my favorite is the Sami's I had mailed to you."

How was she going to afford to buy this all the time? But this was for Kylie, so she'd find a way to make it work. She could start packing her lunches and not eat out so often. There had to be ways to cut back on other things.

They headed for the checkout, and Jon started putting items on the belt. Her phone alerted her to a message, and she swiped it on. "It's Mason. He sent us an address. It's up in Eagle River."

"We don't have anything refrigerated so we can go up there now."

She glanced at the time. One thirty. It was forty-five minutes each way. They should be back by four o'clock, which still left her enough time to fix dinner and spend some time with Kylie.

The total rang up at over a hundred dollars, and she winced before reaching for her wallet. Before she could pull out her debit card, Jon handed his over to pay.

"I can pay for it."

"It was my idea to go shopping. Maybe the treats will have Kylie warming up to me a little. I should never have implied she didn't clean the fish well enough that first day. I'm a little clueless with kids."

"She'll get over it. She still misses her dad."

"I'm sure she does. That had to be hard to lose her father so young."

Was Nathan Kylie's father? The uncertainty was wearing Annie down, but there didn't seem to be a way to know for sure. Jon began to gather up the bags when a thought struck her. She still had some of Nate's things around. Could she get a paternity test done from his toothbrush or something else with his DNA? She'd talk to the doctor about it. Nate was gone, so there wouldn't be the need to get his permission. It would be the logical place to start. Maybe she could lay these questions to rest.

Jon carried the bags out to his car and stowed them in the trunk. Three bags for over a hundred dollars. Pitiful. But she couldn't change the situation.

She got buckled into the passenger seat and stared at her phone. "The address is on Second Street."

As she read off the address, he put it in his GPS. "Did Mason find out any information about this guy? Name, age, arrest history—anything that could prove useful?"

"He was emailing me some details. Let me check. Got it." She scanned the email. "Lonnie Fox, age thirty-two. He's got a rap sheet from his teen years, mostly small-time offenses like breaking and entering and a couple of fights. The charges were dropped."

"No rape or kidnapping charges?"

She studied what Mason had sent her. "Nope, nothing like that. But he did work for the fishery, so we know for sure he's the guy you saw."

"Glad for the confirmation since it's been nine years. I thought it was him, but time can steal details. Anything else?"

"Never married. He's a truck driver now, mostly local. Hauling gravel and dirt for one of the businesses in town. And no other priors for the past ten years. He's kept his nose clean."

"At least as far as the law knows."

She nodded. "True enough. Maybe he just hasn't been caught again."

"Siblings, parents?"

"Born in Eagle River. Looks like he lives with family. At least the property is owned by someone with the same last name."

"How do you plan to question him?"

She'd been considering that. If only she had an outstanding warrant to use, she might be able to get to the truth. Jumping into questions about an event that had happened so long ago would likely get her nowhere. He'd claim he didn't remember. And if he wasn't involved, maybe he wouldn't recall the events.

She was good at reading people, though, and she prayed he'd drop some hints to help her. The one thing she hadn't told Jon was that the judge would likely want to talk to him.

That might not go well.

NINETEEN

EAGLE RIVER WAS ONE OF THE FIRST SETTLEMENTS ON the Keweenaw, and its location on Lake Superior and the quaint buildings around town meant it was a tourist draw in the summer. It had been a copper town back in the day. Now its biggest draw was the monastery and its accompanying business, the Jampot. The monks sold Poorrock Abbey thimbleberry preserves, coffee, and all kinds of treats.

Jon pointed out a billboard for the Jampot as they passed. "I hear they have gluten-free cookies now. Let's stop after we're done and grab some things."

Annie nodded and consulted the GPS on the dash. "We're turning in a mile."

Jon followed the directions and spotted the place. The house was a single-story cottage style with white siding and green shutters. The pristine yard and planting bed showed someone loved gardening or else they hired it done.

Jon parked his Jag behind Lonnie's Camaro. "Showtime."

Annie pushed open her door. "Jump in if you remember something. I won't be offended."

"Roger that."

He got out and automatically locked the doors, though in Eagle River vandalism or theft would be unlikely. He followed

Annie up the flower-lined walkway to the red door. A basket of petunias swung in the breeze from a hook by the front door.

Annie rang the bell, and steps thundered toward them. The door flew open and, jaw outthrust, Lonnie Fox glared at them.

He jabbed a thick finger toward the sign on the door. "Can't you read? No solicitors."

"Park service, Mr. Fox," Annie said. "I'm investigating a cold-case disappearance, and I'd like to ask you a few questions. See if you remember something that could help."

His hazel eyes narrowed. "Cold case? I don't know anything about a disappearance."

Jon heard the curiosity in his voice and realized Annie had hooked him. Most people liked thinking they had some kind of inside information.

Annie pulled out her phone and called up a picture of the missing teens. "About nine years ago, these two girls went missing. Penelope Day and Sophie Smith." She handed her phone to the man. "A witness puts you at Lake of the Clouds that day, and I hoped you might have seen someone talking to them."

He stared down at the phone, and his frown returned. "That's a long time ago. I've been to Lake of the Clouds countless times. There are always teenagers hanging around."

"These girls were very attractive. I think they would stand out."

He handed her the phone. "I don't remember."

"You were with your boss at the time, Glenn Hussert."

His scowl grew thunderous. "Glenn sic you on me? He's the womanizer, not me. If anyone noticed those two, it would have been him. Stinks that he tried to throw off suspicion from himself by pointing to me."

"Did you notice him talking to the girls?"

"He always talked to girls. Even ones too young for him. He's a scumbag, which is why I quit working for him."

"Do you remember who else was at the lake with the two of you that day?"

Fox paused to think. "We went on fishing trips up there a lot, so it was probably the twins, Roger and Rolf Wolstincraft. They still work for him. Birds of a feather, you know?"

A promising clue. "You know where they live?" Jon asked.

"Out on Lampaa Lane outside Rock Harbor. In an old trailer. But watch it. They have two mean rotties that would rather maul you than eat. Nasty creatures."

"Thanks for the tip." Annie handed him her card. "If you think of anything else, please give me a call."

He stuck the card in the shirt pocket of his tee. "Why the interest in the disappearance after all this time?"

"It's no longer a missing persons case—it's homicide."

"Their bodies have been found?"

"Yes."

"I hope you find who did it." He closed the door and the lock clicked.

Jon took Annie's arm, and they went back to his car. "I didn't think we'd get anything from him. No love lost with his former employer."

"Interesting though. Good to learn Hussert is a womanizer. We'll need to talk to him again, but first I'd like to talk to the twins."

"With the mean dogs."

"Not going to be fun," she agreed. "I should have brought pepper spray."

"We could try to talk to them at the fishery. I can call and find out the work hours."

They got in the car, and he pulled out his phone to call Bunyan Fisheries. The automated answering service stated the business hours as seven to four.

He ended the call. "I don't think we can make it back by four. We can go first thing in the morning."

"I'd rather not wait. We can at least assess the situation at the trailer. If they're outside, we can have them call off the dogs."

"If they will." Jon had seen that kind of man before—someone who took pleasure in having mean dogs usually liked to use his fists and throw his weight around.

He started the car. "The Jampot isn't far, and we can grab the food and head for Rock Harbor."

He drove M26 to the Jampot. The small white building with its red door was an icon in the area, and the modest appearance was no indication of the delicious treats inside. There was usually a line, but at least today it wasn't winding out the door.

"You want to wait here while I grab a few things?"

"Yes, I'll call Mason and let him know what we found. He might have an update."

He got out into the sunshine and went inside the small building lined with pots of jam, jelly, cookies, and pastries. The aroma of chocolate and coffee greeted him. He grabbed the things he knew were safe, and the monk behind the register rang him up.

"You know anything about Lonnie Fox?" he asked. "He lives here in town."

The monk ducked his head. "I choose never to indulge in gossip."

"I know him," a woman said from behind Jon. "Lives over on Second Street?"

"That's the guy."

"He used to date my sister. Don't trust him around women. He raped her."

Jon took a step back. "Would you mind talking to the park service about this? It would be very helpful in a murder case."

So, Fox wasn't truthful. He shouldn't have been surprised.

/ / /

Annie had always prided herself on being a good judge of character, but listening to the woman Jon had found recount Fox's behavior to her teenage sister made her question her initial good impression of Fox. It just went to prove that people were good at wearing masks.

She thanked the woman and climbed into the Jag to drive out to the Wolstincraft property.

Conversation between Jon and her lagged as they made the trip back to Rock Harbor. Her thoughts squirreled around her investigation as well as what to do about Kylie's paternity. Discovering that truth was important for her daughter's future, but the thought of finding out something Annie didn't want to know froze her decision-making ability.

Lampaa Lane turned to dirt a few miles out of town. Jon drove slowly along the humped road flanked by oak trees. The pretty view expanded into an open landscape with two cheery red cottages on either side of a finger of a dock extending across the calm waters of a small lake. It was a typical fishing property.

Annie heard dogs barking. A few seconds later two Rottweilers appeared. Snarling and snapping at the tires, they were intent on keeping anyone off the property.

Jon glanced at a tan pickup. "Let's see if anyone is home."

He laid on the horn in long blasts until a man with red hair tied back in a ponytail poked his head through the cabin's door on their left. The man exited the home and came their way. His brown eyes gleamed as he took in the red sports car. He stopped a few feet away and patted the leg of his khaki shorts. "Come!"

The dogs gave a last hungry stare at Jon's face before trotting over to lay down at the man's feet. Jon ran his window down. "You Roger or Rolf Wolstincraft?"

"I'm Roger." He patted the now-dusty hood of the Jaguar. "Sweet wheels. I wouldn't mind taking it for a ride." He glanced down at the dogs lying by his feet as if he was making a threat.

Annie tensed. She already didn't like this guy, and his twin was probably just as bad. Meeting them unarmed in a dark alley might be dangerous.

Jon jerked his head toward Annie. "Park ranger here has a few questions for you if you don't mind. Your brother around?"

"Park ranger. What'd I do, leave a cigarette butt in the wrong place?" His tanned face stretched into a grin that made him look more sinister. "Rolf is inside his place. He lives in the other cabin. I'll get him."

He told the dogs to stay before going to the cabin's door and yelling for his brother. A few seconds later another man who was a dead ringer for Roger appeared, right down to the color of his shorts and blue tee. Did they consciously try to confuse people on their identity? It would make it hard to ID one of them for a crime when you couldn't tell them apart.

Both men walked around to Annie's side of the car. She made no move to get out since the dogs followed the men.

She ran her car window down. "You both work at Bunyan Fisheries?"

"For a lot of years," Rolf said. "So what?"

Annie held out her phone. "You recognize these teenage girls?"

Roger took the phone and glanced at it. "Those girls who went missing some years back. I don't remember their names." He handed back the phone. "Don't know them, never met them."

"A witness puts you at the Lake of the Clouds when they were there. Along with your boss."

"And Lonnie Fox." Rolf's lip curled. "Glad he's out of our hair."

"And Lonnie," Annie agreed. Could she get them to spill something because of their obvious dislike for Lonnie? "Lonnie gave us your names and the fact you were at the lake that day."

Roger's big hands balled at his side. "Yah, sure-hey." His Yooper expression meant, "You've got to be kidding me," and he rolled his eyes. "I'll be sure to thank him."

It was hard to say who would be the winner in a one-on-one fight between the men. They were equally big and muscular, but she had a feeling the twins would gang up on an adversary instead of giving a fair fight. She hoped Lonnie was ready for their animosity. He probably knew what would happen when he'd told her though. He had to know these two men well.

She stared him down. "If I hear he's been hurt, I'll know where to come."

Rolf scowled. "I know how to run the sauce through the attic, ya. I wouldn't waste my time."

"Did you speak to Penelope Day or Sophie Smith?"

"I don't remember," Roger said. "Pretty girls like that—we might have. But they were talking to some teenagers when we left the lake. There was some talk about a party at an RV."

The guy was lying. Annie bit back a sigh. Anything to throw off suspicion. "You have any names or descriptions?"

"Nah," Rolf said. "It was just kids—you know?"

"Did Lonnie or Glenn talk to the girls?"

"Glenn did. Invited them for a drink."

Which was confirmation of what Jon had said. Glenn was moving up on her suspect list, but it was too early to tell.

"Anything else you remember?"

Rolf jabbed a thumb Jon's direction. "I remember that guy. He was with them. They argued and he walked away. Maybe he came back and did them in, ya."

"Thanks for the information. We do know about Mr. Dunstan picking them up when they were hitchhiking. Did you see them along the road yourself?"

"Nope. We would have stopped for them too. Any red-blooded man would have."

"Thank you for your time." She handed a card through the window. "If you remember anything else, please contact me."

One of the dogs got up and leaped at her hand. She jerked it away from its snapping jaws in the nick of time. "Let's get out of here," she told Jon.

These men were making her feel more and more icky. She would need a shower after talking with these guys. None of them would be anyone she wanted to know better.

TWENTY

HE WAS HOME.

A light shone through the windows of the cottage, and Taylor saw a male figure moving around inside even though it was nearly nine at night. She'd taken a chance to walk the shoreline with the warm brownies, but her gamble had paid off.

She'd thought all day about Jon and the way he'd looked at her. He'd been attracted to her. She could tell by the smile that crinkled the outer corners of his green eyes and the way his gaze had lingered on her red hair. She'd known if she dyed her hair bright enough, someone would notice her.

And she was thankful it was Jon.

Such a generous man. Fixing up Annie's pickup, talking kindly to Kylie, helping out with the investigation. Not many men were as solicitous about other people as he was.

She walked to the porch and waved away the bugs buzzing the light by the door, then peered through the screen. Jon was rolling gray paint on the wall, and the smell wafted toward her. She drank in his appearance in his shorts and tee. His brown hair fell across his forehead, and paint smudged his biceps and one knee.

She rapped on the door. "Hey there."

He jerked and turned so quickly he nearly dropped the roller.

"Taylor. You startled me. I didn't hear a car. Kylie and Annie with you?"

"No, just me. I walked."

His gaze fell on the fudge brownies in her hand, and his eyes widened. "Those look good."

"They're gluten free. You never got any on Friday." She set her hand on the door handle. "Can I come in?"

He hesitated, then stepped aside. "It's a mess."

Why was he being so standoffish? She looked around the living room. "This is a nice place. I like it."

"Thanks. Hopefully a buyer will too. It's a lot of work to get it ready to list." He glanced at his watch. "You're out late, especially walking alone. It's not really safe with that hiker being murdered."

Maybe he'd offer to take her home. She let herself imagine sitting in his car. It was small, and their shoulders might touch.

"It was a nice walk in the moonlight. The loons were out, and I spotted some owls."

He frowned. "It's not really safe though. I'll run you home when you're ready to go. I'm about finished up here."

"Want some help? Looks like there's one more wall to paint. We could knock it out, and you'd be done with the room."

He hesitated and glanced at the remaining wall. "Sure. It would be stupid to turn down free labor. This is a bigger job than I expected." He handed her his roller. "I'll get another one. I already cut in the edges and trim."

The handle was still warm from his touch, and his fingerprints marked the handle. It made her feel almost as if they were holding hands. And she liked the smell of him, that masculine, hardworking scent that was all male.

She loaded the roller and began to spread paint on the last

wall. In moments he joined her, painting from the other side and moving toward her. It was almost as if they were a couple working on their home together. Wouldn't that be a wonderful life? What a dream.

They finished the wall in fifteen minutes, and Jon stood back to admire their handiwork. "That was fast. I'm going to clean up and dive face-first into one of those brownies."

She handed him her roller. "They're still warm."

"The smell makes my mouth water." He carried the paint supplies to the sink and began the cleanup.

She watched the way his muscles flexed under his tee and the careful way he scrubbed every bit of paint from the roller and brush. His attention to detail didn't surprise her. He was an exceptional man in every way.

He dried his hands and pulled back the plastic wrap from the plate of brownies. "Want one?"

"No thanks. I made two batches, and there are more back at Tremolo Marina. Why is it called Tremolo? I've been meaning to ask Annie."

He took a bite of brownie and gave her a thumbs-up. "Best brownies I've ever ate," he mumbled past the mouthful. He swallowed and gestured toward the back door at the sound of a loon's call. "It's the sound a loon makes. The loons are all over around here. Annie hates them though."

"I love loons. Why would she hate them?"

"It's just the tremolo she hates. Ever notice she has that noise machine in her bedroom? Her younger sister was kidnapped when Annie was a kid. It was nighttime, and they'd been out on the dock listening to the loons. Annie blames herself for taking her sister out at night."

"Sounds like it *was* her fault."

His brows rose and he frowned. "She was just a little girl. About Kylie's age. No kid that age has a lick of sense, and she was just doing what Sarah asked. And she'd never been faced with evil like that. She had no reason to be afraid. But the tremolo brings it all back, and she can't sleep with the loons sounding off. I'm not sure she'll ever get past it."

Taylor pressed her lips together so she didn't say anything more that would make him defend Annie. Sneaking out had been a dumb thing to do. Taylor had been taught to obey her mother. Always, without question. It sounded like Annie had never learned obedience.

Annie deserved the avalanche of punishment coming her way. No sympathy, no mercy.

Jon rinsed the crumbs from his fingers. "I'll run you home."

The ride back to the lodge was everything she'd hoped. Their shoulders nearly touched, and being in the close confines of the Jaguar allowed her to breathe in the remaining scent of his cologne—something spicy and wonderful.

He stopped in the lot. "Thanks again, Taylor, for the brownies and the help. You're the best."

"You're welcome." She climbed out and smiled. He'd soon find out how good she was at everything.

/ / /

The sun was barely up when Jon parked at the cottage. Sean's truck was already there, and the ring of hammers echoed in the treetops as he got out of his car. He smelled asphalt and spotted a bucket of the sticky black stuff at the foot of the ladder.

Sean hammered shingles onto the roof. He waved, then climbed down the ladder and came toward Jon with a smile. "Today is roofing day."

"I like the black."

"It gives the old cottage an updated look, don't you think? Wait until you see it with new windows with black trim and a new paint color."

"I think it will attract buyers. I painted the living room last night."

"It looks great. The inside's ready for the new cabinets and flooring."

"All ready."

Jon eyed him. Sean had lived here his entire life. Maybe he'd have some insight. "You happen to know Lonnie Fox? Lives up in Eagle River but worked near here for a while."

"Sure, I know Lonnie. He's from Rock Harbor. I went to school with him. Great guy."

"You ever hear about him raping a teenage girl?" It was Annie's investigation, and Jon didn't want to reveal too much.

A frown formed between Sean's hazel eyes. "Where'd you hear that old scuttlebutt? You shouldn't be repeating it. It's not true."

"Not true?" Better not to say how he'd heard it.

"Lissa is only a year younger than Lonnie, but her sister makes it sound like he robbed the cradle. Lonnie caught Lissa in the backseat of a car with one of his best friends. Let's say they weren't wearing much. He broke up with her, and she stalked him for weeks, trying to get him to take her back. When he wouldn't have anything more to do with her, she started telling everyone he raped her."

"How are you so certain what happened?"

Sean sighed and ran a hand through his curly brown hair. "I'd rather not say."

Jon studied his downcast expression. "Were you the friend caught with Lissa?"

The hammer fell from Sean's fingers, and he bent down to retrieve it. "Yeah. Not much of a friend, was I? Lonnie never talked to me again. Lissa was a hottie, but I guess I lost my head."

"How are you so sure he didn't hurt her?"

"She was mad at Lonnie that night. She only made out with me to get back at him for breaking a date with her. After he broke it off, she wanted me to take her to the prom, but I wouldn't do it. Seeing his face that night destroyed any feelings I'd had for her. So she told me we'd both be sorry. She told everyone who would listen that Lonnie raped her and I'd held her down. It was a flat-out lie."

While Jon heard the ring of truth in Sean's words, how did he go about corroborating a story like this? Maybe he'd talk to Lissa and gauge her character himself. Talk to some of her friends.

"Thanks for the information."

"What's this all about?"

Jon hesitated again. This was an active investigation, and he didn't know how much he could tell. "Annie and I talked to Lonnie yesterday. Afterward, Lissa's sister told us he'd raped her sister." With that comment, an innocent conversation had just taken a weird turn.

"See, just like I said. She had a vendetta against him, and it's been years since they broke up. It's weird."

True enough. Jon gestured toward the house. "So, roof today. What's next?"

"Windows. Then I'll put in the new floors for the kitchen and bath. It's moving along. I've got a couple of guys helping me. We should be done in about three weeks. Luckily, it's a small place."

Three weeks. Twenty-one days to help Annie. Such a short time before he had to get back to his real life. Did he even want that other life? He'd only been gone eight days, but it felt a world away. The hustle and bustle of Rochester and his career seemed to belong to someone else.

The more he was around Annie, the more he regretted letting her go. But she'd run right into Nate's arms. They hadn't talked enough about that. Had she ever really loved him? Had Nate completely replaced Jon in her heart?

She was still prickly and kept him at arm's length. Maybe she always would. She hadn't run right into *his* arms, and Jon had to admit that stung. He'd thought the surprise of seeing him might get her to reveal how she felt. But if she felt anything at all, she kept it well hidden.

Maybe he should leave the work all to Sean. Cut his losses before his feelings got too entangled again. But the thought of not seeing Annie's smile light up her blue eyes made his chest grow tight. Those feelings had sprung up like dormant seeds, erupting into vines that spiraled around his heart. It was probably already too late to go back to Rochester without another truckload of regret.

When he'd left, she'd been a girl. Now she was a woman. Mature and wise with an important job she was good at. And she was a mother. A good mother. It felt strange to see her in that role, but she'd been made to nurture. She pursued justice with a single-minded passion, but she could turn off that side and slip into motherhood seamlessly. What other layers did she have that he hadn't seen yet?

TWENTY-ONE

ANNIE HADN'T SLEPT WELL EVEN THOUGH SHE'D TAKEN a shower to scrub off the contact with those twins. Nasty men.

On Tuesday morning she sat across the desk from Kade, with the aroma of burnt coffee wafting around her, and told him what she'd found while up in Eagle River.

"I got a call from Jon a few minutes ago with a message for you. He said he tried to call you and you didn't pick up," Kade said. "According to Sean Johnson, the reported rape is a lie for revenge. I called Mason to check the records after Jon called, and there's no report. Lonnie had some minor teenage infractions but nothing since he turned eighteen."

"Interesting. You going to talk to Lissa?"

"Mason thought she might be intimidated by him and wanted to know if you want to have a casual chat with her to verify? You have good instincts."

"You bet. We have an address for her?"

"I'll text it to you." He leaned back in his chair. "I'm glad you stopped by. I was going to call you anyway. The DNA results for the child's remains came through this morning."

Annie's pulse jumped, and she leaned forward. "It's Sarah?"

He shook his head. "I'm sorry. No DNA match to you. We

don't have an ID yet, but we're working on it. I didn't want you to wait and hope for closure when it's not Sarah."

She sat back. This was a position she'd been in several times. Relief and despair battled for control. While she didn't know Sarah's fate, she could still hope she lived out there somewhere, even though realistically it was unlikely.

"Thank you. I'll keep looking."

Would she ever stop searching for her sister? She couldn't see any way that would happen. Every time she met a stranger, she'd be looking for a blue-eyed blonde with long legs. She'd be listening for a familiar cadence in the voice or a mannerism that stopped Annie in her tracks. But after all these years, even if she found Sarah, would she recognize her or would she walk right past?

Wouldn't her soul instantly know her little sister or was that a fantasy she'd indulged?

Sarah was still out there somewhere, depending on Annie to find her. Even if it was a few scattered bones to bring home and lay beside their parents.

"Thanks for trying, Kade."

"I'll keep an eye out too." He cleared his throat and pulled a paper toward him. "Forensics is done with the campsite where the Willis man disappeared. You have good instincts, and I thought maybe you'd want to walk the area. You might see something they missed. You're used to being in the deep woods."

She took out her phone. "Where's the site?"

"Out west of the Ontonagon Indian Reservation. I'll send you the coordinates." He grabbed his phone and made a few keystrokes.

Her phone signaled a message and she saw two from Kade, one with the coordinates of the Willis crime scene and one with the address of the woman she was going to interview. She had her day cut out for her.

"That's a hike back into the site. I won't be able to take the ATV all the way."

"I know. You don't have to go out there if you don't want to. It's not an easy hike."

"No, I want to have a look. I'll grab some lunch and let Taylor know when I'll be back, then head on out. I should be back by six o'clock, no later than seven."

"Let me call Larry. I don't like you going out there alone." He made a quick call and frowned.

As Annie listened, she could tell the other ranger wasn't free to accompany her. She thought of Jon, but he was painting today, and she didn't want to derail the work on his cottage.

Kade ended the call. "Larry won't be free for a few hours."

"I'll be fine."

"Be careful."

"I will."

When she left Kade, she drove to town to talk to the doctor. She parked on the street and walked toward Dr. Eckright's office where she ran into Bree. "I was going to stop by to ask what I should be doing to train the puppy. When should he start SAR training?"

Bree pushed her strawberry curls out of her eyes and squinted in the bright sun. "You can start as early as about twelve weeks. The puppy is nine weeks so just a little longer. Does he have a name yet?"

"Not yet. Soon. Sign us up when it's time."

Bree studied Annie's expression. "You look stressed. Everything okay?"

Annie hesitated. Could she unburden something so personal? She'd always been private, and this felt like something she needed to hold close to the chest. "I'd thought maybe the remains of my sister had been found, but it wasn't Sarah."

Bree's green eyes softened. "I'm sorry. The not knowing has to be so hard."

"I'm not giving up."

Bree nodded. "I knew you wouldn't." She squeezed her forearm. "Call if you need to talk."

Annie waited until she was out of sight, then jetted across the street to the doctor's office. She found him escorting a patient out the door. She waited until the woman exited, then shut the door behind them.

The doctor gestured for her to follow him over to the desk where he made a quick note before he turned to her. "Annie, I wasn't expecting you. Kylie doing all right?"

"I found her some gluten-free replacements, and she's adjusting." There was no one else in the office this close to lunch, so she pulled out the plastic bag in her purse. "Could we run a paternity check on Nathan? It would be the easiest to do first. I've got his toothbrush and his hairbrush. Would that work?"

His eyes were kind. "We can see if there's enough DNA on the toothbrush. There should be. There are labs that specialize in that."

A weight rolled off her. She wouldn't have to talk to Jon. Once she had proof of Nate's paternity, she could breathe easier. "How long will it take?"

"About a week."

"That's much quicker than I expected. Thanks so much." She handed over the bag.

"I'll get this sent in right away, and I'll email you the bill once I know what it is. I think it's around a hundred dollars."

Well worth it for her peace of mind.

/ / /

Annie swatted away a black fly and knelt to examine the obvious signs of a camp setup. The trail she was following ended in a small lake. This was the place where Christopher Willis had camped before he disappeared.

All of Willis's belongings had been removed for evidence, but she sat on a log by the remains of the campfire and tried to put herself in his shoes. Two trumpeter swans glided on the glassy surface of the water, and birds twittered in the leafy canopy overhead. She could see why he'd chosen this spot. So serene, so full of God's creation and presence.

A rustling sound came from her left, and hand on the butt of her gun, she bolted to her feet and turned, but it was a deer wandering through the brush. The doe bounced away when it saw her, but the adrenaline still pumping through Annie's veins wouldn't let her recapture the quiet moment. She scoured the ground for clues.

Forensics had been all over this area, leaving numerous footprints and scuff marks in the dirt. She wandered closer to the lake, then turned upon hearing a distinctive ticking sound, like typewriter keys, in time to catch a glimpse of a yellow rail. It was rare to see the tawny bird. Had Willis been here birding? She'd already seen several highly sought-after avian sightings along this lake.

She glanced at the sky. It was time to hike out of here or she'd be caught trying to find her way in the dark. After taking a sip of water, she turned back toward the trail. Her right foot slipped into a hole, and she twisted it as she fell onto a bed of moss and mud. A sharp pain gripped her ankle. She cried out and grabbed at her hiking boot.

She untied the laces and loosened the leather around her ankle so she could press on it. It was already discoloring. Had she broken it? She didn't dare take off her shoe or she suspected she wouldn't get it back on again, and she had to get out of here. A large rock was to her right, and she dragged herself over to pull herself up on top of the boulder. She checked her phone. No bars. There was rarely a signal this far back in the woods.

She couldn't call for help and reasoned she would have to get out of here on her own. The hike out was two miles over rough terrain. Could she do it? She struggled to her feet and tried to take a step on the injured leg. Excruciating pain gripped her ankle in a vise. There was no way she could hike out by herself.

Kade knew she was here, so she could only pray Taylor let someone know when she didn't show up tonight. The thought of staying here as darkness fell wasn't appealing. Bears would be out, but even worse, the mosquitoes would come hunting for her tender skin.

She had insect repellant in her backpack, along with snacks and plenty of water, so she would survive it, but it wouldn't be pleasant.

If only she could call Jon. Funny how he was the first person she thought of to come help her. What did that mean?

She pushed the question away and prayed God would alert someone when she didn't show up when expected. Taylor and Kylie expected her home by seven. If Taylor called Mason by eight, someone might be here by ten. Or maybe not. Sunset tonight was around nine forty-five, so it might take them longer to hike in to find her. It wasn't an easy trip.

She ate a Kind bar and took a swig of water. Soaking her ankle in the cold lake water might relieve the pain, but she probably still couldn't hike that far out without help. And it wouldn't be smart to go thrashing through the brush and end up off track where Kade couldn't find her. Best to stay here even though she wanted out.

The minutes ticked by. Seven. By now Taylor and Kylie would be expecting her. How long before Taylor called Mason? Half an hour? An hour? Annie prayed it wouldn't be longer than that.

Darkness fell faster in the woods with the leaves blotting out the fading sun. The mosquitoes buzzed around her ears, and she applied more repellant. It was going to be a long night.

The lake's glassy surface reflected the trees lining its shores. The swans glided past again, and she saw ducks on the other side. She peered closer and inhaled sharply at the shape of the beak. Those weren't ducks. It was a pair of loons.

Dread curled in her belly as the loons swam closer. When one of them waddled out of the water onto an island of vegetation about five feet from her, she realized she was perched near the nest. She cast her gaze around for a walking stick, anything that would help her move farther away, but there was nothing but moss, dirt, and rocks.

The loon settled on the nest and watched her with red eyes that warned her to stay away. No worries about that. The fuzzy head almost looked like fur instead of feathers, and the white speckles on its wings were distinctive. She would give anything to be somewhere else. Seeing the bird up close brought memories from her childhood flooding in. She and Sarah had been fascinated by loons. They watched for nests and guarded the eggs. They watched male loons battle for nesting rights. She could almost hear Sarah's laughter.

Then the loons began to wail. The eerie *oo-AH-ho* of the tremolo made Annie shudder. She hated that sound so much, and there was no way to block it out. She had no headphones with her, and even if she did, she'd deleted the music app. She put her fingers in her ears, but the wail pierced through anyway.

She swallowed hard and peered at the loon on the nest. Its mate swam in protective circles nearby.

She was thirty-three years old. She'd spent the last twenty-four years of her life letting a sound send her running for safety. Was she going to let an incident when she was nine define the rest of her life? How did she get free from this fear? She prayed for strength, but maybe she'd prayed for the wrong thing.

There was a time to turn and face fear. Maybe God had let her fall so she could see it was time to let go of the past.

As the night descended in a dark blanket, she knew one thing—she had to go back to Tremolo Island. Back to that dock where Sarah had been taken. She had to walk those weathered boards and face the past.

TWENTY-TWO

THIS WAS PROBABLY A TERRIBLE IDEA, BUT JON couldn't stay away. He rapped on the screen door of Annie's house at just after seven. His mouth watered at the aromas of roast beef and potatoes wafting out to him, and he could see Taylor lifting the roast out of the Crock-Pot onto a plate. "Knock, knock. I am returning your plate."

Taylor whirled with a shy smile. "Hey, Jon. You're just in time for dinner. Come on in."

He entered, and the screen banged behind him as the puppy launched himself at Jon's leg. He reached down to rub its ears.

Kylie scowled. "We can't eat yet. Mommy isn't back. She said she'd be here at six. *He* can't have her share."

The little girl's snippy words barely registered. "Your mom is late? Has she called?"

Taylor put the white plate on the counter. "No, she hasn't."

"Doesn't she usually call if she's going to be late?" Annie was the punctual sort, and she wouldn't want to worry anyone, especially her daughter.

"Mommy always calls or texts Taylor. I want to go look for her, but Taylor won't let me."

Jon pulled out his phone and tried Annie's number. It went to voice mail. "Maybe she's out of range. Any idea where she went?"

Taylor shook her head. "The sheriff might know. Or Bree. She was going to ask Bree how to train the puppy."

"Or Kade. He's her boss. He should know her whereabouts." He placed a call to Kade, and the head ranger picked up almost immediately. "Kade, this is Jon Dunstan. Annie isn't home yet, and she's not answering calls or texts. You have any idea where she might be?"

"I told her not to go out there by herself."

"Out where?"

"West of the Indian reservation. I'll have Mason send some deputies out to search for her, and I'll go myself."

"I'd like to go too. Can you send me the coordinates?"

"Yeah, but don't go into the woods by yourself. It will be dark in the shadows, and you're likely to get lost."

"I've got a GPS unit and a satellite phone. But I'll wait on the deputies." Jon ended the call, and as soon as he got Kade's text, he headed for the door. "I'll let you know when I find her."

Taylor nodded, but her brown eyes were expressionless. Jon didn't have time to worry about whether she was offended that he didn't stay for dinner.

He felt in his gut that something was wrong. Annie should have been out of the woods by now, and if she was, she would have answered her phone.

He raced back to the cottage in his car, then went to the garage to find his ATV. It was still there, but it seemed so much smaller than he remembered. It was more the size of a motorcycle than the big ATV he'd seen Annie driving.

He hadn't checked it since he got back, but he'd get closer in the ATV than if he tried to take the Jag into the woods. When he unlocked the garage door, the thick stench of dust and disuse swept toward him. He flipped on the light and pulled a tarp off the ATV. It looked fine, but it wouldn't have been ridden in years.

He found the key on a hook and got on. It took some coaxing to get it started, and it ran raggedly. He needed to change the oil and gas in it, but what was in here was old too. He'd have to pray for the best and hope it got him where he needed to go.

He backed it out of the garage, then stopped to get his satellite phone out of the car before he fired up the GPS and headed out.

It seemed to take forever for him to reach the turnoff to deep woods. Before he lost signal, he tried her phone again. Still no answer. If his phone wasn't working, hers wasn't either. He had the satellite phone if he needed to call Mason. And no sign of the deputies. He checked his phone and found a message from Mason that the deputies were running late.

He wasn't going to wait on them, so he switched on the headlamps and entered the deep shadow of the forest. There was less noise than he expected. The birds were beginning to find their nests for the night, and the wind had stilled. It was as if the forest held its breath as he rolled the ATV over the rocky, barely perceptible trail.

One mile into the forest he spotted Annie's ATV. He dismounted and checked it out. No damage or anything suspicious, so she'd probably left it here to hike into the woods. The trail was too narrow to get her ATV through, but his was a smaller one, and he thought he could follow the trail for a while longer.

He got back on his vehicle and let it roll slowly through the darkness. It was hard to see the trail even with the lights on, so he couldn't accelerate like he wanted to. Something was very wrong, and he wanted to reach Annie as quickly as he could. The engine noise reverberated through the treetops and echoed back to him.

Should he stop and call her name? He glanced at the GPS. Only a quarter of a mile to the destination. He'd get there first, and if she wasn't there, he'd circle back and stop every few minutes to shout for her.

His vehicle broke into a clearing, and he saw the glimmer of light on water ahead. He was close. He cut the engine and dismounted. Cupping his hands around his mouth, he shouted, "Annie!"

He paused. Was that an answering shout? He listened again and heard her voice.

"Over here, Jon! I'm here."

He still didn't see her, but he followed the sound of her voice. "Keep talking, Annie, I'm coming!"

"I fell." Her voice quivered and grew choked. "My phone doesn't work, and I can't walk out. I either broke my ankle or I have a bad sprain. And the loons are here."

The loon's tremolo warbled, and the mournful sound even made him shiver. "Almost there. Wave to me."

There she was, her face turned up to the moonlight. He rushed forward the last few feet and knelt to gather her into his arms. "You're okay. I've got you."

She buried her face in his shirt. "I hoped Taylor would call Mason or Kade. How did you find me?"

"I stopped by your house and found out you were overdue. Kade told me where you were. Let's get you out of here before the mosquitoes drain our blood."

He rose and helped her to her feet. "Don't try to put your weight on it. I'll carry you." He swung her into his arms.

"It's two miles," she protested with her arms tightly around his neck.

"My ATV is right over there. It will be tight for both of us, but we can switch to your machine when we get there."

He carried her to the ATV and set her on the seat before he reached for the satellite phone in a case on his waist. "I'll let Mason know we're coming out."

While he made the call, he drank in the sight of her. It could have turned out much worse.

/ / /

The verdict was a sprain bad enough to require a walking boot for a while. Bandaged and dosed with ibuprofen, Annie sat on her sofa with her foot elevated and a cup of green tea in her hand while Jon fixed her a plate of warmed-up meat and potatoes. Taylor had departed for her cabin, and Kylie was curled up against Annie's side with the puppy on her lap.

"We really need to name him," Annie said. "We can't call him Dog or Puppy forever. He won't know his name."

"I like Milo, but Jon suggested it, and I don't want him to think he named *my* puppy."

Annie put down her cup of tea. "Why don't you like Jon, Bug? He's a very nice man. And he saved me today. If he hadn't come looking for me, I might have had to spend the night in the forest. The mosquitoes would have left me as a dry husk." She chuckled, but Kylie didn't laugh.

Kylie pressed her lips together and stroked her puppy's ears. "He's not my boss, but he thinks he is. He's not supposed to teach me things. He's not my dad. I want my real daddy back." Tears formed in her blue eyes and rolled down her cheeks.

Annie pulled Kylie tight against her. "I know you miss your

daddy. I know he wished he didn't have to leave us. But that doesn't mean we can't have friends and people who care about us. Your daddy wouldn't want you to never have any other male influences to guide you and be kind to you. You have male teachers you like. Think of Jon like one of them."

Kylie pulled away from her mother and got up. "I will never like him. I wish he wouldn't come around. I'm going to bed."

Annie suppressed a sigh and kissed her. "Good night, Bug."

Arguing with her wouldn't change her opinion of Jon. He'd have to prove himself to her. And what if the DNA came back showing Nate wasn't Kylie's father? How could she tell her daughter the daddy she loved wasn't her biological father? It didn't mean she couldn't love him just as much, but it would put a big wrinkle in their lives.

Something Annie didn't want to face. The test had to come out the way she wanted. It had to.

Jon came in with the plate of food in his hand. "Hungry?"

Her stomach rumbled at the aroma. "Starving. I only had a Kind bar. Did you eat?"

"I'll get something in a little while." He handed her the plate and settled in the armchair across from her. "How's your pain level?"

"Not bad. I need it to be better tomorrow. I talked to Kade about the rape accusation. He had Mason check it, and it was never reported."

"So you want to talk to Lissa Sanchez."

"I do."

"I can go with you."

"You need to be working on the house," she pointed out.

"I'm done with my part. It's all Sean now. He put on the new roof and is doing flooring and windows next. He'll thank you to keep me out of his way."

"Sure he will." But she couldn't deny the fillip of pleasure at the thought of having him around tomorrow.

"It's your right foot, so you can't drive with a boot on anyway."

True enough. Everything would be delayed while she waited to heal. "As long as you're sure, I'll let you drive. I'll be ready around five."

He nodded. "Those loons freak you out tonight? I'm surprised you weren't a jabbering mess by the time I got there."

"I was for a while, but I think God planned it. I haven't fully faced what happened to Sarah. I realized I have to go back to the island. I have to walk that dock again."

"Are you sure? That won't be easy, I know." His green eyes softened. "And you have to forgive yourself, Annie. It wasn't your fault."

She nodded, recalling how they'd been over this before. It was easier to say you could forgive yourself than to actually do it. But she had to find a way somehow. Every time she thought she'd put it behind her, it resurfaced. And how would she know it was over? She couldn't imagine a time when she stopped looking for Sarah. Surely God wouldn't ask her to do that. She had to bring Sarah to a final resting place.

"When do you want to go?"

"I'm supposed to go to a party on the island on Saturday. I wasn't going to go, but I've changed my mind. It's time."

"Want some company? I could gate crash and go with you."

"I wouldn't say no to moral support."

"What time?"

"Six."

"I'll come at five thirty." He rose. "I'll grab me some food, then head for home so you can rest."

She listened to him banging around in the kitchen. Back in the day, he used to bump around in the kitchen cooking things with her mom. Nostalgia swept over her, and she wished she could call back the invitation. Being on a boat with Jon in the moonlight wasn't the smartest thing she'd ever agreed to.

TWENTY-THREE

LISSA SANCHEZ LIVED IN A MODEST HOME IN Houghton. The roof was missing a few shingles, but the yellow house looked freshly painted. The weedy lawn was overgrown, and thistles poked up through the soil in the planting bed instead of flowers.

Jon held Annie by the arm as she lurched her way toward the front door. "I hope I don't have to wear this thing for long," she grumbled.

She'd been grumpy ever since he picked her up, and he suppressed a smile. "At least you're not on crutches."

She didn't reply but stepped to the doorbell and pressed it. When no one came, she looked around. "There's a car in the driveway. Maybe she doesn't answer the door if she doesn't know who it is."

"She might be working in the yard."

"It doesn't appear she likes yard work."

He glanced at the thistle garden. "True enough." Reaching past Annie, he pressed the doorbell again.

The garage door opened, and a little girl of about two peeked out. A woman with the same brown curls and chocolate eyes stood behind her. "I have to get my daughter to day care and go to work," she said in a clipped voice. "Make it snappy."

Annie smiled down at the little girl, then turned to the mother. "Are you Lissa Sanchez?"

"Yes. What do you want?"

"I'm with the park service, and I had a couple of quick questions for you."

Lissa glanced at the Apple watch on her wrist. "You've got five minutes. I can't be late or I'll lose my job."

"Do you know Lonnie Fox?"

Lissa glanced down. "Sure. Used to date him. What's the scumbag done now?"

"It sounds as if you don't like him."

"Would you like someone who raped you, then dumped you? I haven't seen him in five years, and he'd better hope I never run into him with my twenty-two pistol." She patted the handbag hanging at her waist.

"The rape was never reported."

"What good would it do? Men like Lonnie never pay for their crimes. They flirt with a girl and make her think she's the one, then move on. He made out like we'd get married, but it was all talk."

Something about her manner put Jon off right from the start, but he was trying to keep an open mind. She seemed more upset about being dumped than the rape she'd claimed happened, but then he could only imagine how hard it would be to talk about something like that to a police officer.

Annie shifted to put more weight on her good foot. "What about Sean Johnson?"

Lissa's lids flickered at Sean's name. "The fact you're bringing him up tells me you already spoke to him about me. Is he the one who gave you my name?"

"No, he didn't. We did speak to him though."

"So you know he thinks I was trying to get revenge. I guess it's a matter of who you believe." Lissa scooped up her daughter and turned toward her car. "I have to go now. I've said all I'm going to."

They stepped onto the lawn as she buckled her daughter into the car seat and backed out of the garage without looking their way. They watched her reach the street and zoom off. Her taillights flashed briefly at the stop sign, and she was gone.

Jon took Annie's arm and helped her back to her truck. Once he was behind the wheel, he glanced over at her. "What'd you think?"

"I hate to say it, but I think she was lying. The whole time she was talking about the rape, she didn't look at me. And she talked more about him dumping her."

"You think that clears Lonnie?"

She shook her head. "Not even close. We know he was there with the girls."

"So were the Wolstincraft twins and Glenn Hussert. I wish we could eliminate some suspects and narrow in on the likely culprit."

"We don't know enough about any of them to rule them out."

He nodded and started the truck. "What now?"

"I guess we're dead in the water at the moment. You have any ideas?"

He drove in the direction Lissa had turned as he thought about it. A flash of blue caught his eye, and he automatically braked at the sight of a man and woman on the lawn in front of a two-story house. Lissa's car was parked at the curb.

He nodded at the house. "Look, isn't that Hussert talking to Lissa?"

Annie gasped. "It is!"

He swerved the truck to the curb and parked a few car lengths ahead of Lissa's car, then turned around in the seat to look back at Lissa and Glenn. They were far enough away that the couple didn't seem to notice them, though the red pickup was hard to miss. Lissa gestured frantically with her hands and paced as she talked. Hussert grabbed her on the shoulder at one point, and she shook him off.

"I think she's crying," Annie said.

Jon noticed her wet cheeks too. "You think she's seeing him?"

"Or she's upset we talked to her, and she's venting while he's trying to calm her. We upset her."

"It's odd she'd go straight to Hussert to complain."

Lissa whirled and stalked back to her car. They'd talked to Hussert at his business, but this must be where he lived. Discovering a connection between Hussert and Lissa was interesting, but it might not be related to the murders.

Time would tell.

/ / /

Annie's ankle throbbed from being on it. She sat across the booth from Jon at the Suomi Café as they perused the menu. She normally ordered a sandwich, but she was trying to think outside the gluten-heavy foods so she could help Kylie make wise choices.

"What are you having?" she asked Jon. "If I want to avoid gluten, is soup a good choice?"

He put down his menu. "Unfortunately, no. It's one of those foods where flour might be used as a thickener. It's never safe to assume it's not in there. I'm going to have a grilled chicken salad with balsamic vinegar. You could get a hamburger and ask for it low carb. That means wrapped in lettuce leaves with no bun. Pure meats are safe, but choose your condiments wisely. I often get a burger topped with avocado and tomato. It's delicious wrapped in lettuce."

She laid down her menu. "I'll have a salad, too, then. Watching for gluten is hard."

"It gets to be second nature."

Everything in her life seemed topsy-turvy right now. It was going to be a long week waiting for the results of the DNA test to come back. In the meantime, she worried about the what-ifs constantly. She kept looking at the problem from every angle and wondering how she'd deal with it if the worst happened.

Her mom had always said to never borrow trouble and take each day as it came, but it was difficult in this situation. The results could change their lives in so many ways.

"How's the ankle feeling?"

"Sore."

"You need to elevate it. Or a swim in the cold water first might help too. It's a nice day."

She nodded and waited until Molly took their order. "Maybe I'll go swimming. Want to join Kylie and me?"

"I'd love to, but Kylie won't be happy about it. Any idea why she dislikes me?"

How did she answer that? She couldn't tell him she didn't want anyone to replace Nate. Jon wasn't vying for that position. "Kids can be inexplicable."

"Guess it's a good thing I won't have to deal with one of my own. I wanted her to like me. She looks so much like you, and I keep wanting to make her smile. But she only scowls." He gave a rueful laugh.

"It's been a long time since you were told you couldn't have kids. Maybe things have changed."

He lifted a brow. "It's a strange thing to say, Annie, and it's the second time you've said that. Doctors don't usually make those kinds of mistakes. I had to come to grips with the facts a long time ago. Railing against what is for what could have been is a road to depression. We have to accept what life throws our way."

While what he said was true, she wanted to make sure the groundwork was laid in case the results were unexpected. He would be suspicious if she kept pushing him about it. She should have kept her mouth shut until she had actual test results in hand. Hopefully, there would be no need for a discussion like this.

"Sorry." She glanced at her phone so she didn't have to see his frown. "Looks like I have a text from Mason." She read it. "The judge wants to talk to you, Jon. It appears he's quite insistent. And Mason got hold of the fishery employee list."

Jon sat back. "Great. When and where should I meet the judge?"

"I'm supposed to let Mason know. He said he texted you too."

Jon pulled out his phone. "I didn't hear the alert, but one came through fifteen minutes ago while I was driving."

Molly brought their salads. "Enjoy. Any dessert?"

"No, thanks," they said in unison.

When she walked away, Jon put down his phone. "I can do it after we eat. Let's say at one o'clock."

"Where?"

"Not the sheriff's office. I don't want to encourage the gossip. It should be somewhere we can't be seen or overheard."

She ran through options in her head. "How about my office at Kitchigami? There shouldn't be much of anyone around this afternoon. Or we could meet him at Kade's baby animal sanctuary. There's a bench as you enter, and no one will be around."

"That's sounds perfect." He grinned. "I can run if he gets combative."

At least he was keeping his sense of humor. "There goes our nice swim."

"The meeting shouldn't take long." He picked up his fork and dug into his salad. "We have steered clear of most personal things since I got here. Tell me about your life with Nate. I have no doubt he was good to you."

Her face flamed, and she bent her head down to attend to her salad. "You know how Nate was. Always easygoing and kind."

"I'm sure he was a good father. Why no more kids?"

"It just never happened." They'd wanted more children, but she'd never gotten pregnant. The salad curdled in her stomach at the possible reason why it had never happened for them.

"You lived at the marina?"

She shook her head. "We lived in Rock Harbor."

"You didn't live in one of the cottages?"

"We wanted our own space, and you know how difficult Dad was. After you left, he got even worse."

"Why?"

That was a subject she wasn't ready to tackle yet, so she shrugged and said nothing.

"Where was Nate working?"

"He was a terrific marine mechanic and started his own business out of the garage." She looked up from her plate. "You never contacted him after you left town?"

He sighed. "What was there to say? I picked up the phone to call him a few times, but I couldn't bring myself to do it. I was too hurt."

"It wasn't his fault. He just picked up the pieces of the mess we'd made together."

"That's as good a way of putting it as anything. He called me once, but I didn't pick up."

She hadn't heard that. "When was this?"

"About three months before he died. I almost took the call, in spite of being behind on my schedule, but my nurse was hurrying me along, and I didn't do it. I regretted it after he died."

A lump formed in her throat. "Did he leave a message?"

"Yeah. Just a short one saying he'd been thinking about me and missed me."

"He did. You were his best friend."

"We lived in the same neighborhood growing up, and he came with us on vacation every summer."

She knew all that, but she nodded as if she didn't. She'd met both boys at the same time out surfing on Superior's waters. One look at Jon and she'd been so smitten she barely noticed Nate. But he'd always been there. Steadfast, eager to help, and hungry for belonging. Tears burned in her eyes. At least they'd been happy together. They didn't talk about Jon, but he was always a wall between them.

"So many regrets. Some mistakes you can't fix," Jon whispered.

She stuffed a bite of salad into her mouth so she didn't have to talk about her own regrets.

TWENTY-FOUR

JON LET THE VELVETY LIPS OF THE FAUN SCOOP UP corn off his palm. The little one blew out a breath and looked at him with dark eyes as if to ask where the rest was. "That's it, little guy." He wiped his palm on the side of his khaki shorts.

"The judge should be here any minute," Annie said.

The serene location should keep tempers at bay. The enclosure held baby animals of all types. Fauns, raccoons, squirrels, beaver, even a few birds. The place had been Kade's brainchild from some years earlier, and residents of the area knew to call the ranger if they found an orphaned animal.

Tires crunched on gravel, and they both turned to see a black SUV stop. Judge Frank Day's slightly built form got out, and he walked briskly toward them.

Recognition lit his light-brown eyes when he spotted Annie, then his gaze traveled to Jon. His mouth flattened, and he walked faster. Even on a warm day, he wore a three-piece suit and looked like he'd stepped from the pages of a men's magazine.

Annie stepped forward with her hand out. "Judge Day, good to see you again. This is Jon Dunstan."

What would he do if Jon called him Frank? Jon decided not to test the limits. The guy's narrowed eyes warned him against being too familiar.

The judge didn't extend his hand, and Annie dropped hers back to her side. "Mason said you had some questions for Jon?"

"I understood I was meeting with him alone."

"I had some questions for you as well, so I tagged along." Annie sounded amiable but firm.

"I'd prefer to speak to Mr. Dunstan alone."

"You want me to ask my questions first then? I'm not going anywhere until I get some answers. I'm investigating the murders of your daughter and Sophie."

The glare he sent Annie's way would have quelled most women, but Annie tipped up her chin and stared back at him. Jon wanted to laugh, but it would have set the wrong tone.

"Fine. I'll speak with Dunstan first, then you can ask your questions."

She opened her mouth as if to protest, then closed it and walked off with her back stiff.

Jon went to the bench and settled on it with a nonchalance he didn't feel. "How can I help you, Judge?"

The judge remained standing, probably so he could glare down at Jon. "You were the last person to see my daughter alive. Did you kill her?"

"No. She was alive and well when I left the area. She and Sophie were talking and laughing."

"Why did you leave them alone?"

"I didn't know them. I merely gave them a ride. They were hitchhiking, and I didn't think it was safe so I stopped and found out they were heading to Lake of the Clouds, just like me. They were too young to be out there taking rides from strangers."

"You were a stranger."

"But I knew I wouldn't harm them."

"What proof do you have?"

"You're a judge. I shouldn't have to tell you that innocence is assumed, not guilt."

His eyes narrowed more. "Two young girls are murdered. You have some explaining to do."

"I've told you everything I know. I realize this is traumatic for you, but every minute you spend looking at me as a suspect takes away from finding out who really did this. Think it through, Judge. If I was going to harm them, I wouldn't have taken them to their destination. I'd have taken them to a deserted place."

"Like the abandoned cabin. We don't know you took them to Lake of the Clouds. How can you prove they didn't go with you to the cabin where they were found?"

"I have a witness. LEO Pederson saw me there with them." He held the judge's gaze. "I didn't hurt your daughter. She and her friend were nice girls. Young and sweet. I'm helping Annie investigate. Number one, I liked the girls. Number two, I want to clear away any suspicion about me. Number three, I want the real killer brought to justice."

"I'm not convinced. The girls had matching friendship necklaces. Penelope's was still around her neck, but Sophie's is missing. I spoke with her parents, and they haven't found it in her belongings."

"And what? You think I kept it as a souvenir?" Jon wanted to sigh, but maybe he'd react the same way if it were his daughter lying in a grave. "I'm sorry for your loss, Judge Day, but I didn't hurt your daughter or Sophie. I don't even remember the jewelry they wore, and I sure didn't keep any necklace. I'm going to do everything I can to find out who did though." He rose and gestured to Annie, who stood on the other side of the enclosure feeding a raccoon.

She waved back and came their way. "All done?" she asked when she reached them.

"It appears he is. I'm not so sure I am," the judge said. "What do you want to know?"

"Did you ever rent a cottage from Tremolo Resort? Or a boat or have any other contact with the business?"

The judge pursed his lips. "The summer before my daughter went missing, we rented a boat for a week and parked our RV at the park. Why do you ask?"

"I wanted to see if your daughter would have known about the cottage where her body was found."

"I see. You think someone on your resort had something to do with it?"

"I'm trying to examine every angle of who knew it was there and unlikely to be entered. Maybe your daughter met someone and brought him to the cottage."

"My daughter wasn't the wild type, Ms. Pederson."

"I didn't mean to imply she was. Not many people know about that cottage. It's off the beaten path without a driveway or path to it, and I needed to know if Penelope knew it was there. That's all I have."

"I know one way to find out. Her sister was with her every minute while at the marina." He pulled out his phone and tapped out a message. In moments it signaled a reply. "It appears the girls found it while hiking but didn't go in."

Jon stepped back and bit his lip as he waited for Annie to handle it. This was her investigation.

The judge glared at Annie. "Keep me posted." It wasn't a request but an order.

"I'm sure Mason will keep you informed."

The judge stalked off, and Jon turned to Annie. "So now he thinks I'm some kind of serial killer and kept Sophie's necklace as a souvenir."

Her eyes widened. "What necklace?"

"I don't know, some kind of friendship necklace. Both girls had one, and Penelope's was still around her neck, but Sophie's is missing."

"I'll ask Mason about it."

Annie was a good investigator and knew how to handle interrogations. At least it was over. For now.

/ / /

Annie felt self-conscious in her one-piece swimsuit. She'd never been awkward about being around Jon in a suit before, so why now?

She sat on the edge of the pier and removed her boot to dip her foot into the waters of Lake Superior. The cold wrapped around her ankle like an ice pack. "Cold!"

Jon dropped beside her. "Wuss. I remember the time when you jumped in without testing the waters first. You never screamed or shouted about the temperature back then."

"I was young and dumb."

When had she last gone swimming in the lake? Years, probably. She often sat on the dock and watched Kylie frolic in the waves with Nate, but she resisted being coaxed into the frigid water.

"Here goes nothing." She slid from the edge of the dock into the water that rushed up to her waist. "Whoa, it's freezing! You talk a big game, Mr. Dunstan. Let's see how you handle the cold water. I'll bet you haven't been in it in years yourself."

"You'd be right about that." He stood and walked back to take a running leap off the pier into the deeper water. He disappeared into the waves for a moment, then came up shouting. "Cold!"

"Told you." She paddled out toward him.

Her ankle was already feeling better. This had been a good idea for her ankle, but maybe not a great idea for her heart. But Jon was magnetic to her, and she was helpless to resist swimming closer to him.

So many times she'd gone swimming with him and exchanged kisses in the cold water. The lake was the embodiment of their relationship: turbulent and calming, exciting and steady. She could look at Lake Superior on a stormy day and remember that last violent argument. She could glide on its glassy surface on a calm morning and remember how his strength would calm her fears.

Why did Jon have to come back into her life like this? Things had finally gotten steady and predictable after the trauma of losing her parents and Nate. Now she had no more control over her life than a boat in a squall. He confused her and drew her.

She reached him, and he took hold of her hand to pull her closer. His skin was warm after the cold embrace of the lake, and his scent was so familiar, so beloved. A hint of his cologne, Eternity, still clung to his skin.

She should pull away and swim back to safer waters, both figuratively and literally, but she couldn't resist the memories. Not just memories, but emotions that had never died. They'd just cooled to embers in her heart. It had taken one spark from his eyes to ignite them again.

She probably would never get over him, so she might as well store up as many memories right now as she could. One of these days the cottage would be finished, and he'd leave her again. But she didn't want to remember their last fight. She wanted to remember this moment with his warm arm around her waist, pushing back the frigid waters. She intended to drink in the warmth of his green eyes and that crooked smile that implied he knew what she was thinking.

Did he? Or was it all an illusion?

He drew her closer, then closer still until she was resting on his chest and staring up into his face. His head came down, and she closed her eyes.

The other day when he'd kissed her, it had been tentative, as if he couldn't quite remember how they fit together. But his lips settled on hers now with confidence and the passion she'd almost forgotten was still alive between them. When he pulled away, she reached for him again until Kylie's shrill voice broke the spell.

"Mommy! What are you doing?"

Annie backpedaled and pushed herself away with her palm flat against his chest. When she looked at the dock, Kylie stood with her arms crossed over her chest and tears standing in her eyes.

"It's okay, Bug," she said, still breathless. "Want to come for a swim?"

"You never swim when I want to, but you came in because *he* asked you to?"

"I was letting the cold water help my ankle." What was she doing apologizing to her daughter? Who was the adult here? "Don't be impertinent, young lady."

"I hate you!" Kylie whirled, and her bare feet thumped on the dock boards as she ran back to shore and darted for the house.

Tears burned Annie's eyes. Kylie had been through so much, and this wasn't the way to introduce a new man into her life. What a mess.

Jon touched her hand. "I'm sorry, Annie. I'll work hard on getting Kylie to like me."

"She's not normally so irrational." She curled her cold fingers around his. "I should go talk to her."

"How's your ankle?"

"Better."

Better than her heart right now. Even if things worked out between Jon and her, how could she subject him to her daughter's tantrums? How could she cause more trauma in her daughter's life after all she'd been through? Annie was stuck in the middle between two people she loved and there seemed no way to reconcile the two.

She wanted to linger and kiss him again, but things felt hopeless in this moment. He let go when she tugged away and started for the dock. After hefting herself up, she dried off and slipped on her boot. Jon climbed up beside her and toweled off too. He was silent as well, probably as much at a loss for words as she was.

He rose and held out his hand. She let him help her to her feet. "Thanks. I'll talk to you tomorrow."

She limped away before she stepped into his embrace like she wanted. Better to stay away from more heartache. Kylie's hostility seemed an impossible obstacle to overcome.

Kylie didn't want to talk the rest of the day so Annie spent a few hours comparing the list of employees Mason texted her with the resort records. She found no match.

She still had a knot in her stomach by the time she went to bed.

TWENTY-FIVE

ANNIE HAD ACTUALLY KISSED HIM. JON COULDN'T STOP smiling. After showering, he left his room at the bed-and-breakfast and went to find his dad in the living room. The aroma of fried chicken from dinner still lingered in the air. His dad dozed in a chair by the fireplace. His pale, spindly legs splayed out from denim shorts, and the collar on his blue shirt was awry.

Jon smiled at his father's slack-jawed face and closed eyes. Dad had gotten stronger while they were here, but by evening, his age caught up with him. Jon settled into another armchair, then flipped on the hurricane light on the table beside him.

His dad stirred at the slight *click*, and he straightened, blinking at the light. "You're home."

"Just got back."

"How'd the day go?"

Jon told him about tracking down Lissa and how the judge had grilled him. "I'm not sure he believed me. He wants to find the killer, and right now, I think anyone will do."

"He knows better. He's sentenced innocent people before. His streak of justice sometimes needs to be tempered by real evidence."

"You know him?"

"I've tried cases before him. I've always said he gets things backward. With him, it's guilty until proven innocent—not the other way around."

"That's what I told him too."

His dad yawned and stretched. "Anyone else around tonight?"

"I haven't seen anyone, but Martha might be cleaning up in the kitchen."

"Great woman, Martha. I like her a lot."

Jon grinned. "I noticed."

"What would you think if I asked her out?"

"It's not up to me. It's your life, Dad." But his gut clenched at the thought of his dad with someone other than Mom. "Just be careful. I don't want to see you hurt."

"No one could ever replace your mother, but an old man gets lonely. I'm happy here. Maybe I'll move into the cottage and not sell it after all. Would that make you mad after all the work?"

"I hated the idea of selling it myself." Jon hesitated. What would his dad think if he knew this was his happy place too?

"You've been spending plenty of time with Annie. Anything brewing there?" His dad's tone was too casual.

"We have a common goal of clearing my name. I'm thankful to have someone on my side."

His dad smiled. "Why do I have a feeling that's not all it is? I've watched you with Annie for a lot of years, son. And I've seen you in Rochester working your fool head off. I like you better when you're here with Annie. You have a light in your eyes I don't see any other time."

His dad wasn't often in this talkative of a mood. "Some mistakes can't be undone."

"And sometimes they can. Have you tried? Ever had an honest talk with Annie about how you feel?"

"I'm not sure myself how I feel."

He should be ashamed for fudging the truth to his dad. He knew exactly how he felt when he was with Annie—alive, really alive. Not plodding through his days doing his duty and existing. Being with her was exhilarating. It was like breathing pure oxygen after being deprived of air. It was like riding in a convertible with the wind in his hair and an exciting but unknown destination ahead.

It felt too personal to discuss, even with his dad, though his dad had been married for thirty-five years before Mom died nine years ago. He'd probably felt like that before he married Mom. Jon had seen pictures of the two of them smiling at each other at their wedding. His dad's face had glowed with an inner joy. Did Dad see that same light in Jon's face?

"Jon?"

He jumped and realized his dad had been talking to him while he was daydreaming. "Sorry, what did you say?"

His dad chuckled. "I was talking about when I met your mother. I was twenty-one, and she was twenty. I was smitten the minute her blue eyes met mine. Annie reminds me a little of your mom. That same exuberance and ability to extract every bit of joy from the day."

"I guess you're right about that."

"So, what are you going to do about it?"

"Do about what?"

His dad lifted a bushy white brow. "You love her, Jon. You've never stopped. You tried to fill your life with other things, but it makes for a flat existence, doesn't it?"

Jon averted his eyes and focused on the fireplace's antique tile. "Like I said, Dad, some mistakes can't be fixed."

"I've never known you to be a quitter. You won her once. You can do it again."

"Her daughter doesn't like me. Annie wouldn't do anything to hurt Kylie."

"You've never been around kids much. We wanted more children, me and your mom. But the good Lord didn't see fit to bless us with another one after Robert died at birth. It's too bad you didn't have a little brother to pick on. But kids respond to love and attention. I bet you can win her over if you put your mind to it."

"What's my end goal, Dad? Even if Kylie and I get along, we have the same obstacles ahead of us. Annie loves it here. I do, too, but I don't think I could make a good living here. Rock Harbor is too small."

"Houghton is within driving distance, half an hour." His dad heaved himself to his feet and went toward the kitchen.

Jon had already admitted that to himself. Dad kept knocking down his arguments, and Jon wasn't sure why he kept erecting new ones. While he could make a living in Houghton, things like a Jag and an expensive house would be out of reach. In Rochester he was an elite and sought-after surgeon. Up here he'd be starting over, building his clientele.

Where did he find his worth? In how much money he made? He knew that was wrong. His character and faith were the most important parts of him. He pulled out his phone and searched for the verse he thought he remembered. He found it in Hebrews 13:5: *"Keep your life free from love of money, and be content with what you have, for he has said, 'I will never leave you nor forsake you.'"*

When had love of money and prestige taken over his life? He thought back and realized he'd felt more worthy when he'd landed a place at Mayo. The longer he'd basked in that elite spot, the more he'd craved things and what money had to offer. It had to stop.

He could step out of that wrongheaded thinking and return to the roots of his faith. With Annie. But the crux of the matter was he was afraid of rejection. Their last fight had struck at a deep core, and that wound still seeped blood. If she walked away again, the injury might be fatal.

/ / /

Another sleepless night. The clock flipped to 1:00 a.m. Annie rolled over and slipped out of bed without her boot. It did no good to toss and turn for hours. She might as well get some work done. Hopping along to protect her ankle, she scooped up her laptop and limped back in bed with it to settle it on her lap.

Her noise machine emitted the soothing sound of waves rolling to the shore. Maybe one of these days she'd be able to sleep without it. While she'd endured the wail of the loons out by the lake, she still shuddered at the eerie tremolo and didn't want to listen to it tonight.

The web link was the first one on her Favorites list. How many times had she called up this missing persons website? Too often to count. Sometimes she thought she saw the same MO of other missing children, and other times she found notices of remains found. But nothing had led her to her sister.

It often felt like an exercise in futility. Tonight was one of those times. She scrolled through the cases, but they were all younger or older kids and none of them had a kidnapper choosing between two children. Most of the time someone close to them was the suspect, and they were generally found—eventually.

None of them had been up here in the U.P., though that didn't mean anything. In this day and age, a perp could get from here to Illinois in a few hours. Or on farther west. She was searching for patterns and similarities that might stand out to her.

But tonight there was nothing. Or maybe she was too restless to concentrate.

She touched her lips. It was that kiss. It had shaken her to her core. So had Kylie's response to seeing it. What if Jon was Kylie's father, and she hated him? Though she'd told herself countless times the hereditary component wasn't always the cause of celiac disease, the fear continued to haunt her.

She could see Kylie's face in her mind's eye if Annie had to tell her something so devastating. But did she have to reveal it? If the news was bad, couldn't she keep quiet about it and let Kylie continue with the warm memories of her father? She didn't have to know what her mother had done, did she?

Annie shook her head. What if Kylie needed to know her blood heritage for other medical reasons? It wasn't just celiac disease. It could be cancer, heart disease, or other hereditary illnesses. Her daughter had the right to know even if she never had a relationship with Jon.

She flopped back against the pillow. Why couldn't she let this go until she knew the truth?

There was one good reason why. She'd wondered a few times. Kylie weighed over eight pounds, yet she'd been born four weeks early. She and Nate had jokingly said it was a good thing Kylie was impatient to be born because she might have weighed over ten pounds if she'd gone full term. But Jon himself had told her he couldn't have children. Of course she assumed Nate was her daughter's father.

But the questions had niggled at the back of her mind. Had Nate ever wondered? If he had, he'd never said anything.

A flickering light caught her eye, and she raised her head off the pillow toward the window. The blind blocked out the landscape, but illumination shone around the edges of it. She got up and hobbled to the window and pulled back the blind.

Flames licked at the pavilion and shot through the roof. Embers floated in the black sky toward the well house. She gasped and grabbed her boot and shoe. She threw on her robe, seized her phone, and hobbled to the door as fast as her awkward gait could go. As she went she called 911 to report the fire.

Outside, she found the water hose reel and turned on the water. The pavilion couldn't be saved, but if she wet down the roof of the well house, maybe it wouldn't catch fire. She trained the stream of water onto the shingles and saturated them as best as she could. Campers came running from all directions, and one of the men took the hose from her while another tried to guide her back to the house, but she shook him off.

This was her property, her responsibility. Taylor, still in her pajamas, ran from her tiny cabin, and Annie directed her inside to watch over Kylie.

It seemed forever before the volunteer fire department arrived, but the structure was smoking debris by the time they hauled out their hoses. The firemen put out the last of the smoldering logs and made sure the fire hadn't spread to any of the other buildings.

Her dad had built the pavilion himself. It had special memories for Annie, and she blinked back the sting of tears. Another change to deal with. And more work. The cleanup was one more thing to add to her list.

One of the firemen joined her. "You see anyone out here tonight?"

She shook her head. "The flames alerted me. I didn't see anyone. Why?"

"An accelerant was used. Typical burn pattern, and I could smell it." He handed her a soot-covered paper encased in plastic. "This was nailed to a nearby tree. I'll turn it over to the sheriff."

Stop poking around or the house is next.

Her hand shook as she read it a second time. "You mean someone set it on fire?"

He nodded. "I'll have the fire inspector come out and see what he can uncover. But be careful all the way out here. The arsonist might strike again." He left to rejoin his crew.

Her entire body trembled as she thought of the warning. Someone didn't want her poking into the murders. This had all started with the discovery of the bodies. It had to be about that.

It was after four when she finally made her way back to the house. Her hair smelled like smoke, and she had soot all over her. After checking on Kylie and finding her sleeping peacefully, Annie stripped off her pajamas and climbed into the shower.

How did she keep her daughter safe?

TWENTY-SIX

ROCK HARBOR BUZZED WITH NEWS OF THE ARSON AT Annie's on Thursday morning, and Jon heard it at the Suomi Café. He didn't bother placing his order but jumped in his car and zoomed out to the Tremolo Marina.

Several people picked through the ruins when he parked and got out. The stench of smoke mingled with that of water, and he scanned the area for Annie's blonde head. He spotted her standing in the shade off to the left side of what was left of the pavilion.

She stood with her arms crossed as if to protect herself from what she was observing. When he got closer, he saw moisture shimmering on her cheeks. He touched her shoulder. "Hey."

She blinked and focused on his face instead of the blackened ruins. "Someone torched it, Jon. They left a warning." She told him what the note said.

"You doing okay?" He wanted to pull her into his arms, but he suspected Kylie was somewhere around, and he didn't want to cause Annie more heartache.

She hugged herself. "I'm fine, just shocked. I didn't get much sleep. The firemen were here until after four a.m."

"Have you eaten this morning?"

She shook her head. "I came out as soon as the investigators arrived."

He took her arm. "Let's go inside. You can't do anything here anyway. They'll come get you if they need you. I'll make you some pancakes."

She took one last longing look toward the demolished structure but let him lead her back to her house. She lurched along in her boot. "Kylie was asking for pancakes yesterday, but I didn't know how to make it safe."

"Almond flour, buckwheat flour, baking powder, eggs, and milk."

"Buckwheat? I thought she couldn't have wheat."

"It's a seed not a wheat. I'll teach you." He opened the door to her house, and she went inside first. He followed her through the entry to the kitchen. "Is Kylie around? Maybe she'd like to learn."

"Taylor took her to visit a friend. I didn't want her watching everything today. She was upset when she woke and saw the charred ruins. Things upset her easily since her dad died."

He slid a glance her way. Did Annie ever think about the night his mother died? The comfort of her arms had been the only thing keeping him from falling apart that night. Even though they both regretted it later. The shame had pushed them apart instead of pulled them together. It had been a catalyst for everything that followed.

Her lids flickered, and she looked away. Maybe she was thinking about it too. Or maybe he was indulging in wishful thinking. It was something they needed to talk about eventually.

But right now pancakes beckoned. "Got a bowl?"

She reached into her gray cabinets and got out a bowl, measuring cup and spoons, as well as baking powder and the flours he'd bought in Houghton. "I'm going to watch everything you do."

"I don't measure." He eyeballed equal amounts of almond and

buckwheat flours into the bowl, then added a teaspoon of baking powder and a pinch of salt and sugar. After stirring it, he got eggs and milk out of the fridge. "You want to whisk up two eggs?"

"I can do that." She cracked the eggs into a cereal bowl and grabbed a fork to beat them.

He dumped milk in the bowl with the eggs and stirred them up, then poured it all into the flour. He stirred and added more milk until it was the right consistency. "You've made pancakes before. You just add enough milk to get the right thickness. Got cinnamon? A little of that is good too."

She got it out of the cabinet, then sprinkled some into the mixture for him. "It looks good. I'll get the skillet." She pulled out an iron skillet and put coconut oil in it.

He adjusted the heat and spooned batter into the hot oil. The aroma of the pancakes wafted into the small space, and he tended to the cooking before he lost his cool and pulled her into his arms. The mundane task of cooking caused her eyes to lose their sadness, and her color was returning. Last night's trauma had been hard on her.

While he cooked, she got out maple syrup and butter as well as cheery yellow-and-blue plates. He'd seen them before. "Your mom's plates."

She nodded. "I don't use them a lot because I don't want to break any, but right now, I miss her. She loved that pavilion." Her voice quivered. "My dad built it before they were married, and he added that fireplace about ten years ago. Our wedding was . . ." She broke off and began to rummage in the drawer for forks.

They'd planned to be married in the pavilion too. He'd forgotten that detail, but wedding planning was important to women. He'd have been happy to tie the knot on a boat or in the forest. It didn't matter to him. All he'd wanted was to have her to himself.

Had she married Nate in the pavilion? It sounded like that's what she was about to say, but there was no way he would ask her that.

All the things he wanted to say gathered in the back of his throat, and he thought he might summon the courage to spit them out. Then the door banged, and Kylie called for Annie.

Busted.

He plated the pancakes and put more batter in the skillet. "I'll make her some too."

Kylie, all long limbs and wild blonde hair, bolted into the kitchen. She stopped dead when she saw him. "What are you doing cooking in our kitchen?"

Annie frowned. "Kylie, watch your manners and your tone."

Kylie pressed her lips together and stared down at the floor.

"I'm showing your mom how to make pancakes you can eat." He gave her a calm smile. "She said you'd been wanting some. Did you try some of the treats I got you the other day? My favorite are the Kind bars."

"You got them?" Her gaze darted from him to her mother, who gave a quick nod. "They're good." Her grudging tone didn't match the dislike in her eyes.

He handed her a plate of pancakes. "See what you think of these. Your mom has maple syrup."

"I'd rather have thimbleberry jam on them."

"We have some." Annie got it down and grabbed a plate of pancakes for herself. "That's sounds really good."

And just like that, his romantic breakfast was a bust. But had he made a bit of headway with Kylie? He couldn't tell, but at least she was eating the pancakes.

/ / /

Annie was actually doing it. If someone had told her she'd be heading out to Tremolo Island this evening, she would have told them they were crazy. She rode the waves in her boat and let the wet spray hit her face.

"You okay?" Jon asked from his seat at the helm.

She wiggled her ankle. "Feels good to finally be without the boot." She swiped her hair out of her eyes. "A little exhilarated that I'm facing my fears and a whole lot terrified. I haven't been out here since we lost Sarah."

"I'll be right there with you."

"I appreciate it more than you know. Oh, and I spoke to Mason about the necklace. The girls were best friends and wore matching necklaces all the time. Mason sent me a picture."

She showed him her phone, and he studied the photo of a dangling piece of sea glass shaped like half a heart. A top silver piece spelled out the word FRIENDS. "Sophie's necklace had BEST at the top of the sea glass."

She smoothed the folds of her tropical-blue dress over her legs.

He looked impossibly handsome tonight with the white shirt contrasting with his tanned face and arms. Water had splashed up onto his navy slacks, and his hair was just tousled enough that she wanted to run her fingers through it. His green eyes were grave and filled with compassion.

It meant a lot that he cared enough to go with her. She wasn't sure she would have been able to do it on her own.

She turned back to face the bow of the boat so she didn't beg him to go back. Just a few more minutes and the worst would be over. Once she stood on those old weathered boards and let the memories wash in, maybe she could expunge them for good.

The island grew closer. Was it always so lush and green? Massive trees stretched out leafy arms over the landscape, and color burst out of every spot with all types of flowers. Maybe Max had planted them. Mom hadn't cared for gardening, and the island had always been in its natural state.

And there it was. The dock where the man had snatched away her sister. Her gaze lingered on the long spit of boards poking into the blue water of Lake Superior. It wasn't as weathered as she remembered, and it seemed shorter, too, but that was probably her own size in contrast to back then.

Several boats had already docked, and Jon aimed the boat toward a generous opening to tie off. She gripped the railing so tightly her knuckles turned white. Deep breaths, in and out. She could do this. Almost there.

The boat bumped gently against the rubber tire at the dock, and she reached out with numb fingers toward a post to tie it off.

A figure moved toward them. "I've got it."

Annie hadn't noticed Anu until the older woman spoke. Her blonde hair tousled by the wind, Anu grabbed the rope and tied it to the post, then went to the stern to tie up the rope there. Once the boat was stable, she reached out a hand to help Annie onto the dock. Annie's knees trembled, and she might have fallen except for Anu's help.

Annie struggled to catch her breath as she looked up and down the length of the dock. They'd been out at the end of the dock when it happened.

Anu patted her hand. "I'll let you have some time." Her brisk steps faded away as she headed for the shore.

Jon was at Annie's side almost instantly, and he took her hand. "We can talk about it, or I can just be quiet."

She raked her hands through her tangled hair. "I don't know. I never thought I'd be here." Her gaze was drawn to that far end where another boat rocked in the waves. "There was a family of loons out there. The fledglings had hatched, and they were already fishing and swimming around with their parents. We saw a fledgling riding on its mama's back that night, which was a new sight for us. I felt guilty for coming out when we weren't supposed to, but Sarah couldn't get enough. I wanted to go back to the cabin, but she begged to stay a little longer. If only—"

"Don't let yourself think that way. You were a little girl indulging your little sister. There wasn't a thing wrong with that."

"We snuck out. I knew Mom and Dad wouldn't want us down here at night by ourselves. That was the first thing my dad said. It was my fault. I-I forgot that until now. He was so angry."

"He was an angry man."

She lifted a brow and turned to stare up at him. "Yes, yes he was. I didn't let myself think about that very often. Most of my childhood was spent trying to placate him and make sure he didn't lose his temper with me. He never got mad at Sarah. I don't think I ever heard him raise his voice to her.

"Life hadn't turned out the way he wanted. He told me once he wanted to go off to college himself, but his parents expected him to take over the marina. He'd thought he would run it a few years, then follow his dreams. That never happened.

"Looking back, I can see that now. He hated working on the boats, and he especially disliked dealing with customers. He wasn't good at it. Mom was the face of the resort. Everyone loved her."

Talking about her parents made it easier to stand here, but it wouldn't accomplish her reason for coming. She took a step out toward the end of the dock, and her knees trembled even more. The ache in her throat deepened, and she swallowed hard when she finally reached where the boards ended and the water took over.

"Right here. We were sitting on the edge of the dock with our legs dangling in the water as we threw bread crumbs to the loons. They didn't much care for them, but the fish liked them."

She forced herself to settle down in the same position again and closed her eyes. Right here where she'd last touched Sarah and seen her bright smile. "We heard the splash of oars in the water and this big canoe glided up. I heard, 'Two to choose from. I think the younger one would be better.' Before I could figure out the meaning of the words, a strong hand grabbed me, and I felt a pain in my neck. The next minute I was in the water. It was so cold I couldn't breathe, and I had to fight the waves. It seemed forever before I was on the shore. Then I realized Sarah was gone."

She opened her eyes and found Jon beside her on the dock. "I never saw her again."

"Do you remember what the boat looked like or the person in it?"

She started to shake her head, but a face swam into her memory. "I always thought I never really saw the kidnapper, but that voice. I-I think it was a woman."

What did it all mean? Her father had tried to force her to remember. He'd tried to make her come out here, but her mother had stepped in and insisted he let her alone. If she'd come out here sooner, would they have found Sarah?

TWENTY-SEVEN

JON KEPT HIS ARM AROUND ANNIE, AND HER HEAD WAS on his chest. "Did you see any details about this woman? Did you hear Sarah cry out or anything? Any details of the boat?" The sweet aroma of her hair mingled with the fresh scent of the lake.

"I was panicked trying to swim after being yanked into deep water. She cried out my name. I remember fighting the water and trying to get to her." She buried her face deeper into his chest. "I almost wish I couldn't remember her crying for me. I failed her."

He hugged her tighter. "Would you blame Kylie if this had happened to her? No, you wouldn't. You can look at her size and know she could never overcome an adult. I suspect you were about Kylie's size at age nine too."

"I had always protected her." The words were muffled with her mouth against his chest. "It's hard to let go of that."

"You have to, though, or you'll never heal and move on from this."

She nodded into his shirt. "It wasn't my fault." She inhaled and said it again. "It wasn't my fault."

"Louder."

"It wasn't my fault!" She lifted her head. "People will think we're rude. We should find the party."

The sound of music and laughter floated toward them as he

helped her to her feet, and they walked toward the lights strung up in a large grassy area. White linen-clad tables lined the perimeter, and delicious Mexican aromas wafted toward them. He spotted enchiladas, a taco bar with various meats and fillings, a quesadilla press, and fixings like guacamole, sour cream, and all kinds of cheese.

"My kind of buffet," he whispered.

Beyond the clearing was a grand two-story log home. "Did your dad build that?"

She shook her head. "Max did. He has a lifetime lease with permission to make any improvements he wants. We had a little cabin farther into the trees. I've heard Max's home is very grand."

Jon scanned the crowd. "Bree and Kade are here. And Anu is with that dark-haired man. There are lots of people I know. Sean, the lady who runs the coffee shop, your doctor."

His gaze lingered on the famous Max Reardon. The man looked distinguished in crisp khaki slacks and a red shirt. Anu wore a lilac dress that highlighted her silvery-blonde hair, and she was smiling up at him.

"That's Max. You think they might be dating? They have their arms linked, and he just leaned down to kiss her. I didn't know they were seeing each other. They look good together. He's very attractive."

He caught the adoration in her voice. "And he's too old for you."

She let out a low chuckle. "I know that, but he's still a hunk. I'd like to see Anu happy as she's about to change up her life a little."

Bree gave a little wave and smiled as she came toward them with Kade in tow. "You actually came. Good for you! How are you doing?"

"It was hard, but I needed to do it." Annie glanced at Kade. "I remembered it was a woman who took Sarah."

"A woman? That's a surprise."

"I know. I'd always thought it was a man, but I remember her voice, husky and amused. She didn't know which one of us to take but decided Sarah would be less trouble."

Jon's gaze went to the scar on her neck. "You nearly died from blood loss."

She fingered the scar. "I think she thought I wouldn't survive to identify her. I couldn't ID her, but at least I lived. Though I often thought Dad would rather I got taken and not Sarah."

Jon clenched his fists at the thought of her childhood spent realizing her dad wished she'd died instead of her sister. How horrific. He'd never liked her dad. There was a coldness in him that was like biting on ice. It set Jon's teeth on edge.

Bree's face mirrored Jon's shock, and she shook her head. "I'm sorry, Annie. That had to be hard."

Annie shrugged. "I gave up trying to earn his forgiveness for failing Sarah." She squinted toward the west. "Looks like Anu is dating Max, or am I reading it wrong?"

"They've gone out about four times. I think Anu is smitten. In all the years I've known her, she's never dated. Max walked in her shop one day, and they hit it off. When he asked her to dinner, she said yes. She told me she was as surprised as I was. Max was the only one not surprised. I think he thought it was his due. He's younger than her, but he doesn't seem to care."

Annie glanced at her. "Do you like him?"

"I like him in spite of his acting like he's the king around here. It's just his way. And if he's good to Anu, that's all that matters to me."

"I hope it works out. They make a sweet couple."

"They do. Davy is a little jealous, I think. He thought he was her main man." Bree laughed. "The twins haven't said much yet, but the first time they can't stay overnight because she has a date, the war will be on."

The Kalevas came their way. Mason's wife, Hilary, was a perfect foil for his bulky frame. Slim and professional with her blonde hair in an elegant French roll, she had been the mayor of Rock Harbor for some years now. The powerhouse couple was an icon in the area.

Jon sidled over to Mason as Hilary slipped past him to chat with Bree and Annie. He nodded to Sean who was talking to Max and Anu.

"Did the judge report back to you after he interrogated me?" he asked Mason.

Mason nodded. "You're still at the top of his list, but at least he listened when I discussed other possible suspects."

Just as Jon feared. The judge held a lot of power, so it was imperative they figured out the true killer. "Any other campers missing so far this summer?"

Mason shook his head. "All quiet on that front."

So where did they go next with finding the girls' killers? He looked around for Annie and didn't see her.

He checked with Bree. "Any idea where Annie went?"

"She said she was going to get some food."

He thanked her and checked the food tables. No Annie. Unease shuddered up his spine. Where was she?

/ / /

The loons wouldn't be out for a few hours, but Annie couldn't resist the temptation to sneak away to walk the island and see if she could remember more about that awful day. Talking about it left her vibrating with the need to pierce the darkness surrounding her hidden memories.

Jon would have come with her, but she felt a strong need to do this alone—to walk the paths she'd trod as a little girl, to see the cabin where they stayed through adult eyes. Everything seemed different now too. Like something from a dream or a long-forgotten movie.

The sound and smells of the party faded into the drone of insects and the chirping of birds overhead. Max had planted roses along the path to the cabin, and their sweet aroma wafted along the walkway. She stopped and stared at the cottage. It looked so much smaller than she remembered. In her mind's eye she envisioned the path from their bedroom to the kitchen as a long way away, but she could traverse this tiny cabin from one end to the other in seconds.

The cedar structure had been recently stained, and the metal roof was new, wasn't it? She didn't remember a green metal roof. The unfamiliarity of the surroundings didn't trigger any latent memories, so she left the cabin behind and wandered along the path to the small pond where she and Sarah used to hunt for tadpoles. The frayed edge of the rope they used to swing out over the water and drop in still hung from the tree.

She remembered stretching out in the sun right here. She and Sarah had matching *Little Mermaid* swimsuits, and their skin was as brown as nut butter. It had been an idyllic summer until that night.

Though sunset hadn't come yet, it was darker here in the

woods. The scent of pine and dead leaves wafted from the vegetation under her feet as she wandered deeper into the gloom. They'd had a tree house out there somewhere, and though she couldn't quite remember the path, her feet knew the way.

There it was, the great oak with its massive limbs spreading out over the understory. The boards nailed to the tree were mostly missing with only a few hanging on by a couple of rusty nails. It wasn't something she'd dare to climb now in its current condition, but she remembered being perched within its leaves and eavesdropping on her parents.

Eavesdropping on her parents.

An image flashed into her memory of hearing them shouting at one another. Her mother had yelled something like, *"I don't want him around the house!"* But Annie had no recollection of who "he" might have been.

It wasn't until she turned to go back that she heard the noise. It sounded like someone breathing heavily. Watching her. The hair prickled on the back of her neck, and she turned toward the sound even as she reached for the gun she'd left behind in the safe at home.

A deer darted from the underbrush and broke into a run as it dashed past her to vanish into the shadows. She smiled and exhaled. Just an animal.

The shadows were darker on the path where the deer had disappeared, and she had to watch her step so she didn't stumble over branches and rocks. Another tumble would wreck her mostly healed ankle, and she didn't want to go back to wearing the boot.

Another rustle sounded to her left, and she whirled. Another deer? She paused and listened. Nothing. The setting made her so jumpy tonight. She started along the path again.

When the attack came it was too fast to see more than a blue blur. In the next second she was on the ground with her face pressed into last year's dead leaves. Her mouth was full of mud and debris, and her arm burned as if she'd scraped it on a branch or rock. A hand that smelled of soap was over her mouth. She struggled to place the scent of the soap. Irish Spring maybe? She struggled to free herself, but the man kept her pinned.

"The fire was your first warning. This is your final one. Stop poking around, or next time your face will be in the lake, and I won't let you up."

She quit fighting and lay still with the roar of her heartbeat in her ears. She wanted to ask what he meant, but his hand remained tightly over her mouth. The only thing she'd been poking into was the murders of Penelope and Sophie. Or did he mean searching for her sister?

When she quit struggling, his grip eased a fraction. "If I hear you're ignoring me, your pretty little girl is my next target. Want to lose her like you lost your sister?"

Annie froze, and her mouth went dry. Tears burned her eyes. How could she do her job and protect her daughter?

"Close your eyes now. Time for a nap."

In the next instant, something struck the back of her head, and the world went black.

TWENTY-EIGHT

THE LONGER HE WENT WITHOUT FINDING ANNIE, THE more Jon's heart raced. Where could she be? She wasn't at the dock, which was where he checked first, and no one had seen her at the party. He checked the house in case she'd gone in to use the bathroom, then dashed back outside when he didn't find her.

He eyed the shadows of the woods. She wouldn't have had any reason to go there, would she? But since he'd exhausted the other likely places, he set off down the gravel pathway deeper into the forest. The light gave way to shadows and gloom. Birds fluttered in the leaves overhead, and he heard a splash in the distance. A stream or pond of some kind?

He pulled out his phone and turned on the flashlight. It was bright enough to illuminate some of the darkest shadows under bushes and overhanging branches. "Annie!"

His shout startled a deer from its bed under a bush, and he continued down the path, pausing to call her name every few feet. In the distance he caught the glimmer of the sunset on the water. "Annie!"

Was that a groan? He shone his light around the ground. "Annie, where are you?"

No answer, but he caught a glimpse of blue, then spotted a bare foot. Annie was lying facedown on the ground. He rushed to her side and touched her. She moved slightly so he knew she was alive. The back of her hair was matted with blood. His phone didn't work here so he couldn't call for help.

He pulled off his shirt and pressed it against the wound. Once the bleeding slowed, he ran his hands over her arms and legs, looking for broken bones and contusions, then moved to her spine and neck. Everything seemed to be in alignment. The wound on her head had stopped bleeding. He slipped his hand under her neck to support it, then gently rolled her onto her back. Her eyes were closed, and she had mud and scratches on her face.

He palmed her cheek and leaned closer. "Annie, can you hear me? Open your eyes, love."

Her lips moved, and her lids fluttered, then she opened her eyes and blinked. "Jon? Where am I?" She moved her arm and lifted her hand to her face. "My head hurts."

"It was bleeding. Lie still and let me check you out." He shone his phone flashlight into her eyes and watched the pupils contract. They dilated to equal size, a good sign.

"Let's see if you can sit up." Supporting her back, he raised her a few inches.

She moaned again. "My head."

Not good. He eased her back onto the ground. "Where does it hurt? All of your head?"

"No, just here." She touched the wound. "I want to get up."

"Let's wait to move you until the pain eases. Do you remember what happened?"

Her blue eyes widened. "Someone jumped on top of me. He told me to quit poking around or Kylie would disappear like my sister."

Jon winced. "Did you recognize him?"

"When he jumped me, I went face first into the ground so I never saw him. I didn't recognize the voice either."

"He wants you to quit looking into the murders of Penelope and Sophie?"

She nodded and winced again. "Can you help me up again? I need to get home and make sure Kylie is all right."

He knew better than to ask if she was sure. Nothing was more important to her than her daughter. Supporting her back again, he eased her to a sitting position. When she was steady, he helped her to her feet, then swung her into his arms.

"I can walk," she protested.

But he'd seen the way she wobbled and how white she went. "It's better if I carry you out. I don't want you to start bleeding again. If you need to lie down and rest along the way, just say so and we'll stop."

He set off down the path. Good thing he liked working out in the gym. Her one hundred twenty pounds was something he could handle, but his muscles began to tire by the time he saw the twinkling lights put up around the party.

He exited the trees, and Mason saw them first. He ran to intercept them. "What happened?"

"She was attacked. Let Max know there's an intruder on the grounds." But was it an intruder? Or someone they thought was a friend? Jon didn't know everyone here, but Annie probably did. Could the killer be someone they knew and trusted?

Mason nodded and rushed over to talk to Max while Jon carried her to a chair and set her down. "Let me get you something to drink, then we'll head back to the resort."

She was very white, and her lips looked a little blue. How much blood had she lost? He wanted to get her to the hospital for an evaluation, but she would insist on making sure Kylie was all right.

Max and Mason came over with Bree and Anu behind them. The women clustered around Annie, and Anu took out a hanky to dab at the mud on Annie's face.

"Dr. Eckright is here somewhere," Max said. "I'll try to find him."

"I'm a doctor," Jon said. "I've checked her out, but we need to get some blood work and X-rays. I'll take her back as soon as she catches her breath."

Max frowned and glanced around at his guests. "I can't believe someone here would attack her. I know every person personally."

"Someone could have sneaked onto the island," Mason said. "What happened exactly?"

Jon told the sheriff about the threat the attacker made. Anu's and Bree's eyes both widened and they moved closer to Annie.

Max glanced into the shadows of the woods. "I have guards all around the shore. My security is top-notch because I've had kidnapping attempts in the past. I suppose it's possible for someone to sneak ashore, maybe a diver. But it would take some skill."

"And a heavy wetsuit with the water so cold," Mason said.

Annie took Jon's hand. "I'd like to go now. I want to check on my daughter."

"I have a satellite phone," Max said. "Let me call and make sure she's all right, then Jon can take you straight to the hospital."

Relief lit Annie's eyes, and she nodded. "I would appreciate it so much. I'm worried."

Max gestured to a man standing on the perimeter of the clearing. "Phone." The guy went into the house for a few seconds, then reappeared with a satellite phone.

Max took it. "Number?"

Annie rattled off the number, and he punched it in, then handed her phone. "You'll feel better if you hear your daughter's voice."

The relief lit her eyes as she spoke into the phone. "Everything's fine," she mouthed to him.

But it wasn't. To protect her and Kylie, Jon needed to back off and do this poking around by himself.

/ / /

Her head stitched and bandaged, the blood and mud cleaned up, and her tummy full of hot chocolate, Annie was finally able to unclench her fists and relax. She sat on the sofa at her cottage with her head against the high back. Watching her closely, Jon was in the chair across from her.

Kylie sat snuggled up against her right side with her puppy in her lap. "You sure you're okay, Mommy? You still have blood in your hair."

"I'm going to be fine, Bug. Don't worry."

Kylie threw her arm against her mother and buried her face in Annie's chest. "I don't want you to die like Daddy!"

Annie exchanged a glance with Jon, and she hugged her little girl. "I'm not going anywhere, Kylie. You don't have to worry."

Kylie lifted a tear-stained face to Annie. "Where would I go if something happened to you? There's no one to take care of me except Taylor, and you pay her. If you're gone, no one would pay her."

Annie's gaze met Jon's, and she saw the compassion in his green eyes. How did a mother answer that? Her daughter would be orphaned if something happened to her. Though Nate's parents were alive, they lived in California now, though they'd lived in Chicago when Nate was younger. Nate and Jon had met and become best friends in grade school.

Kylie had only met Nate's parents a handful of times. Nate had been an amazing dad, and he'd vowed never to let Kylie feel as neglected as he had growing up. But that also meant the hole he'd left had been huge.

Nate wouldn't want Kylie to be raised by his parents. Maybe his brother? Annie hadn't spent much time with Matt since he was several years older, but Nate had loved him. She should make an effort to visit. Maybe she could offer Matt a cabin for a few weeks this summer so Kylie could get to know him, his wife, and his two children, and Kylie wouldn't feel so alone.

She pressed a kiss on her daughter's head. "I'll make sure you're okay. I'm fine, Kylie, really. I'm not going anywhere."

Nate hadn't planned to die either, but things happen. There were plans she needed to make, and she couldn't put it off.

"Time for bed. It's after ten. I'll come tuck you in shortly."

Kylie pouted for a minute, then scampered down the hallway.

Jon was silent for a long moment. "I never thought how a kid would react after losing a parent. She's terrified of losing you. You can't let Nate's parents have her."

"I was thinking the same thing. I need to assign a guardian just in case. Not that I think death is lurking around the corner, but you never know."

"Your uncle Jeff maybe?"

She shook her head at the mention of her dad's brother. "He has a temper like Dad. I don't want Kylie subjected to that. There's no family member I can think I'd be comfortable with. Other kids would be good."

"Maybe Bree and Kade?"

It wasn't a bad thought. Bree and Kade had been in Kylie's life from the beginning. They were the type of people who could love other children like their own. Davy was Bree's son from a previous marriage, but he and Kade were tight. Kade made no distinction between Davy and his twins.

"I think I'll talk to Bree about it."

She didn't dare let herself think about the possibility of Jon being Kylie's biological father. So many pitfalls awaited her if that happened. She couldn't even imagine how to navigate that kind of minefield. Right now, going with Jon would be the last thing Kylie would want to do. And Annie didn't know how to fix that. She'd never known her daughter to have such irrational dislike.

"How's your pain?"

She touched the back of her head. "Better. Just sore now. No headache."

His eyes intent, Jon leaned forward. "You can't afford to continue this investigation, Annie. Not when that dirtbag threatened Kylie. I'll poke around on my own. Mason seems to believe in my innocence, and he'll help me. You can settle back into your normal duties. This isn't really your battle."

The concern in his eyes touched her, but she shook her head. "Don't think I'm not tempted to agree, but if I let myself be blackmailed—because that's what it is—I might as well find a new line of work. Law enforcement officers need to be above being manipulated. The more I've thought about it, the more I've realized the guy had to know something about me. He knew I had a daughter, and he knew how to push my buttons. But I don't believe he'd seriously do anything to Kylie. The search would intensify, not dissipate."

"But what if he had something to do with Sarah's disappearance?"

"I don't think that's possible. It's been too long since Sarah disappeared. This is all about Penelope and Sophie, and we need to put our focus there. The threat tells me we're close. Someone we interviewed is responsible for their deaths. I have to bring justice to those girls."

His eyes warmed. "You're a remarkable woman, Annie."

She looked down at her hands and reminded herself Kylie hated him. Keeping her distance was imperative. He'd soon be gone and they'd be on their own again.

TWENTY-NINE

JON EXITED THE CHURCH INTO THE LATE-MORNING sunshine. Annie and Kylie had been in the third row, but he'd slipped into the back so he didn't upset the little girl. Taylor had blushed when she glanced behind her and saw him, and he sighed. She definitely had a crush on him, and he needed to nip it.

When she'd brought the brownies, he hadn't thought much about it, but he must have been obtuse to miss the moonstruck expression in her brown eyes. He should do something about it before she got hurt, but this kind of thing was not easy for him.

He looked up and down Quincy Street to the hill that overlooked the blue water of Lake Superior. It would be a gorgeous day, and waves were high with a storm arriving tomorrow. Perfect for surfing, if he even remembered how after so many years. He'd have to rent a wetsuit, but that was doable.

"Hey, Jon."

He turned at the sound of Taylor's voice. Bright sunlight gleamed on her red hair. "Good morning."

She fiddled with the new edition of the weekly newspaper in her hand. "What are you doing today? I have the next few days off, and I thought I'd go out looking for agates. Want to come along?"

"You might have better success if you go after the storm that's coming in."

Her face fell. "I don't want to wait until tomorrow."

"Kylie would probably like to go." He was dancing all around her invitation, and he needed to just spit it out. "I think I'll go surfing today."

How did he get across to her that he had no romantic interest in her? His gaze went to Annie's blonde head off to the right. She stood with Kylie, who was talking to Anu and Bree. Maybe letting her know how he felt about Annie would be appropriate.

"It's too cold to surf," Taylor said.

"You have to wear a wetsuit for sure. Annie is really good at it. I asked her to marry me after surfing, so it's special to us."

She took a step back. "You're engaged to Annie?"

"We were once, but things didn't work out. I'm hoping for a different outcome this time."

She gulped, and her eyes filled. He felt like a heel. The wind gusted over them, and debris from the gravel parking lot whirled in the air.

She blinked rapidly and rubbed her left eye. "Something in my eye."

"I've got eye drops in the car if you need them."

She shook her head and rubbed more at her eye. Something hung on her lashes, and he caught a flash of a blue eye as she blinked. A contact lens was on her lash. "I think your contact lens came out."

She snagged it before it could fall off her lashes, then rummaged in her purse for a bottle of lens solution. When she looked up from the search, he saw clearly her blue eye. Not brown. Why would a woman cover up vivid blue eyes like that? There was no accounting for taste. Maybe she hated the color blue or thought it clashed with her hair.

She put the lens between two fingers and washed it off, then laid it in her palm and cleaned it off front and back before she popped it back into her eye. "Well, I guess I'll let you go surf. Have fun."

Her lackluster voice and avoidance of eye contact told him his comment had been taken to heart. It gave him no pleasure to hurt her, but better a small scrape now than an open wound later. Had he unwittingly encouraged her early on? No instance of that came to mind. He watched her scurry away and wished this hadn't happened.

How would she treat Annie now? Would she be sullen and angry or ride back to the marina in silence? He couldn't warn Annie without Kylie overhearing. If she heard that he'd told Taylor he wanted to get back together with Annie, Kylie would be even more upset.

Better to just let it ride.

He walked over to join Annie and Kylie. "Hey, Kylie, you want to learn to surf?"

"Surf? You mean in the lake?"

He nodded and gestured down Quincy Street to the waves rolling onto the pebbled shore. "Your mom is really good at it."

"Mommy doesn't surf."

Annie pushed windblown hair out of her eyes. "I haven't gone in years."

"I haven't either, but we both learned at about Kylie's age. Today's a perfect day for it."

Kylie turned an eager face to Annie and nearly bounced with excitement. "Could we, Mommy? Your old board is still in the storage shed."

"We'd need wetsuits."

"The outfitter shop has them for rent," Jon said.

"Please, Mommy."

Annie finally smiled. "As long as the rentals aren't too expensive."

"My treat since it was my idea. I'll go see what I can find, then meet you back at the resort."

"I can pay our way," she protested.

"I know, but I want to do it. Nostalgia and all that. You used to be better at surfing than me. We'll see if you've still got the moves."

"I'll probably wipe out now. It's been a long time." Her gaze tracked Taylor's movement as she went toward the truck. "Taylor is off for a few days. She's been working hard, and I, um, wanted to stay close to home for a few days. She might want to join us."

Good idea to stay close to Kylie. Jon turned away from Taylor's pensive face. "She told me she wanted to go agate hunting."

And she wouldn't want to watch him interact with Annie. He couldn't say that though.

Kylie hung on Annie's arm. "Let's go home and get ready!"

Maybe he was making headway with the little girl. But she was mercurial so only time would tell. He could bring cherry Popsicles too. Maybe that would be the final winning pitch.

/ / /

Surfing used to be Annie's solace from her dad's anger and condemnation. Why had she avoided it for so long? "Think you can get the boards out of the shed?" she asked Kylie as Annie pulled into the resort's parking lot.

"Sure."

"I'll fix a quick lunch and get our swimsuits ready." Something light like turkey sandwiches on gluten-free bread.

Kylie nodded and went past the house, heading for the shed. Her daughter was more excited than Annie had seen her in a while. This would be good for all of them. Maybe learning to surf would help heal her broken heart over losing her dad. A hobby like that could become a passion, and Annie would love to see Kylie recover her zest for play.

When Annie started to insert her key into the lock of her cottage, the front door swung open. She gasped, and her hand went to her throat. She backed away and scrabbled for the gun in her purse. After shooting a quick text to Mason, she approached the door again. It swung open farther when she pushed it with her foot, and she entered slowly with her gun at the ready.

There was a strangely familiar odor in the air, and it took a second for her to register it was the soap she'd smelled on her attacker. Her pulse ratcheted up, and she eased through the house, searching for the intruder. No one in the living room or kitchen. Her bedroom seemed undisturbed. The bathrooms were empty, and so was the spare room.

It was only when she entered Kylie's room that she found evidence the intruder had been here. All Kylie's clothing had been pulled off hangers and out of drawers. Most of it looked shredded by scissors, and ink had been dripped on all her shoes.

She knew the man intended to frighten her again, but she pressed her lips together and marched around the room, hoping he was still in here. But he was long gone.

Kylie! She ran through the living room and out the door to the yard. Dragging the surfboard in both hands, Kylie exited the shed, and Annie exhaled. The guy hadn't gone after her. This had been a scare tactic.

She moved to intercept Kylie so she didn't find her room in

shambles. Her phone dinged with a message, and she saw Mason was on his way. She stuck her gun in the waistband of her slacks and tucked her phone into her purse, then went to help Kylie with the board.

Her daughter's face was red with exertion, and she was huffing. "It's heavier than I thought."

Annie lifted it and tucked it under her arm to carry it to the front yard. "It's an old one. If you like surfing, we'll get a lighter, sleeker one."

She caught a flash of red out of the corner of her eye and saw Jon's sports car pulling into the parking lot. After dropping the board in the yard, she went across the grass to meet him where Kylie couldn't overhear.

He got out and opened the trunk to lift out the wetsuits. As he came toward her, his smile vanished. "What's wrong?"

He always knew how to read her. Keeping her eye on Kylie, she lowered her voice. "That guy who attacked me yesterday—he was here in the house. I know it's the same guy because I smelled the same scented soap. He destroyed all of Kylie's clothes."

"He wanted to drive home his warning."

She nodded. "He wanted to scare me, but he made me mad instead. I *will* find him, and he'll pay for this."

"Did you call for backup?"

"I texted Mason. He's on his way."

"Good thing I did a little shopping." He waved at Kylie. "I got you a new swimsuit too. Want to see it?"

She nodded and came to join them. "I have a swimsuit."

"I thought we should commemorate your first surfing lesson with a special suit."

Kylie sniffed. "I like my old one."

He handed her a white bag. "See what you think."

As soon as Annie caught sight of the green color, she knew Kylie would hate it. She willed her daughter to at least be polite. She answered Mason's text with one telling him to check out the house while she kept Kylie busy with a surf lesson.

"It's *green*. Did you get the right size?" She glanced at the tag. "It's a size ten. How did you know my size?"

"I saw Anu in town and asked her. She is good at knowing sizes."

Kylie glanced at Annie, who narrowed her eyes in warning. "Thank you. It was very nice of you."

"We can exchange it for another color."

"No, this is okay. It's cute for a green one. I'll go put it on."

Annie grabbed her arm as her daughter started past her. "Um, Kylie, use my bedroom to change. I'll go with you."

"Why? I want to get my mermaid beach towel."

No way to break it easily. "Someone broke in while we were at church, and your room is a mess."

Kylie turned toward the door. "Did they take my stuff?"

Annie took her hand and walked with her. "Let's just say you get to pick out all new clothes and shoes."

"It's all *gone*?"

Better to let her think it was gone than ruined with such malice. "Think of all the fun things you can buy."

"But it will be expensive to get all new stuff."

"I have insurance. We'll have a fun shopping trip. Anu has some new things in, and we can go to Houghton too. You love shoe shopping. We'll see what's out there."

Kylie's eyes filled with tears. "My shoes too? I just got new sandals."

"I know, sweetheart. Sometimes we have to roll with the punches, and this is one of those times."

"I'm tired of punches. First we lost Daddy and Grandma and Grandpa, and now this. Is life ever going to be normal?"

Annie stopped and pulled her into a hug. "Normal life is not ever perfect. What kind of people would we be if God never allowed our faith to be tested? Adversity makes us stronger. I'm sorry you had such bad things happen so early in life, but God never wastes these kinds of things in our lives. Bad things are never permanent, but neither are happy times. Life changes. It's supposed to."

Kylie sniffled and pulled away. "I don't like that."

"You will someday when you understand it better. We have to learn to adapt to change."

Here Annie was trying to buck up Kylie into embracing change when she had let Jon walk away so she could keep life the same. What a hypocrite.

THIRTY

ANNIE DROPPED HER ARM AROUND KYLIE'S COLD, WET shoulders as they followed Jon away from the water toward the cottage. "You are a natural at surfing. Good job, sweetheart. Your dad would be proud."

In spite of the wetsuit, Annie was chilled all the way to the bone. Her hair smelled like the lake. Kylie's lips were blue, and even Jon was shivering. Hot chocolate and gluten-free pizza was in order to warm up.

Kylie stopped and twirled a strand of wet hair in her fingers. "Do you think Daddy sees me when I do stuff like that?"

"No one really knows, but the Bible says we're surrounded by a great cloud of witnesses, meaning those who have gone before. I think God lets Daddy know things about you because that would make him happy to see you growing and thriving. He mostly wants to see you get even closer to Jesus."

Kylie nodded, and they continued on toward the house. Annie still had to clean up the mess in Kylie's room, but now that a little time had passed, she hoped her daughter would deal with the loss better. So far, it hadn't seemed to occur to her that the vandalization was a threat, and Annie hoped to keep it that way.

The best break for surfing was off to the right of the house, and their walk back took them by the burned-out pavilion where a cleaning crew worked. Eager to get inside and warm up with a hot drink, Annie veered through the ashes of the old building. The place reeked of soot and burned timbers.

The teenagers she'd hired had hauled away the charred rafters and picnic tables, and all that remained were the concrete floor and the fireplace where she used to roast marshmallows.

She'd asked them to knock down the old fireplace, and two of the boys were pounding at it with sledgehammers. The bricks began to fall onto the ground on the far end, and one of the boys hollered at her.

"Hey, Mrs. Pederson, there's something here."

Annoyed at the interruption, she turned their direction. Knowing how boys were, it was probably a dead animal. But as she stepped closer, she saw a small box lying among the bricks. It was only about a foot square, and it appeared to have been installed behind the brick.

Jon came with her and studied the remains too. "Looks like a fireproof safe."

"My dad built this fireplace himself. If anything had been installed here, he would have done it." But why wouldn't he have mentioned it? Wouldn't he want something important found after he was gone? Unease rippled down her spine.

"It's probably heavy. I'll get it." Jon bent over and lifted it in both hands. "It's heavy all right. Where do you want it?"

"On the porch is fine. Is it locked?"

"Yeah. It has a tumbler. You'll need to figure out the code or get someone to drill into it."

Could it be worth all that trouble? Maybe. What secret could Dad have wanted to protect so much that he hid it in a fireplace? She and Kylie followed Jon to the porch where he set the safe down, then knelt beside it. Kylie watched with fascination. Secrets were exciting to her.

"Any idea which set of numbers he might use?" he asked.

When had she seen him building it? Maybe when she was around fifteen. "Let's try his birthday." She rattled off the numbers, but the handle didn't budge. "Mom's birthday is in September." Jon keyed it in, but that didn't work either. Neither did her birthday.

"Maybe Sarah's birthday. It's February twenty-second."

Jon rolled the dial, and Annie heard a *click*. The lever moved and the door swung open. She should have guessed that first. Sarah had been everything to her father. She used to be hurt by it, but she couldn't change the past.

"What's in there?" Kylie asked.

Jon swung the door wide and peered inside. "Looks like some kind of notebook." He pulled out a letter-size hardback notebook.

The cover had pictures of rocks along Superior. Annie didn't remember ever seeing this book.

Jon handed it to her. "Maybe it will tell you where his fortune is hidden."

She laughed. "Wouldn't that be nice?"

She opened the front cover and leafed through it, but her dad's handwriting had always been nearly incomprehensible. "I'm going to need food and drink to decipher this. He had the most atrocious script in the world. Who feels like pizza and hot chocolate?"

"I'm starving," Kylie said. "I want the hot chocolate first. I'm cold."

"Maybe go take a hot shower while I get everything ready."

"What am I supposed to wear?"

"You could put on some of my sweats. They'll be too big, but they'll be warm."

"Can I wear the pink ones?"

"They're all yours."

The door banged behind Kylie, and Annie followed with Jon. The book held some kind of mystery, but what? Her dad had been a hard man to get close to, but his purpose in hiding a book felt ominous somehow. Why not simply keep this book in his bedroom? Was it a list of his affairs? Or maybe money he'd kept from Mom? Maybe he'd blackmailed people over the years, and this was the master list.

She almost laughed at such nonsensical thoughts. Her dad was difficult and hotheaded, but she couldn't see him blackmailing anyone. Even the thought of him having an affair was ludicrous. He wasn't the type ruled by passion. Methodical, authoritarian, hardheaded all described him, and she didn't see him ever losing his head over a woman.

Once she was fortified, she'd tackle that journal and see what secrets it held. After Kylie went to bed. Some secrets might be better if her daughter didn't know.

/ / /

Jon washed down his last bite of pizza with a sip of water. He was finally warming up from the cold water, and he couldn't wait to take a look at that book hidden in the fireplace. Annie glanced at her watch again, and he knew she was dying to dig in as well.

Annie's phone rang and she picked it up. "Hey, Bree." She listened for several minutes, then glanced at Kylie. "Bree's twins want you to come stay a few nights. Are you too tired?"

Kylie's blue eyes widened. "Oh yes! I want to go. I bet Bree heard about my stuff." She hugged the puppy in her lap.

"Kade told her, and little Hannah wants to go shopping with you. Anu has already brought over a bag of things she thinks you'll like. She said to tell you to send back anything you don't like or that doesn't fit and she'll bring more. Oh, and bring the puppy."

"I love Anu."

"We all do." Annie glanced at Jon. "Would you mind running her to Bree's while I clean up the mess in her room?"

He forced himself not to let her see his worry. "Sure."

"I want you to take me, Mommy."

"I have things to do, Bug, and they're waiting on you. Jon will have you there in a jiffy in his sports car. It will be fun. You want some of your stuffed animals?"

"My koala bear and my bunny," Kylie said.

"I'll get them." Annie left them alone and went down the hall.

What was he going to say to this hostile little girl on the ride in? Maybe he could turn up music she liked, and he wouldn't have to make small talk with someone who didn't want to speak to him. She'd thawed some during the lessons, but now she wasn't looking at him again.

Annie returned with the stuffed animals. "They were in my room from this morning so they escaped."

Kylie hugged them to her chest. "Thanks, Mommy. I'll talk to you tomorrow?"

"You bet." Annie walked her to the front door and kissed her before smiling up at Jon. "Thanks for the help."

"Anytime." He escorted Kylie and her puppy out to his car and unlocked it as they got close.

His phone dinged, and he smiled when he saw Annie's text about coming back to her house after he'd dropped off Kylie. She must not have wanted to aggravate her daughter by making the invitation in front of her.

He fiddled with the radio after starting the car. "What kind of music do you like?"

Kylie's chin rested on the puppy's head. "Me and Mommy listen to the Christian station, but I like the country station too."

"Does Mommy let you listen to it?"

"Sometimes."

Uh-oh, he might be walking into a minefield here. He found a country station on Sirius radio and fastened his seat belt. If he was doing the wrong thing, Annie would let him know. In the meantime, at least Kylie was smiling.

She'd put her dress from church back on, and her blonde hair gleamed in the late-afternoon light. Cute little girl and so much like Annie. He was beginning to understand that kids weren't just extensions of their parents. Even though she looked like her mother, her likes and dislikes were all her own. Annie loved green and Kylie hated it.

He had a lot to learn about kids.

He glanced over at her and decided to risk having a conversation. "You had a really special dad. Did you know he was my best friend growing up?"

Her eyes widened. "Are you telling me the truth?"

"Yep. Our favorite Popsicles were cherry. Your dad loved Snickers ice cream bars, and he was the best checkers player I ever saw. He could filet a fish in seconds, and he made the best fried shrimp in the world. He loved to watch the Braves, and his second toes were longer than his big toes. Want to hear more?"

"If you were such good friends, how come you never came to visit?"

Now he'd done it. How did he explain that one? "I live in Rochester, and I am always working. I'm an orthopedic surgeon. That means I treat bones and operate when I have to. I'm sorry now that I never got up here to watch him be your dad. I'll bet he was the best dad in the world."

She ducked her head. "I miss him. He made people laugh. He gave the best hugs and used to carry me on his shoulders. We went thimbleberry picking and fishing all the time. In the winter we'd play board games, and he always let me win."

"Your dad always looked out for other people." Jon's voice wobbled, and he realized he hadn't let himself grieve the loss of his best friend. He'd give anything if he could go back a few years and be part of Nate's life again.

When Nate had married Annie, he had done what was in his nature to do—he'd taken care of her. Yes, he'd loved her, but if he hadn't, Nate would still have stepped in and tried to help her—whatever that looked like. Even if it meant marrying her to make her smile again.

"I miss your dad too. I'm sorry I didn't see him these past years. I wish I could change that."

Kylie's gaze softened, and she turned to stare out the window without answering. Had he made any headway? It was hard to tell, but he'd had a breakthrough in his own heart. All the anger he'd carried toward Nate was gone. Nate deserved the very best in life, and it wasn't fair he'd died out there on that water.

The only thing Jon could do now was try to make sure he didn't make the mistake of carrying a grudge ever again.

THIRTY-ONE

THE DIFFICULTY IN READING THE JOURNAL WASN'T just Annie's dad's sloppy writing—words were missing, initials meant something she was having trouble deciphering, and there were obscure statements that made no sense. Annie was ten pages in and still had no idea why it was so important.

She'd opened the windows to let the cool evening breezes blow through the house. The scent of woodsmoke wafted in along with that of the lake, and she was glad for a different smell in here. That man's soap wasn't something she wanted to deal with all night. Though it was a clean scent, it brought back the memory of the taste of mud in her mouth.

And she still had no idea who had jumped her. He'd felt heavy and strong, but the soap smell was her only clue. She hadn't caught even a glimpse of his face or clothing.

She poured a cup of coffee and settled at the table with a blank piece of paper. Maybe if she wrote down what she could make out, they would begin to form some kind of pattern. She stared at the black slashes of letters on the page.

Curse words jumped out at her. She couldn't remember ever hearing her dad swear even though he had a temper. He would throw things and shout, but he never used bad language in front of her.

He appeared to be angry with someone called Woodman. Was that a last name or something else? She read a little further.

No friend of mine.

The words took a moment to penetrate. *His dad would be ashamed. There's a reason I don't let him around my girl.*

A friend's child? Who could it be? She grabbed her laptop and looked up Woodman. There were no Woodmans in the Houghton or Ontonagon areas and just one over in Chassell, a woman. Maybe the woman in Chassell had a son.

She went back to the notebook. Dad hadn't wanted him around her. Why? Was he dangerous, or was it because Dad was afraid he'd blab the truth to her and Mom would find out?

She tried to decipher more text. There were letters missing in words, and nothing was jiving in her head.

How to hide what he did. Not easy. Stupid. Owe his father.

Alarms began to scream at her. What had this guy done? Theft? Burglary? And why would her dad try to hide it? Dad was all about taking your lumps for what you'd done and facing things. She couldn't imagine him letting this friend's son get by with something.

Unless maybe it implicated Dad, too, or would alter his life in some way.

She flipped through the pages to see how much more text was in it. Only about two pages of her dad's cramped cursive. Her head began to ache at trying to decipher the letters. Her mom probably could have done it almost instantly.

Stupid girls.

Was it really what it said? The word *girls* clearly had an *s* on the end, but she wasn't positive about the word *stupid*. It might be *silly*. Or some other S-word because that was the only clear letter.

A knock came at the screen, and Jon stood there. "Come on in."

"She happily went in to play. Bree told me she thought Kylie would be safer in town for a few days. Smart thinking." He stepped inside. "Looks like you're deep into the notebook. What's it all about?"

"I'm not sure yet. Know anyone with the last name of Woodman?"

He shook his head. "Doesn't sound like a common name around here."

"I found one over in Chassell, but no one else. And the one there is a woman."

"What's so important about the name?"

"I think Dad was covering up a crime a friend's son committed. I might be wrong, but it looks that way to me." She slid the journal over to him. "What do you think that phrase says?"

He frowned and studied it. "Something girls. Stupid maybe? Sexy? Silly? Hard to tell. His handwriting is atrocious."

"You should have seen his signature. No one could ever duplicate it."

She pushed her notepad over to him where she'd jotted the clues, and he looked it over. "Maybe the woman in Chassell is this Woodman's mother."

"I think we need to talk to her and see if we can find out anything."

He glanced at the clock on the wall. "It's already seven. It would be an hour over there. You want to chance going that late?"

"We'd likely find her home, and it's going to be light awhile. Let's take my truck so she's not intimidated by your fancy car."

He grinned and lifted a brow. "My car is intimidating?"

She returned his smile. "Let's say it's a little ostentatious."

"It wasn't in Rochester, but I've been thinking maybe I need to get rid of it."

She wasn't going to touch that hot potato. If he wanted to get rid of it, that was his decision. But was he beginning to long for the simpler life they enjoyed up here? How would she feel if he ever admitted it? It wasn't something she wanted to linger on. Heartache led in that direction.

/ / /

The agate in Taylor's fingers wasn't like the smooth, polished ones she'd seen in rock stores in the area, and she tossed it back onto the sand with disgust. Nothing was turning out like she'd planned when she came up here. He had promised her so much more when he coaxed her into coming. Was life ever going to turn around for her?

She plopped onto the beach and seized a handful of sand, then let it trickle through her splayed fingers. That's what her days felt like right now—an hourglass she couldn't slow down and enjoy.

Angry tears burned her eyes. She'd thought Jon was the one, but he'd fallen under Annie's spell. Taylor didn't understand why men couldn't see past that pretty face. Annie had everything, while Taylor had only crumbs. All her life had been leftovers. She'd been an afterthought, and for once she'd thought she might build a life of significance.

It wasn't fair, and Jon should have to pay for encouraging her love when he didn't care. He'd taken every bit of her attention and enjoyed it before tossing her away like the agate by her feet. Men were pigs, just like her mother had said.

He'd deceived her, and he had to pay for it.

She stared out at the deep blue of the water and thought about what she could do. There had been gossip Jon was suspected of hurting those girls. Could she throw more suspicion his way? That would be poetic justice. He'd killed her heart, and now that she thought about it, maybe he really had killed those girls. If he was capable of what he'd done to her, he was capable of anything.

She ran over the options in her head. Any accusation had to have teeth. The girls had been found in that abandoned cabin on Annie's property. She could plant evidence from there. Even though the remote cabin had been checked for clues, she could claim he'd told her something and she could corroborate it in some way.

But how?

She sighed and grabbed the newspaper she'd gotten after church. The front page showed a picture of the murdered girls. They stood arm-in-arm, smiling at the camera. Her gaze fell on the necklaces around their necks and she gasped. She pulled her lucky necklace from her pocket and stared at it. It was exactly like the one around Sophie's neck.

She'd stolen it from *him* when he came to help after her mother died. Her cousin was the murderer?

An idea clicked into her head, and, smiling, she rose to carry out her plan. He'd be sorry he destroyed her heart. She'd implicate Jon and protect her cousin at the same time.

Annie had loaned her a small moped to ride while she worked for her, so she bumped along the narrow road back to Jon's cottage where she found the unlocked shed just as she'd remembered.

Perfect.

She sneezed at the dust motes and stale air as she wandered the interior of the shed, looking for the right place to plant the necklace. An ax leaned against the far wall, and she dropped the sea glass piece down behind it.

Now all she had to do was tell the sheriff where to find it.

/ / /

Chassell was one of Jon's favorite U.P. small towns. Nestled along Portage Lake, the town held a strawberry festival every July that pulled in people from all over the Keweenaw. It was once a stop on the Duluth, South Shore and Atlantic Railway that serviced the logging industry back in the eighteen hundreds and early into the twentieth century. Jon loved the old houses and the friendly people.

Jon recognized their destination immediately. "I've been here before with my parents. It used to be the Hamar House Bed-and-Breakfast, and the owner, Barbara Ryland Wells, put on a lavish breakfast for us. She was a wealth of information about the area and the monastery up in Eagle River. She'd once been a famous concert pianist, and my mom persuaded her to give us a short concert."

"I've been here before too. Barbara and her daughter, Kathryn, sold beautiful agate items and jewelry. I have some at the house."

The red-and-white Victorian was just as charming as he remembered. As soon as they got out of Annie's truck, a woman stood up from where she'd been weeding a tomato and herb garden. She appeared to be in her thirties, and Jon knew without asking that this was probably going to be a dead end. Unless she had a brother maybe.

"Can I help you?" she asked. "This isn't a bed-and-breakfast any longer."

Annie's smile was on full wattage. "I noticed the sign was gone. We're here to talk to Emily Woodman."

She pulled off muddy gloves. "That's me. How can I help you?"

"You're not what I was expecting," Annie said. "So I might be wasting your time. But by any chance did you know Ted Vitanen? He owned the Tremolo Marina and Cabin Resort near Rock Harbor."

She shook her head. "I've heard of the marina, but I never met him."

"Do you have a brother?" Jon asked.

The woman's dark brows rose, and she shook her head. "That's a strange question, but no. I have two sisters."

"How about any relatives with your same last name?" Annie said.

"Not in the Keweenaw. I have some second cousins down in Tennessee, but I don't believe they have ever been up here. What's this all about?"

They'd discussed how to handle questions, and it was uncomfortable to be digging into such private matters without giving away too much information. Jon decided Annie could answer that one. This was her family matter, not his.

Annie's smile faltered. "I'm Ted's daughter, and the only one left in my family. I'd heard he might have a good friend named Woodman, whom I didn't know. The only information I have about him is that this friend had a son. You were the only person with that name I could find. I knew it was a long shot, but I couldn't resist the chance to see if there were more of us around than I knew. Thank you for your trouble."

"I hope you find what you're looking for. Sorry I couldn't be of more help." Emily bent and snipped a white rose from a nearby bush, then handed it to Annie. "But no matter what, you're never alone because God is with you."

Annie took the rose and held it to her nose. "I know he is. Thank you for that encouragement. And for the rose."

"You're so welcome."

Jon walked with Annie back to the truck parked along the street. "Could Woodman mean anything else? A nickname of some kind?" He opened the truck's door for her, and she slid into the passenger seat.

He went around to the driver side and shut the door behind him. "Check on your phone. See if it is a common nickname of some kind."

Her mouth curled into a wry twist. "Woodman doesn't seem like a nickname, but I'll check."

He drove out of town on the Chassell-Painesdale Road. He'd barely left the city limits when he heard two pops, and the truck veered toward the ditch. "Hang on!"

The vehicle careened as he fought to keep the truck from rolling into the ditch. His breath was coming fast, and his fingers were clenched on the steering wheel by the time the vehicle stopped inches short of a deep ravine.

Annie shoved open her door and got out. "That was close."

He climbed out to assess the damage too. Around on the passenger side the front tire was in shreds. At first he assumed it was a normal blowout, but just above the tire he spotted a round hole.

He touched it. "Look here, Annie. A bullet hole. I heard two pops. Did you hear them?"

"Someone shot out my tire."

"I think they might have been aiming at you since there were two shots. Would the workers have mentioned the safe you found to anyone?"

"They might have. They are teenage boys and wouldn't have known to keep it quiet."

"We need to talk to them and see who they mentioned it to. Someone knew we were coming over here tonight. A drive to Chassell isn't in your normal routine."

She frowned. "Unless someone followed us. Or tracked us in some way."

"Let me look under the car." He got out and peered under the front. Nothing there. But he hit pay dirt under the back bumper. A tracking device.

He carried it back to the front of the truck to show her. "This is how the guy found you."

"Hang on, let me contact Mason." She pulled out her phone and called.

A pattern of attacks on her were escalating in intensity. This could have turned out badly if he'd run the truck into the ditch. With the steep embankment, the vehicle likely would have rolled over several times.

"Mason is sending out a team to search for evidence."

He feared Mason wouldn't find anything to help track down this phantom. Kylie's terror of losing her mother wasn't unfounded. "Someone is determined to stop you from investigating, Annie. You need to take this seriously."

Her gaze hardened. "There's always an element of danger in law enforcement. It's the job I picked. I'm not walking away from it, Jon. I can't."

"This guy shot at you while I was driving. There's no way

to protect against that. I know you said it's only made you more determined, but you have to think of Kylie. I would never get over it if something happened to you because of me."

He barely stopped short of telling her he still loved her and always would. "What happened to us, Annie? I'm still not sure I know. I'm going to change your tire, and then we're going to talk about what went wrong."

Was that fear that flashed through her beautiful eyes? If so, it matched the terror in his heart too. Things might be said that could never be unsaid.

THIRTY-TWO

THE SUNSET OVER LAKE SUPERIOR LIT THE SKY WITH red and orange. Annie's heart wanted to leap out of her chest as she settled on a rock under the strobe of Bree's lighthouse. She'd texted Kade and asked if he'd keep an eye out while she and Jon had this conversation, then had left her phone with Mason. Jon had driven them to the Matthews's residence after changing the truck's tire.

This conversation was long overdue, and she still wasn't sure if she was ready for it. Talking about it would rip the scab off the wound.

Jon touched her shoulder briefly as he moved past her to settle on another rock a couple of feet away. Close enough for her to catch a whiff of his spicy cologne but far enough away to be able to settle her thoughts and emotions.

The sunset's glow on his brown hair made it appear auburn. His expression was as hesitant as she felt. If neither of them wanted this conversation, why were they having it? Pain awaited them no matter what they said now. They couldn't go back and undo the past.

Jon cleared his throat. "That last night. How did we go so wrong?"

They were really going to do this. She prayed for peace, for honesty. Nothing could be gained from this unless she left pretense behind. "I blamed you for my own weakness. I'd really wanted to wait for our marriage night, but when your mom died and I saw you crying, I lost my resolve. When I got home and looked in the mirror the next morning, I saw the failure my dad had always seen."

"You're not a failure. Your dad saying it doesn't make it so."

He'd skirted what she'd said. Was this going to end up in another fight when he couldn't be honest too?

"I knew you'd been accepted into an internship at the University of Wisconsin in Madison, and I thought you'd go there, a-after that night. You would have been less than five hours away." She drew in another deep breath and prepared to lay bare her heart. "When you said you couldn't turn down the chance at Mayo Clinic, it felt like you'd taken everything I'd given to you and tossed it out the window. It made me feel like that night meant nothing to you."

He looked down at his hands. "I'm not proud of that night either, Annie. I'll be honest—it felt like we'd crossed a line, and we couldn't go back. And we did, I guess. I thought about how that one night could change my whole life, and I wasn't sure I was ready to give up my dreams. I should have been ready—I'd loved you for years. But I was hurting from losing my mom, and the thought of walking away from the dreams she and I had shared about my future felt wrong. She'd been so excited when the letter came from Mayo. It felt like a betrayal of everything I'd worked for."

"So you walked away from me instead."

His green eyes sparked. "You are the one who made it an ultimatum. You made it clear if I left, our relationship was over. And it hurt that you'd do that on the heels of my mom's death. It felt like you didn't take into consideration all the sacrifices I'd made to get where I am."

With nine years of distance now, she could see where he would feel she'd put too much pressure on him when he was grieving. But there was one important thing she'd never told him.

She took and deep breath and looked down at her hands. "There's something you don't know. My dad saw us that night through the window of the cabin when we were buttoning up our clothes. The morning after our fight, he told me to get out. That I was no daughter of his. I was already ashamed that I'd disappointed God, and Dad's anger destroyed what self-respect I had left. Which wasn't much."

She could still remember her disbelief at her dad's announcement. Where was she supposed to go on a moment's notice? Luckily, Bree had been there for her as always. When Bree heard her dad had thrown her out, she'd immediately told her to stay with her.

Jon's eyes widened. "I'm sorry, Annie. Why didn't you tell me? I was still in town then."

"And force you to stay? To expect you to marry me just to make my dad happy? What kind of relationship would it be if you didn't go into it willingly?"

He gave a jerky nod. "We sure messed up what had been a great relationship. I never really talked to you about my mom's dreams for me. She didn't just want me to be an orthopedic surgeon—she wanted me to be one of the best in the country, something impossible to do up here."

"And I didn't understand why you didn't want to go to school in Madison. You could have come to see me every weekend."

"There was no comparison between Madison and Mayo as far as Mom was concerned. The week before she died, I promised her I wouldn't let anything stand between me and going to Rochester."

The secrets between them had ripped them apart. What would have happened if they'd both been honest about what had happened? Maybe nothing would have changed, but maybe everything would have. She could see the same realization dawning in his eyes.

"So Nate knew you were living at Bree's. He wanted to help."

She nodded. "He'd moved permanently to Rock Harbor in May, and he felt steadfast and strong. I was a mess. I thought my life was over, and he honestly was worried I might harm myself." That wasn't something she wanted to admit, but she'd promised God she'd be truthful. "Nate swooped in, made me eat, told me life wasn't over, and that my dad was wrong."

"Why didn't your mom stop him from throwing you out?"

"She told me I didn't have to leave, but you know how my dad was—an immovable object. He would have made life miserable for me and Mom. I didn't want to put her through that. I think I wanted to punish myself. And Nate was there."

"You fell for him?" His voice was tight.

She had to be honest, so she raised her gaze to his. "We'd always had a special friendship. I knew he'd always loved me, and when he said he'd always be there for me, I thought it was the right thing to do. I knew he'd never hurt me, and I didn't feel right staying with Bree for long."

"He wouldn't desert you like I did."

"That's what I thought at the time. I blamed you for everything, and it took a long time for me to see where I'd been wrong. It's always easier to blame the other person. And maybe there was an element of getting back at you by marrying Nate. That was wrong of me too."

He rose and came to stoop in front of her. "I wish I'd told you everything. I'm sorry. I hope you can forgive me, Annie."

She nodded. They should have talked this out a long time ago.

"I never got over you, Annie. Not ever. I hope we can start over."

The raw honesty in his words brought tears to her eyes, but she couldn't promise him that. Now when Kylie disliked him so much. Not when there was still a secret to tell if it became necessary.

/ / /

Annie never agreed they could start over.

Jon parked his car in the drive in front of his cottage and slumped in his seat. He and Annie had finished trying to decipher the rest of her dad's journal without any success, then he'd gone to the bed-and-breakfast but tossed and turned until after three. His eyes were tired and dry this morning.

Sean's truck was already here, and the ring of hammers pounding nails echoed in the treetops as the last window was fastened into place. Jon got out and went inside where the smell of sawdust and paint mixed with the scent of pine through the window screens.

Sean turned toward him with a grin. "Making progress, eh? Tomorrow the cabinets get here and counters two days later. The bathroom is already done. You should be able to sell this place in another week."

Jon looked around and smiled. "*If* I sell it. It looks good, and honestly, my dad is talking about moving here."

Sean tipped his head to one side. "You're serious about keeping it? I thought you were joking."

"It's hard to think about letting it go."

Sean's hazel eyes held a knowing look. "Trying to get back with Annie, eh? She's definitely a keeper. She has *sisu*."

Sisu was the Finnish Yooper term for grit and determination. "She's amazing."

They weren't close enough for Jon to feel comfortable talking about something so personal, so he shrugged. "It's been in the family since my grandpa built it sixty years ago. I've been enjoying being up here again."

"Fair enough." Sean put down his hammer and gestured to Jon. "I'll show you the bathroom, eh?"

"Sure." Jon followed him into the bath, which now had two sinks, a new toilet, and a larger shower in a marble-like tile. The floor was a black and white retro tile. "I like it."

"It turned out great. Once the kitchen is in, we're all done. And on budget."

"Thanks for getting it done so quickly." But it meant he would have to make a decision fast.

If he was honest with himself, he'd already made the decision. He'd walked away from Annie once. He couldn't do it again, even if it took years to get past her defenses. Something told him the love she had for him hadn't died. Maybe it had gone underground, but it was still there. She was afraid, but he could prove he wouldn't flake out again.

"How's the investigation going?" Sean asked when they got back to the main room. "Annie having any luck tracking down who was out at Lake of the Clouds the day the girls went missing?"

"Not yet. She's got a few leads." Jon glanced at Sean, who had lived here all his life. "You know any Woodmans?"

Sean blinked and bent down to put his hammer in his toolbox. "Woodman. That's not a common surname. Where'd you hear it?"

"Someone mentioned it. I don't know any."

"I can't think of any either."

"Annie will figure it out. She's smart and dogged. She was going to see if it's a nickname for something. That might lead somewhere."

Sean picked up his toolbox. "I'm going to run to the hardware store for cabinet pulls. If you see anything else you want fixed or is not to your liking, text me, eh?"

"You bet." With Sean gone Jon wandered out to the back deck and stared out over the sparkling blue of Superior.

Should he move in here permanently or keep it as a summer home? Could he even win Annie back if he was only here part time? It might take full commitment. With him being her closest neighbor, she couldn't ignore him. If he'd realized he might change his mind, he would have put in double-paned windows.

He pulled out his phone and looked up orthopedic doctors in Houghton. There were several. Should he start his own practice or join another one? He'd gotten lucky with an offer in Rochester and had quickly moved up to full partner when the owner retired. If he was part of a team, he'd have more personal time. It would take time to start a practice and recruit other doctors.

After studying the reviews and stats of several surgeons, he called the office number of the top one listed and told the receptionist he'd like to set up an appointment with the head doctor about a possible partnership. To his surprise she informed him the doctor was actively looking.

Was God leading him to this point? Jon wanted to believe it. He wanted to trust this would all work out, but right now it was the biggest leap of faith he'd ever taken and it scared him to death.

THIRTY-THREE

BY NINE ON MONDAY MORNING, ANNIE FINISHED TALKing to Mason about the gunshots. As expected, the deputies had found nothing. The shooter could have been anywhere. She ended the call and went out to the pavilion.

The teenage boys were putting the last wheelbarrows full of debris into the Dumpster. "Good morning. You guys ready for some coffee?"

"We'd take a soft drink," one of them said.

She hadn't gotten their names. "I can handle that. Hang on."

She went back to the house and packed a cooler with assorted canned drinks. They were washing their hands in the outside shower when she lugged out the cooler for them. "Have at it."

"Thank you," the same young man said. "We're all done here."

"You did a great job. I have a quick question for you before you leave. You know that safe you found? I wondered if you'd mentioned it to anyone."

The shortest of the three boys frowned. "I didn't say anything about it to anyone. Why? Did you find treasure?" His brown eyes gleamed with interest.

"There wasn't anything in it but some old family records. I just wondered who knew about it."

He lifted a skeptical brow. "Then why ask us about it?"

She couldn't tell him there might be incriminating evidence in it. "I wondered if it might lead to something else." She glanced at the other two. "Either of you mention it to anyone?"

"Just the boss. No big deal," the talkative one said. "Listen, we have to go. Sean has another job for us."

"Thanks for your help!" she called after them.

So that was a dead end. She already knew her phone had been tracked. Mason had cloned it, then given it back to her, but it would take time to figure out who'd put the program on there. She'd wondered if someone knew a safe had been found and worried there was something incriminating in it. Jon was worried, and to be honest, so was she.

She went back inside to grab her laptop and call up a search engine to check if maybe *Woodman* was a nickname for something. It didn't sound likely, but it was all she had at the moment. Her query had immediate hits. It was a nickname for *cabinetmaker*, *journeyman*, *craftsman*, *carver*, *furniture maker*, and *carpenter*.

That didn't seem likely to be pertinent. Deflated, she closed the lid on her computer and leaned back. While she was used to chasing down leads and investigation, she'd never been the brunt of someone's animosity this way.

Knuckles rapped on her screen door, and she turned to see Sean Johnson standing on the porch. "Knock, knock."

"Good morning." She rose and went out to join him. "Were you looking for your workers? They just left for another job you had lined up."

"I saw them on the way in. I actually came to see you. I wanted to rent a boat if you have one available. Mine sank last night. I knew it had a small hole and had patched it, but it must have given out. I wanted to take out a small boat and try to float it." He wrinkled his nose. "Though it's going to be a challenge."

"Where's it located?"

"I'd anchored it a little offshore at Ten Mile."

She made a split-second decision to help. "I've got the equipment to make it easy. I'll go with you. Let me grab my dive gear."

"What equipment do we need?"

"Air compressor, a couple of inner tubes, a tarp to repair the hole temporarily. I have that in a kit in my personal boat. We'll take it. You have your dive gear with you?"

He nodded. "I was going to rent a boat and go out to assess it before giving it a try. Thanks so much for the help."

"It's what neighbors do."

She led the way across the parking lot to the dock and her boat. It rocked when she stepped aboard, and she moved out of the way for Sean to join her. "We should have that boat raised in an hour. You'll need to get it up on your lift for repair right away. The tarp won't keep the water out for long."

"I'm pretty good at repair usually. I was shocked when I got up this morning and realized it was underwater. There's a storm due in a couple of hours, and I knew if I didn't get salvaged, it would be battered to pieces."

She winced and nodded, then went to start the engine. "We'll bring it up before then."

Though the glowering clouds were bearing down on them, she was certain she could raise it quickly. The engine roared to life, and she chugged away from the dock before accelerating to full speed toward the boat's location. It took fifteen minutes to reach the site, and there wasn't another craft on the water, not with the choppy waves and increasing wind.

"It's there," Sean yelled over the wind whipping along the sides of the boat.

She nodded and throttled down the engine to idle while she tossed her equipment overboard in a net supported by buoys. Her boat chugged close enough she could see down through the clear, cold water to the boat listing starboard under the waves. "That doesn't look like *The Princess*."

The wind changed directions, and she caught a whiff of a familiar soap scent. Something with pine. When she turned to look at Sean, she found herself staring down the barrel of a Glock. Her breath seized in her throat, and her gaze went from the gun to Sean's face. She'd known him all her life. Why would he want to harm her?

Woodman . . . carpenter. "Are you Woodman? Dad was protecting *you*?"

He winced. "I was afraid there was something incriminating in that safe."

"Why did he help you and why did it make him angry?"

Sean shrugged. "He embezzled money from an employer when he was young, in his twenties. My dad got him off, and your dad swore he'd do anything to help him. When Ted saw me at your abandoned cabin, he felt obligated to help, even though he could cheerfully have killed me and fed me to the fishes."

His smile sent a wave of cold over her. The truth came from somewhere inside, and she wasn't sure how she made the deductive leap. "You killed Penelope and Sophie. Dad saw you hide the bodies."

/ / /

Metro Espresso was hopping this morning, and Jon carried his caramel latte outside. The clouds had rolled in quickly, and thunderheads rose high into the stratosphere. The storm was supposed to hit by noon, but he wasn't sure it would wait that long.

"Jon, wait up."

He turned at Mason's deep voice. The sheriff wore a solemn expression as he hurried to catch up. "Good morning."

"I need you to come into the office to answer some questions."

"Mason, I've told you everything I know about the girls. You're wasting your time."

"We have a new witness." Mason glanced around. "Look, you don't want people in town to see me questioning you and wondering what's going on. It's better to have this conversation in private."

"You think people won't notice me going in for an interrogation?" Jon knew better than to argue though, so he followed the sheriff over to the jail. Hopefully people wouldn't think he was being arrested.

Instead of taking him to his office, Mason led him to an interrogation room smelling of fear and despair. He gestured to the table flanked by two chairs. "Have a seat."

"Am I being arrested?"

"No, but I've got to ask some serious questions."

Jon sank onto the red vinyl seat and folded his arms across his chest. "So ask your questions. I have things to do."

"A witness has come forward who claims to have seen you with Sophie's necklace."

"What? That's impossible. Who would have said that? I've never even seen that missing necklace." Jon blew out an exasperated breath. "I didn't kill those girls. I think you know that deep down, Mason. Who is this so-called witness?"

"Taylor Moore."

The sheer lunacy of that rocked Jon. "Look, Mason, she has a crush on me. She brought me brownies and kept asking me to do things with her. I made it clear to her a couple of days ago that I'm not interested. I let her know Annie and I had been engaged and I wanted to rekindle that relationship. This is some kind of revenge."

A flicker of compassion lit Mason's eyes. "It's your word against hers so I went where she told me I could find the necklace. It was there just like she said."

"And where was this?"

"The shed at your lake cottage."

"It's not mine. The lake cottage belongs to my dad. Are you going to accuse him of killing the girls?"

"It's a strong piece of evidence, Jon. You can't dismiss it."

"Did you check the necklace for fingerprints? You won't find mine there."

"I'd like to get a sample of your fingerprints to compare."

"Sure. Bring in your tech. I have nothing to hide."

That was a stupid thing to say. Innocent people went to jail all the time.

Mason rose and left him alone in the interrogation room. Jon rubbed his forehead, then pulled out his phone to call Annie. It rang several times before it went to voice mail. Where could she be? She'd planned to do a little more investigation on the computer until he came to join her at lunchtime, and it was nearly that time now.

There was no concrete reason for alarm to begin raising the hair on his arms. No real explanation for the way his chest tightened. But he felt an urgent need to make sure she was all right.

Bree. Maybe she'd gone to visit Kylie. He called Bree, and she answered on the first ring. "Hey, Bree, is Annie with you?"

"No, she's not. I've been trying to reach her for the last fifteen minutes. Kylie wants to talk to her. She's been very fearful for her mom's safety, and I'd like to reassure her. You haven't talked to her this morning?"

"No. You left a message for her?"

"Three of them."

Jon rose and went to the interrogation room door. It didn't budge when he yanked on it. Locked. "I'll try to get out there right away and see where she is. Mason has me locked in a room right now."

"What? That's crazy."

"I should be out of here shortly. Try to keep Kylie calm. I'll call you when I know more."

He ended the call and banged on the door. "Mason! I need to get out of here. Mason!"

It seemed an eternity before the lock clicked. He stepped back as Mason entered with a woman carrying a fingerprint kit.

"I need to go check on Annie," Jon said. "Bree can't reach her and neither can I. You know she's being stalked. Something is wrong."

"I'm sorry, but this is serious, Jon. I need to follow through." Mason nodded to the woman. "This will only take a minute. Have a seat."

Jon couldn't do that. He feinted left as if he was going back to the table, then leaped around both of them and ran down the hallway. Mason shouted after him, but he kept going. He exited the building to face a glowering sky as a few drops of rain fell. In seconds he was across the street and in his Jag. A few more seconds and he had the speedometer up to eighty when he left the Rock Harbor city limits behind.

He might have heard a siren behind him, but a patrol car would never keep up with him. Mason knew where he was headed, and he would need the extra manpower to find Annie.

Because something was very, very wrong.

THIRTY-FOUR

THE WIND INTENSIFIED TO A BANSHEE'S HOWL, AND black clouds swirled overhead. The scent of ozone followed a flash of lightning. Rain began to patter on the water.

The gun in Sean's hand never wavered. "My, my, how on earth does your mind work, eh?"

"I knew when I met Glenn Hussert that I'd seen him before, but I couldn't remember where or when. You'd had a breakdown in your truck, and I was with Dad when he stopped to help you. Hussert was in the truck with you. The two of you were hunting partners."

"Glenn didn't want anyone to know we'd talked to the girls, but he didn't have the guts to take what he wanted." His eyes narrowed.

"Why did you kill them?"

His glare went colder. "I'm not stupid, Annie. I know you're trying to drag out the conversation to delay the inevitable, but we don't have much time here." He gestured to the sky overhead. "While I'd love to take the time to share the details, I'm afraid you'll need to go overboard now. In these waters the cold will take you without too much pain. In you go, eh."

She shook her head. "I won't make it easy for you, Sean. You want to make it look like an accident, but you'll have to shoot me."

His jaw flexed, and he rushed toward her. She sidestepped him and slipped behind the captain's chair. What could she use for a weapon? She'd left with him in such a hurry, she hadn't grabbed her gun. There was a harpoon onboard, but it was safely stowed below and hard to reach. Same with her dive knife.

Her gaze fell on the red fire extinguisher. Its weight could knock him out, but to get to it she'd have to evade him in a rush across to the port side of the boat. Not an easy task because he was so much bigger and stronger.

He grabbed at her arm, and she evaded him again, then shoved at his chest and dashed for the extinguisher. She wrenched it free as he roared and came at her again.

She swung the extinguisher at his head, and he ducked enough that she only landed a glancing blow that slowed him down for an instant.

She leaped to his right, and his fingers grazed her arm as she slipped away and ran toward the starboard side of the boat.

It was her against this maniac, and he'd be on her before she could call up anyone on the marine radio.

"I've been your friend," she hissed as he came toward her again. "Why would you try to hurt me?"

"This friend, that friend, it's all the same to me. Your dad found that out."

His sinister grin made her gasp. "You sabotaged Dad's boat, didn't you?"

"I couldn't trust him."

"Couldn't trust him after he helped you hide two bodies? You must demand a lot of blind faith from people."

"He thought I put them in Superior, and he would have had a meltdown if he'd known they were in the abandoned cabin."

"Why didn't you put them in Superior? They would never have been found."

He smirked, and the glint in his eye held smug satisfaction. "I wanted to be able to stop in and see them sometimes."

She shuddered at the macabre revelation that he had an ego Lake Superior couldn't fill. "Then why kill Dad?"

"I got tired of hearing him yammering at me to turn myself in. I think he was getting ready to call the sheriff if I didn't."

Sean might be right. Dad held everyone to higher standards than he did himself.

The thoughts swirled so fast in her head that she missed the way his muscles tensed until it was too late. He lunged to her left and clasped her upper arm. She tried to twist out of his grip, but he was too strong.

His viselike grip made her cry out as he forced her back against the railing. The metal bit into her waist as he bent her backward. She reached behind her with her free hand to brace herself enough so he couldn't push her overboard, but her hand couldn't find purchase. In the next moment she was flipping over the rail in what felt like an awkward backflip.

Her head hit the water first. The cold squeezed her in a breath-stopping grip. Waves rolled over her head and forced water into her mouth and nose. She went under and came up sputtering. Her limbs went numb from the water's temperature. Her movements were already slow and lethargic from the lake's merciless grip.

She spotted Sean staring at her from aboard her boat with a grim yet triumphant expression. She turned away, and she heard the engine roar to life before it began to recede in the distance.

The lyrics to the old Gordon Lightfoot song "The Wreck of the Edmund Fitzgerald" played in her mind in a nonstop litany.

And anyone who lived on the lake knew it was true. The lake was so cold bodies didn't decompose, which also meant they didn't float to the top. It was deep here, and her body would go down, down to the depths if she didn't find a way to survive.

Would that be her fate? Would Kylie watch and wonder what became of her? No, she couldn't let that happen. She struggled against the cold lethargy that weighted her down. Kylie needed her mother to come home. Annie couldn't let Sean win.

Another wave crashed over her head, and she spiraled down into the blue depths before fighting her way back to the top. Her lungs were near bursting by the time she got her nose into the air to draw in precious oxygen. She couldn't feel her limbs any longer, and she struggled to maintain her desire to live when all she wanted to do was sink into the lake's embrace and sleep.

She smacked herself in the face. "Stay awake. Fight! Don't let him win."

A buoy caught her attention, and she saw her boat-raising equipment. Was she even moving toward it? She couldn't feel her feet well enough to know. The netting was in her hand before she realized she'd reached it. Consciousness came and went as she clung to a buoy with all her might and prayed for Jon to come find her.

/ / /

Jon reached the parking lot of Tremolo Marina as the clouds let loose with buckets of rain. He got out beside Annie's truck into the downpour, not even able to see two feet in front of his face. He veered to her truck and yanked open the door to check inside.

Empty. No keys in the ignition either.

He stood in the pouring rain for a long moment trying to decide where to go first. He'd check the cottage and make sure she wasn't lying injured inside. He was chilled to the bone by the time he reached her house.

All the lights were out, so he knew she wasn't home even though her truck was here. That piece of information didn't sit well. He took the time to enter the unlocked house, and everything appeared normal. Nothing out of place, no sign of a struggle.

He went out onto the porch and peered through the curtain of rain toward the dock. He couldn't see a thing from here, so he dashed through deluge to see if she might be out on the boat. His feet hydroplaned along the dock boards, and he nearly went headlong into the water but managed to grab hold of a piling to catch himself.

He had to traverse the length of the dock to visually inspect every boat since visibility was so poor. Her boat wasn't here.

She was out on the lake in the worst storm of the past few years.

He gulped at the thought, but she was an excellent sailor. She knew boats inside and out.

But even good sailors drowned.

Superior was a hard mistress, as capricious as any ocean on earth. She could change from smooth as glass to raging waves in a few minutes.

The bigger question was why would she have gone out on a stormy day like today? Had someone forced her to go? Had she gone to rescue someone? Knowing Annie, it could have been either option.

There were several boats tied up at the marina, so he opted to take the biggest one on the end to search for her. She kept the keys in her office, so he ran back through the huge puddles in the yard to the house and found the key he needed.

As he reached the parking lot, he spotted a man running for a pickup from the direction of the dock. The guy yanked open the vehicle door and slid into view under the dome light. Sean. His truck tires spun in the flooded lot, and his engine roared as he accelerated away as if he were being chased.

What had he been doing out on the dock?

That question could wait. Jon ran back to the dock and stopped short when he spotted Annie's boat parked in its usual slip. It hadn't been there five minutes ago.

He cupped his hands to his mouth. "Annie!"

When he stepped aboard her boat, he found nothing amiss. And no Annie. Had she gone back to the house and he'd missed her? He jogged back to the cottage again, but the lights were still out. No Annie.

Sean. Had *he* been using her boat? If so, why? Was Annie out there in another boat? Something told him Annie was out there on those mountainous waves.

Sirens screamed through the pounding rain, and he spotted a red light pulsing through the limited visibility. He couldn't let Mason stop him from getting to Annie, so he raced back to the dock and took her boat instead. The key was still in the ignition. It would weather the storm better than any of the other boats.

He started the engine and motored out from the dock, then paused to shoot a text to Mason.

> Annie missing. Sean Johnson just came in with her boat. I'm going to look for her, but please go after Sean. I think he might know something.

Once he pressed Send, he accelerated out into the wild and choppy waters. He thought he heard Mason shout his name, but the roar of the water and the wind snatched away the sound. All he could do was pray Mason listened and got more information on Annie's whereabouts from Sean.

The waves battled for supremacy with him, and his arms were tired from fighting the wheel. For every five feet he moved forward, the waves battered him back three feet, so progress was slow. The rain finally began to let up a bit, but thunder and lightning still crashed overhead. He was thankful for the lightning because it illuminated the water better. He didn't see another boat or anything that indicated someone in the water either. Which would be a good thing. The thought of Annie trying to survive in these waters was heart stopping.

How far should he go out here? He might be jumping to wrong conclusions and Annie was in danger somewhere else. For all he knew, she could be back in the woods somewhere. Or in the deserted cabin where the bodies were found.

The truth was he was flying blind.

He'd search out here for ten more minutes. If he saw nothing, he'd turn around and go back. But after those ten minutes ticked by, some inner turmoil he took to be an urging from God pressed him to stay the course. To continue to search.

He squinted through the gray curtain of rain. Annie had been attacked at Tremolo Island. Could she be there? It was worth checking out, so he headed for the island. He prayed for her safety and help finding her. The sense of danger overwhelmed him, and he knew in his heart she was in trouble.

THIRTY-FIVE

ANNIE COULD BARELY KEEP HER EYES OPEN IN THE glowering storm. Waves rolled over her, and she'd gone past cold to a strange warmth that coaxed her to spiral down into a deep sleep. But knowing it would be a permanent sleep, she fought its hypnotic power with all her might for Kylie's sake. She couldn't leave her daughter orphaned.

Of all the legends, she'd always been most intrigued with Michibeichu, the great serpent of the lake. There had been alleged sightings all through history, with a picture actually being taken in 1977. The account was of some kind of creature with humps covered in spikes undulating out of the water. It was said to have a horse-shaped head with a neck fifteen feet tall.

Was it even now under her, tracking her for its dinner? The lake held many secrets, many dangers. The last time the lake had nearly drowned her was the night Sarah was taken, and the attacker had thrown her into the waves. She managed to lift her head and stare out through the rain. Was she anywhere near Tremolo Island? It might be the nearest land mass, and the dangerous rip currents out here jetted right past the island.

She could no longer feel the buoy she clung to as the waves tossed her and the buoy to and fro. The rough waves had torn it loose from the netting, and she had no idea where she was in the vast waters of Superior. She'd gone past being able to pray to simply accepting whatever God chose for her in this moment. But she wouldn't just give up without a fight for her daughter.

A huge wave lifted her and tore the buoy from her arms, then slammed her down into the depths again. She feebly fought her way back to the surface, but in her heart she knew she wouldn't be able to do it again. All her strength was gone. Only enough of her will lived to encourage her to scissor her legs and try to keep afloat.

Another surge lifted her and rolled down what seemed to be a mountain with her in its arms, but her head didn't go under. Instead, she felt something under her feet. Her toes were too numb to sense anything, but she tried to support her weight on whatever was under her and staggered forward. The waves receded, down from her chest, to her hips, to her knees, to her ankles, and she finally fell onto solid ground.

With no idea where she was, she lay in a stupor for several long minutes. Feeling began to creep back into her frozen limbs, but it was more painful than welcome. Tingling nerve pain radiated from her hands and feet, and she forced herself to crawl away from the water. The thought of finding a blanket and being able to curl up somewhere and sleep drove her on.

Where there was land, there should be people. Warmth, light, laughter. *Life.*

She was alive, at least for now. It didn't seem possible after she'd given up real hope.

She turned her head and looked into the sky. What time was it? Morning? Still nighttime? Lightning still flickered in the swirling clouds, but it was of less intensity and brilliance. She rubbed her face and tried to focus. Everything was a jumble in her head. Her struggle felt like it had lasted for days, but it was hard to truly evaluate her ordeal.

An ordeal that wasn't over.

The wind raced over her skin, making her teeth chatter. If she didn't get warm, she could still die of exposure. Did she have the strength to walk?

She struggled to her knees and tried to rise, but her legs wouldn't support her, and she collapsed back on the rocky sand. If she couldn't walk, she would crawl. Maybe she could find a cave or some cover from the wind that whistled through the trees and raked across her wet hair and skin. The rain had left a fresh scent in the air that made her feel renewed and focused. She had to do this.

Rocks cut into her forearms and hands as she dragged her mostly useless legs and torso forward. It was too dark to see much of what lay ahead, and she wasn't sure she was going in the right direction. All she knew was she had to find shelter somehow.

A bit of green caught her attention to her right, and she moved that way, but when she reached what she'd hoped would be some kind of shelter, she found only weeds poking up out of the thin soil.

Maybe she could rest just a minute here. She settled her cheek on the mud and closed her eyes. The conversation with Jon yesterday flooded in. It had been long overdue, and she wasn't sure how she felt about it yet. To hear his side had at least let her glimpse the turmoil he'd been in.

She'd expected too much from him after losing his mother. Now that she had the perspective of grief at the loss of her own parents, she knew emotions weren't always rational. She'd grieved her father, too, in spite of his harshness through her life. In the end, he was still her father.

A daughter's emotions didn't always make sense, and they didn't really have to. He'd been a hard taskmaster, but he'd taught her to work, to have morals, and to own up to her mistakes. There was the good side and the dark side.

And Sean.

She still didn't know the extent of her father's dark side, but he'd covered up Sean's murders. What had happened with Penelope and Sophie? While she knew Sean was the killer, she didn't know his motive or what had happened. And she had to know. If she survived, he'd be arrested for attempted murder, but there wouldn't be full justice until he paid for the murders. And to arrest him, she'd need evidence. His confession would be his word against hers.

There had to be more.

Justice required her survival.

She lifted her head again and realized it had gotten darker even though the storm was abating. That meant it was evening, not morning. Gauging from the sky, she thought it might be around ten, but until the thick, swirling clouds dispersed, she couldn't be sure.

Was anyone looking for her? Had Sean survived the storm to return to shore? If she was lucky, maybe God himself had punished him and he was in a watery grave.

Confusion flooded in again, and she couldn't think any longer. Her lids grew heavy, and she rested her cheek onto the cold, wet sand and sank into its embrace.

Were the mountainous waves subsiding a little? Jon hoped it wasn't his imagination as he rode the boat into a trough and up the next surge. Checking the boat's GPS, he knew Tremolo Island should be just ahead. It was his sign to turn around, but even now his spirit rebelled against giving up, even though he wasn't positive Annie was out here.

What was he supposed to do? He couldn't make up his mind.

As the curtain of rain began to part, he caught a glimpse of the island ahead. The dock would be around to the west side. Should he land and check out the island in case Annie had come here? But why would she? Logic dictated he turn around and go back to talk to Mason to see what he'd found out from Sean.

His gaze fell on the satellite radio. He could contact Mason on that before he returned. Once he had more information, he could decide what to do.

In the next trough he spotted something red and grabbed the binoculars. It took him several minutes to find it again. A red buoy, a common enough sight. But what was it doing out here? He caught a flash of black on it and tried to make out what it was. Lettering? No, it was a loon. The Tremolo Marina's logo.

Galvanized by the proof Annie had been out on the water, he dropped the binoculars and strained to see more of the water.

"Where are you, love?" he muttered. "Hang on, I'm coming."

The land grew closer, and he narrowed his gaze, searching for movement or anything that might tell him where to search. He hadn't seen Annie today, so he didn't know what she was wearing.

Should he head for the dock and search the shoreline over here? The buoy out there had filled him with hope, and he didn't want to turn back. Not until he was sure she wasn't here.

A wave tossed the boat to the left, and it seemed a sign that his decision was made for him. He steered the craft for the dock. Anchoring would be difficult in this weather, but he had to try. He was close enough to spot the dock. He could tie up to a slip offshore a bit and try to swim, but with the waves so high, he wasn't sure he could make it. If he knew for sure she was there, he'd run the boat aground and try to anchor it in place, but he didn't want the boat to break apart in the surf unless he was sure it was necessary.

He studied the dock for his final approach. There were bumper tires along the south side of it. Maybe he could come in there. He had to try it in spite of the waves still battering the boat. Praying for proper timing, he steered as best as he could toward the dock.

The starboard side bounced off the first tire and skidded along the dock to the next one. He grabbed a post and hung on for dear life as he looped the rope around it. The rope burned his fingers as he yanked it fast and tied it up, then rushed to the stern. When the stern veered back toward the dock, he managed to tie it up too.

The boat rocked hard in the waves, but he thought it would hold fast. He shut off the engine and hurried to disembark. It took three tries before he managed to leap to the dock without falling into the water. His feet slipped on the slick boards as he ran for the shore, and he nearly fell but managed to hold his footing.

With the rain slackening, he could hear better too. He ran along the shore calling Annie's name. Searching for any sound or a flash of movement, he moved as fast as he could back toward the area where he'd seen the buoy. The currents could have carried it here, but it was the best clue he had for her whereabouts, and he had to follow it.

He paused and checked his location. This should be close.

"Annie!"

The rain started pounding the surf and sand again. He'd never hear her if she called. It was going to take a foot-by-foot search through here. He swiped water out of his eyes and began to search in a grid, though it was hard to see.

Two feet out from a line of weeds, he saw something on the ground and went to investigate. As he neared he saw a bare foot extending out of a pair of khaki pants. Soaked blonde hair lay all down the blue shirt. He'd found her!

His heart leaped, and he knelt beside the figure praying she was still alive. "Annie?"

His gut clenched at how cold her skin was when he touched her. Was he too late? Tears burned his eyes, and he rolled her over gently to look in her beautiful face. Would it be for the last time?

Please, God, let her be alive.

He cupped her face in his palms and leaned down to kiss her lips. Cold, so cold. "Annie, open your eyes. Please, love. I'm here." He brushed sand from her cold cheeks, then moved his fingers to her neck to check for a pulse.

Nothing. He moved his fingers to another spot. Was that a slight pulse? He held his fingers in front of her nose and mouth, but with the wind still howling, he couldn't tell if she was breathing. He placed his palm on her chest wall. It felt like there might be some movement up and down.

He ran his hands over her arms and legs. No broken bones. No bleeding on her head or anywhere he could see, so he slipped his hand around to support her neck and lifted her in his arms. Max's house was back that way. She was suffering from hypothermia, and he needed to warm her if she was going to survive.

THIRTY-SIX

WARMTH CURLED AROUND ANNIE'S LIMBS IN A DELIcious state of well-being. She stretched and sighed at the comforting sensation of being in a toasty bed snuggled by quilts.

"Annie? Can you hear me?"

Jon's voice. Eager to see him, she swam up toward consciousness. She opened her eyes and blinked at the bright light before she slammed them shut again and turned to bury her face to escape the glare. The rough texture of a shirt under her cheek told her that Jon held her. She snuggled closer and sighed. She was tired, so tired.

"Annie, wake up, love."

Love.

He used to call her *love* all the time, but she hadn't heard him say that in so long. Maybe she was dreaming.

Something touched her cheek, and she realized he'd brushed his lips across her skin. "Jon?"

"I'm here. You're safe. The storm is over."

The storm.

Her eyes popped open and she came awake as she remembered fighting the massive waves and never-ending cold. "I'm alive?"

His smile swam into focus, and he nodded. There was still a shadow in his eyes. "I didn't think so when I first found you."

"Where are we?"

"At Max's house. He isn't here, but his housekeeper let us in."

Everything came flooding back, and she struggled to sit up. Jon helped her, and she saw she was on a beige leather sofa in a large, comfortable living room. A fire flickered in a massive stone fireplace that extended to the vaulted wood ceiling. She'd never been in the house Max had built. It was beautiful.

"Sean threw me overboard."

Jon's eyes went wide, then narrowed with a warning glint. "Bree and I both had been trying to call you. When you didn't pick up, I thought something was wrong so I went to your house. When I got there, your boat was gone, but when I checked the house before returning to the dock, I saw Sean running away and your boat was back. I had a gut instinct he'd done something to you and went out to look."

She clung to his hand. "Thank the good Lord you did. I would have died out there in the wind and cold if you hadn't come."

"Let me get this straight—he tried to drown you by throwing you in the water?"

She nodded.

"Sean killed Sophie and Penelope?"

She nodded again. "He wouldn't tell me why, and it's my word against his so I can't prove he admitted it to me."

"We can get him for attempted murder."

"Again, it's my word against his. He's a respected member of the community. We need more. My accusation should be enough to get a search warrant though. Did Mason talk to him?"

"I haven't talked to Mason. I texted him to go after Sean. There's another problem." He told her about the necklace Taylor claimed to have "found" in the shed. "She had to have planted it."

"Why would she do that?"

Color ran up his neck. "She had a crush on me, and I let her know I wanted to renew my relationship with you. I guess she wanted revenge, but I haven't talked to her yet."

She'd fire her on the spot. Annie couldn't abide lies. "The bigger question is how did that necklace get into the shed?"

He nodded. "I haven't had a minute to think about it, but if Taylor planted it, where did she get it? She isn't from around here. Did she know the girls? Does she know Sean somehow?"

Annie thought back to what little Taylor had told her. "She's never mentioned Sean."

"We can't get back to the mainland until the storm abates," Jon said. "The wind is still howling out there."

"Max has a satellite phone if it's still here. Try calling Mason and tell him what's happened. And you said you took my boat. It has a marine radio, so you could call the Coast Guard and have them relay a message."

"I'll see if Max left it here. Hang on."

She felt cold when he left her, and she pulled the quilt up around her shoulders. Bree needed to know too. Kylie would be frantic with worry if she knew Bree hadn't been able to reach her mom.

Jon returned with a phone. "The housekeeper found it. He took one with him, but he always keeps a spare. Want me to call?"

"Let me call Bree first. I want to reassure Kylie."

"Of course."

She took the phone and punched in Bree's number. At the sound of Bree's voice, her eyes filled with tears. "Bree, it's Annie."

"Annie! You're all right. The whole county is engaged in a massive search for you. Kylie hasn't stopped crying. You're all right?"

"I'm fine. Let me talk to her."

"Kylie, come here. Your mommy is on the phone."

Kylie's distant voice called out, "Mommy!" Then she was sobbing into the phone.

"Settle down, Bug. I'm fine. As soon as the storm is over, I'll be home. I got caught in it, and I'm out on Tremolo Island. Don't be afraid, okay? God was taking care of me. He sent Jon to rescue me."

Kylie's sobs tapered off. "Mommy, you should always have your phone when I need to talk to you."

"I was in a dead spot, baby. I'm sorry you were so worried. When I get home, we'll snuggle up and eat popcorn while we watch *Moana*, okay? I'm fine. Really. Bree will tell you."

"Okay. Promise you'll come get me. I want to see you."

Annie promised and ended the call. She hadn't realized she was crying until Jon dabbed her cheeks with a tissue. She took it and mopped her face. "Thanks. The thought of leaving Kylie orphaned terrified me as I fought the waves."

"It's probably why you're still alive. A mother's love drove you on."

She nodded. "I'm exhausted. Can you call Mason?"

Jon nodded and took the phone to place the call. She lay back against the pillow and snuggled deeper into the quilt. She might never leave the warm, comforting folds of this quilt.

Once Jon announced he'd found her alive and that Sean had tried to kill her, he listened more than he spoke. From the gist of what she heard, it sounded like Mason hadn't found Sean. The thought of him still on the loose out there wasn't an encouraging thought. He was dangerous, very dangerous.

Jon ended the call. "Mason chased Sean from your place, but he managed to evade them as the rain intensified. There are so many small fire roads he could've disappeared into. At least

Mason's not looking at me as a person of interest in Penelope's and Sophie's deaths anymore. But he's looking for Taylor to find out how she knows Sean. She had to have gotten the necklace from him and planted it. There's a manhunt going on for Sean right now. He won't get away."

But this was thick backcountry. He could disappear and live off the land for years or make his way to Canada. She couldn't rest easy while he was out there somewhere. He had to be brought to justice.

/ / /

By morning it was hard to believe the water had been so ferocious. Annie still felt wiped out, so she let Jon pilot the boat back to the marina. Approaching from the water, the resort had never looked so beautiful. The cabins glistened after the heavy rain, and she drank in the sight of her home. She hadn't been sure she'd ever see it again.

She spotted Kylie and Bree waiting on the dock. Her daughter jumped up and down when she noticed the boat's approach. Bree grabbed the rope and tied them off, and Kylie leaped aboard to run into Annie's arms. The warm, solid body of her little girl was the best thing Annie had felt in a long time. She drank in Kylie's sweet smell and relished the kisses she rained on Annie's cheek.

When Kylie pulled away, tears swam in her eyes. "I was so scared, Mommy."

"I know, Bug. I'm sorry I worried you. The phone wouldn't work out there."

Did Kylie know Annie had nearly died? She knew Bree wouldn't have mentioned it, but Kylie probably knew Annie had been missing and everyone was searching. Hopefully Kylie never learned the full story—at least not for a long time. She'd eventually know a bad man had tried to kill her mother, but by then the fear would have faded.

Jon got off the boat and turned to help Annie and Kylie off too. Annie still felt so wobbly and weak. She didn't feel capable of taking Sean on right now. Somehow she needed to gather her strength and get him behind bars. She'd never sleep knowing he was out there somewhere.

All he'd have to do is get rid of her, and there'd be no one to testify against him. No one saw him throw her overboard. The thin case concerned her.

When Jon tried to help Kylie disembark, she called to her mother instead. Annie turned and held out her hand, but the little girl's pull on her arm was nearly enough to make her tumble into the water, and Jon steadied her.

"Be careful with your mommy, Kylie. She needs to rest today."

Kylie's glare held a suspicious glint. "She was just out at the island. She's fine."

Bree hugged Annie in a tight grip. "I'm so glad you're all right," she whispered. "I'm going to get out of here and let you have some time with your girl. I kept the puppy, which she finally named Milo, even though she didn't want to because it was Jon's suggestion. My kids thought the name was perfect so she went with it."

"Thank you for everything."

"We're always here for you. Get some rest. I'll talk to Mason and see what's going on there."

Annie gave her a final hug and took Kylie's hand to lead her to the house. "Jon's right—I'm pretty tired. I think we should fix popcorn and watch a movie while we snuggle in bed."

"Ice cream first?" Kylie suggested.

Annie didn't want to crawl under a steering wheel. Not right now. "We're out of ice cream, and I need a nap. Maybe ice cream later."

"I'll go get you some," Jon said. "What flavor?"

"We have different favorites," Annie said. "I like Rocky Road, and Kylie likes Superman."

"I can handle that. I'll be back in about an hour. Take care of your mommy, okay, Kylie? Make sure she rests."

Kylie's frown deepened, but she gave a short nod and squeezed Annie's hand. The kid didn't seem inclined to give Jon any kind of break, no matter what he did. Kylie hadn't thanked him for saving Annie either. Maybe she hadn't caught that on the phone last night, but Annie would make sure she knew.

If it hadn't been for Jon, the situation today would have been very different. Her phone dinged with a message from Bree.

> Mason says Sean was seen near the Soo so he's likely out of the country by now. In touch with Canadian officials.

Annie walked to the house with her daughter, pausing long enough to grab the mail, then had Kylie get the movie ready while Annie put popcorn in the microwave.

While it popped, she sorted through yesterday's mail, and her heart jerked. An envelope from the paternity company. Kylie's results were back.

She stared at it for a long moment and had a wild desire to burn it without reading it. Once she knew the results, she couldn't ever go back. This could change everything or nothing, and she didn't know if she was ready.

Without consciously thinking about it, she flipped over the envelope and ripped it open to extract the single sheet of paper. The black letters bled across the white sheet, and she couldn't make out the words until she inhaled and blinked away the terror that blurred her vision.

If she knew what to pray, she'd be doing it, but this was beyond her ability. All she could do was assume God knew best right now, just like he always did.

There was a confusing chart of all kinds of details at the top of incomprehensible numbers. She shook her head and scanned down toward the bottom where she found a box that read *Statement of Results.*

The alleged father is excluded as the biological father of the tested child. The conclusion is based on the nonmatching alleles observed in the STI loci listed above with a DI equal to 0. The probability of paternity is 0%.

All the strength went out of Annie's legs, and she had to catch the edge of the counter to prevent herself from sinking to the floor.

Nate wasn't Kylie's father. How could she ever explain this to her little girl? And how could she even get Jon to believe her when he was convinced he couldn't have children? The road ahead had suddenly taken a twist that left her breathless and afraid.

What was she going to do?

THIRTY-SEVEN

ANNIE'S CONDITION HAD DETERIORATED WHILE JON was away getting ice cream. Her pale face and nervous movements alarmed him. Should he insist she go to the hospital? He touched her skin. Warming up. He pressed his fingertips against her carotid artery. Good, strong pulse of sixty beats per minute. She would fight him if he tried to take her to the hospital, and she really just needed rest.

He carried the ice cream bowls to the kitchen and rinsed them before he put them in the dishwasher.

He went back to the living room in time for the closing song from *Moana*. "Kylie, I challenge you to a game of Yahtzee while your mom takes a nap."

Kylie's eyes brightened for a moment, then she shook her head. "I only want to play if Mommy does."

He squatted in front of her and held her gaze. "Look at your mommy. She's falling asleep on her feet. She had a hard night. Rest would do her a world of good. Can you be a big girl and help her by doing something else while she naps?"

She regarded him with suspicion. "You want her all to yourself."

"No, I want to spend some time with you. What if we go fishing? Or swimming? It's a nice day. I'll take you to do anything you like."

A soft expression filled Annie's eyes while she watched him try to coax her daughter into doing something else. There was no question that he had to win over Kylie before there could be any future with Annie, but she would want more than reconciliation. She'd want true feelings between them.

He didn't know kids well enough to know how to get there, but he was game to try. Kylie was a cute kid with her mommy's blonde beauty, and he knew he could love her if she gave him a chance. At least he thought he could. It was hard to tell right now when she constantly pushed him away. It often raised his back, but it would be difficult for anyone to face constant rejection.

"Where's Taylor?" Kylie demanded.

Jon exchanged a glance with Annie. "I haven't seen her."

"I haven't either. I gave her a few days off, and she said she was going to explore the area a little. She might be back, but I haven't seen her," Annie said.

Anger simmered in her eyes. Taylor would face Annie's wrath when she returned. At least she'd been good to Kylie.

Kylie jumped to her feet. "I'm going to go look for her. Maybe she's in her cottage. If she's not, I want to play with some of the kids at the playground."

"I don't want you outside alone," Annie said. "Go play in your room while I rest for a bit, and we'll do something together after awhile."

Kylie scowled, but she went down the hallway, and her bedroom door slammed.

Jon sighed. "I'm getting nowhere fast."

"She misses her daddy." Annie's voice was low.

What was that note in her voice? Grief, nostalgia, hope? He couldn't quite tell, but he knew it was all about his relationship with her daughter. The pressure was on to do something about it, and he didn't know what it would take to break through Kylie's wall.

You'd think him saving her mother would do it, but Annie had shushed him when he'd wanted to elaborate on it. Probably because she didn't want to scare Kylie with how close to death Annie had come.

He walked to the sofa and settled beside Annie. "You can put your head on my lap and take a nap. Or go to bed for a while. I'll try to keep Kylie quiet while you rest."

She rested her head against the back of the sofa. "I'm tired but wired. I keep waiting for Mason to call with news about Sean. He has to be out there somewhere."

"Maybe he left the state. He has to know there's a BOLO for him. Sean isn't stupid—I don't think he'd hang around until Mason shows up with an arrest warrant."

"Mason texted me that he was executing a search warrant on his residence and business this morning. It's likely to take hours before we hear if he found anything though."

Jon leaned over and caught a golden curl around his finger. "You look beautiful this morning. I wasn't sure I'd ever see you again. When I found you on the beach cold as death, I was sure you were gone." His voice went husky, and he blinked away the moisture.

She scooted closer to him and snuggled against his side. It was the first overt movement toward him she'd made since they talked about their breakup. He dropped his arm around her shoulders and pulled her closer.

"You'd make a great dad," she said.

This whole dad thing again. What if she wanted more

children? Her mama-bear feelings for Kylie had shown him how important motherhood was to her. What if all her comments about him making sure he couldn't have kids was because she wanted another child? That was something he couldn't give her.

They could adopt. Or maybe do in vitro with a sperm bank. He hated that thought though when he'd love to see her carry their own baby. It would be hard to know he couldn't give her what she wanted most.

His gut roiled at the thought of that disappointment. The future was wrought with quicksand, but she was worth every bit of the danger.

She sat up and glanced at the clock on the wall. "I'm surprised Kylie isn't back out here. Would you check on her?"

"Sure." He gave her a final squeeze, then went down the hall to Kylie's bedroom. He rapped his knuckles on the door. "Kylie? Your mom would like to see you."

When she didn't answer, he opened the door. "Kylie?" The curtains blowing in the breeze through the open window caught his attention.

She'd sneaked out.

He raced back down the hall and told Annie that Kylie had gone out. "I'll find her."

She hadn't liked being told she couldn't look for Taylor. Maybe she'd gone there.

He reached her cabin and tried the door. Locked. "Taylor? Kylie?" No answer. Frowning, he found the key under the mat and went inside. "Kylie?"

The room was tiny, but Kylie could be hiding in here, so he peered under the bed and in the closet. No little girl. But as he started to close the closet door, a picture caught his attention.

Two little blonde girls stood with their arms around each other. He recognized the marina's dock. Was this Annie and Sarah? He loosened the tape and took it with him to show Annie, then went outside to check the play area.

A young woman with a little girl smiled at him. "You looking for Kylie? She left with Sean, the contractor whose team did the pavilion cleanup. They were going for ice cream."

His chest squeezed in a painful grip of dread. Pulling out his phone to call Mason, he turned and ran for the house.

/ / /

The screen door had just banged behind Jon when Annie's phone rang. Sean's name flashed on the screen, and she gasped. He must have heard she'd survived. Why would he be calling? "Hello?"

"Mommy? Why didn't you want to get ice cream with Sean? I'll bring you back some."

An icy sensation ran down Annie's back. Sean had Kylie. He wasn't out of the country at all. It had been a ploy to throw them all off his tail.

Sean's voice sounded in her ear. "What happens to Kylie all depends on you, Annie. I'll make a trade—you for your daughter."

"I'll come right now. Where?"

"There's an old fishing cabin on the west side of Loon Lake. Meet me there in half an hour or you know what will happen."

"I know it. I'll be there. Don't hurt her. Please, don't hurt her."

"She's a cute kid. Someone would pay good money. Come alone." The call ended.

The horror of what he implied left her numb. Sean had played them all. After grabbing her purse, she ran for her truck. Jon would wonder where she went, but she couldn't let him come with her, not when Kylie's future was in Sean's hands. Whatever Sean planned for Annie herself wasn't something she wanted to think about now.

She jammed the key into her truck's ignition before tearing out of the parking lot. She drove with one hand and reached for her switchblade in the glove box. Where could she hide it? Along the side of her sneaker maybe? It was small and would probably ride there okay in its sheath. She removed the gun from her purse and tucked it into her bra. She put another one in the waistband of her jeans.

He'd probably frisk her, and with any kind of luck, he would assume the one he easily found at her waist was the only weapon on her person.

Her phone rang, and she glanced at it. Jon must be back at the house. It was too early to talk to him. His fast car would catch up to her way too easily. She had to be almost to the cabin before she told him to come get Kylie there.

The ringing finally stopped, and a few seconds later her voicemail notification sounded, but she didn't listen to it. Hearing his concerned voice might weaken her resolve to carry through with her plan.

Jon didn't understand a parent's love yet, but then he didn't know the news that awaited him. It wasn't a conversation she was looking forward to either. If she died tonight, would he ever know he was a father? Would he find the test results and realize Kylie was his?

She reached the turnoff to the lake, and nausea roiled in her stomach. *Please let Kylie be all right.* If Sean touched her daughter . . . Shaking her head, she concentrated on what was ahead.

Her plan was to talk Sean into leaving with her while Kylie waited to be picked up by Jon. She'd shoot him a text where to get her, and they'd be gone by the time he arrived. If she set it up before she saw Sean, he'd be forced to go along with her plan or Jon and Mason would descend on him before he could escape. If he didn't leave Kylie behind, she'd refuse to get in his truck.

It had to work. She was out of other options.

Half a mile from the cabin, she paused and sent the text to Jon, then accelerated to the cabin. Sean's truck was parked in front of the cabin, and she spotted Kylie sitting on a rock in front of the broken-down porch.

She exhaled. "Thank you, God."

Jamming on her brakes, she cut the engine and leaped out of the truck. "Kylie!"

"Mommy!" Kylie leaped to her feet and rushed into Annie's arms. "He's not a nice man. We didn't get ice cream at all."

Annie held her close and relished the scent and feel of her. She imprinted the moment in her heart in case it never came again. "I have to go with him, but Jon will come get you. It's going to be okay. If I don't come back by tomorrow, there are some papers on the kitchen table I want you to give to Jon. He'll take care of you until you see me again."

Her assurances sounded hollow in her own ears, but she tried to cling to hope. Sean was six-four and strong as a bull moose on a rampage. She'd have to choose the right moment.

Sean strolled out of a copse of trees. "What a sweet reunion. You're a good mother, so I was sure you'd follow my instructions." He frisked her and found the gun in her waistband and took it as well as her phone. "As I expected. You can't stop trying, can you? Get in the truck, both of you."

At least he hadn't found the other weapons. Annie faced him with her fists clenched. "You said exchange."

"I lied."

"I thought you might so I have backup coming in a few minutes. We have just enough time to get out and leave her here or you'll be arrested."

His face darkened, and he grabbed her arm. "You said you wouldn't involve anyone else."

"I lied." She felt a stab of satisfaction at the shock on his face. "I'll go with you willingly if you leave Kylie. If you try to take her, I'll fight you tooth and nail, and Mason and Jon will be here before you can get away. You can make it easy or make it hard."

He shoved her. "Fine. I don't need the kid anymore. Get in the truck."

Annie hugged her daughter one last time. "Wait by the porch for Jon and Mason. I'll be okay, Bug."

Kylie clung to her. "No, you won't," she wailed. "I want to go with you."

Annie pushed her away and set her down on the rock again. "I have to go now, Kylie. I'll talk to you soon."

The heartbreaking sound of her daughter's sobs accompanied her to the truck, but she didn't look back. It had to be this way.

THIRTY-EIGHT

JON READ THE TEXT AND SHOOK HIS HEAD. THIS couldn't be happening. Why would she follow that maniac's orders? She was walking into a yawning trap. He tried to call her again, but it went straight to voice mail so he called Mason and told him what was happening.

He ran for his car. "I think we need the Kitchigami Search-and-Rescue team just in case. I'm heading for the cabin right now."

"I'll call Bree and meet you out there. I'll alert state law enforcement to watch for his truck and someone matching his description. And Annie's. If they're even in the same vehicle. He's wily and threw us off the trail by letting himself be chased over by the Soo. I thought for sure he'd escaped to Canada."

Jon ended the call and accelerated his car out of the parking lot. He was vaguely familiar with the lake's location, but Annie's text held a pin location that told him where to turn and how to find the cabin. As he drove as fast as he dared on the curvy roads, he prayed for Kylie and Annie to be safe. And for Annie to have insight on how to handle that psycho.

The minutes ticked by like hours before he reached the turnoff to the lake. He passed no other vehicles on the narrow, rutted road, and his fists clenched on the steering wheel. Sean was likely long gone with Annie. Maybe Kylie too.

If he hadn't asked Annie for help clearing his name, she wouldn't be the target. If only he'd known what he was getting her into.

He reached the barely visible track back to the cottage and took it. Branches scraped the sides of his car, but he didn't care if it removed all the paint as long as he got back there and found out what was happening. The car broke through the vegetation into the small clearing with a ramshackle cabin crouched at the edge of the encroaching woods.

It was mostly overgrown with vines, and his frantic gaze swept the area as he parked the car. He jumped out. "Kylie! Annie!"

"Here!"

He whirled and saw Kylie leaping out from some vegetation. Tears tracked down her dirty face, and she burst into loud sobs when she saw him. "He took Mommy! She made me stay here. He's going to hurt her."

Did he embrace her or honor her warning stance of arms crossed across her chest? He started toward her, but she took a step back, which answered that question.

"Mason and Bree are on their way. Did you overhear anything that might tell us where he was taking her?"

She shook her head. "He seemed nice at first. This is my fault. Mommy always said I shouldn't go anywhere with strangers. We had the code word *tremolo*, but I didn't ask him for a code since I knew him and Mommy liked him."

"It's not your fault, Kylie. Sean is the one at fault. We'll find your mommy. You want to sit in the car and listen to the radio?"

She shook her head again. "I want my mommy."

He wanted to see Annie's bright-blue eyes and wide smile more than anything in the world. "I know you do. I won't rest until we find her. Neither will Bree and Mason."

The sound of an engine came from behind him, and he turned to see Mason's SUV pull into the clearing. Right behind him was Bree in her search vehicle, and he caught sight of Naomi as well as Samson and Charley, Naomi's golden retriever. Bree opened the back hatch, and the dogs jumped out.

When Bree turned toward the cabin, Kylie ran into her arms. "You have to find Mommy."

Bree gave her a hug, then pulled her away to peer in her face. "Did they walk into the woods?"

"No. He took Mommy away in his truck."

"What color was it?" Mason asked.

"Blue. It had a sign on the side about Johnson Construction."

"His work truck," Mason said. "I can guarantee he'll have another vehicle parked somewhere to switch out. Bree, take the dogs into the woods and see if you can find where he had the alternative vehicle parked."

She nodded and snapped her fingers for Samson to come. Naomi flipped her brown braid over her shoulder to her back and called Charley to her. The two women and their dogs hurried into the forest and disappeared into the foliage.

Jon couldn't just wait here. He'd spent more time with Sean lately than anyone. Surely there was something, some clue he'd mentioned of a possible place to take Annie. He ran back through their conversations.

They'd talked about surfing and skiing as well as mountain climbing. A memory clicked of Sean mentioning a mountain cabin his uncle owned near Freda. He said when he wanted to be alone, he went there because his uncle had dementia and he could be alone. Could he have taken Annie there?

He told Mason what Sean had said. "I can't remember his uncle's name."

"Mort Johnson." Mason pulled out his phone. "I'll find the location of the property."

Jon stared into the woods and willed Bree to walk out with some kind of evidence. The minutes of Annie's life trickled through an hourglass. They had to find her.

/ / /

Annie watched out the window as the black truck climbed the slope with ease. Sean would never let her see where they were going if he planned to let her live. She would have one shot to take him down. The scent of his soap was beginning to give her a headache, and she struggled to stay focused when she was so exhausted from her ordeal in the water.

The panorama of huge trees and valleys melded into the deep blue of Lake Superior in the distance.

"I've never been up this mountain," she said. "It's a beautiful view."

He shot her a glowering glare. "Friendly talk won't work. You'd just as soon shoot me as look at me."

She suspected if she asked about Penelope and Sophie, he'd refuse to answer like he did before. Was someone else involved with him? Her gut instinct was he hadn't done this alone. Who else had been at Lake of the Clouds with him?

"Is Lonnie up here waiting to help you dispose of me like you did the girls? Or maybe Glenn?"

Sean turned his head and lifted a brow. "I'm perfectly capable of handling you by myself. It will be my pleasure."

"Just like you did last night?"

His hands tightened on the steering wheel. "You're resilient—I'll give you that. But a fall down a rocky cliff should take care of you."

At least now she knew what he planned for her demise. This was definitely backcountry, and it was unlikely her body would ever be found. Which meant her own deliverance rested on her shoulders. And God's. While she doubted her own ability, she knew God had the power to turn this around.

And she'd watch for any opportunity he gave her.

He turned onto a narrow fire road that went straight up the mountain. Trees brushed the truck and the tires lost purchase a few times as they spun, then grabbed hold.

"Home sweet home." He put the truck in Park and turned off the engine. "If only we had your little sis here, it would have come full circle."

"Little sis is dead."

He laughed. "Sure she is."

Her throat convulsed, and she stared at him. What did he mean? "Do you know Taylor Moore?"

"Better than you do."

He'd parked in front of a tiny log cabin with a lean-to porch. The green metal roof blended into the pines surrounding the small clearing. Even in the winter it would be difficult to distinguish from the trees.

"Get out."

She climbed out of the truck and started for the cabin. "What did you mean about Sarah?"

"You'll find out one of these days. I might tell you before I kill you."

He took way too much pleasure out of taunting her, so it was best to change the subject. "Is there a ski run up here too?" The scent of pine was as strong as his soap.

"Nah. Not enough people come up here. The cliffs are too steep, and it would cost a fortune to groom ski trails and build a lift. I'm usually the only one up here."

"What do you hope to gain by killing me? I already gave Mason a statement."

"There's no evidence, and with you gone, no one to testify at a trial."

"You're delusional. You think a jury won't convict you when I come up missing after I charge you with attempted murder? That's a strong indication I told the truth. And we suspect Hussert is involved. Mason will get him to talk."

"Hussert knows nothing. He would have gone straight to Mason if he suspected anything. He might seem like a rebel, but he doesn't even like to speed. Besides, I plan to disappear. Getting rid of you is insurance."

When he grabbed her arm, she knew it was time. She took a step back and dropped her shoulder so his hand slipped off. At the same time she turned on one heel and brought other leg up behind his kneecap. He went down with a yell, and she was off the porch and running for the woods.

He'd taken the keys to the truck so she couldn't drive out of here. She had to find her way down by herself, which seemed daunting, but she had her hidden gun and knife. He knew this area well, but she had an innate sense of direction. He was bigger, but she was faster.

Her breath puffed out of her mouth in short bursts as she ran. Dodging lodgepole pines and cedar trees, she worked her way back toward the fire trail. He'd expect her to try to hide deeper in the woods, but she'd get down faster if she could avoid the heavy terrain.

She'd thought she made it until something caught her by the ankle. In the next instant, she was hoisted upside down by her leg and hung suspended in a tree. Her gun fell out of her bra, and she tried to reach her knife before having to take a rest.

Sean's voice came from below and to her right. "I always knew my traps would come in handy."

"Let me down."

"In a minute. I'm enjoying the moment."

He stepped into view with a knife and cut the rope at the tree that held her. She crashed down into the pine needles and darkness claimed her.

THIRTY-NINE

AFTER FINDING SEAN'S ABANDONED BLUE TRUCK, BREE and Naomi had taken Kylie with them to Rock Harbor. The men still stood in the yard of the abandoned cabin. In the silence of Kylie's absence, Jon could focus on finding Annie.

Mason sketched the route on his phone with a thick finger. "He'll see us if we take the main fire trail up to the cabin. But Kade pulled up some obscure trails and found us an alternate ATV route. Let's take two machines so there's room to bring her back that way if necessary."

"How long will it take to get up there?"

Mason glanced at his watch. "An hour. I'm having the machines brought to the base of the mountain. We can drive there and leave my SUV behind while we climb up in the ATVs."

"Let's get going. She's already been gone an hour, and we don't know for sure he's up there."

"We actually do know. As soon as I got the location, I had a drone sent up to take a look at the fire road and the property. There's a black truck parked outside the cabin. That's got to be the truck he'd swapped out for his blue one."

The reassurance was what Jon needed. "So let's go get her."

He headed for Mason's SUV and the sheriff followed him.

Jon wished he could drive because the sheriff piddled along at a much more sedate pace.

"Can you turn on the siren or something?"

"It's going to take a few minutes to get the machines there and ready. We're in good shape time wise."

Jon drummed his fingers on the door's armrest. Every second that passed felt like agony when he didn't know what was happening to Annie. Mason leaned over and turned up the music, probably to drown out the sound of Jon's impatience.

Jon turned the radio back down. "Is the drone still surveying?"

"Yeah, for a few more minutes. It will be out of power and have to return soon."

"Can you send up another one? It might show us when he makes a move outside the cabin."

"I only have one at my disposal. I've told my team to inform me of any movement." Mason gave him a long glance before turning his attention back to the road. "You really love her, don't you? Once we find her, make sure she knows that."

"I will."

Mason braked. "We're here, and so are the machines."

Finally, they'd be able to take action. The SUV had barely come to stop when Jon opened his door and sprang out to rush over to the ATVs. He threw himself onto the closest one and got ready to go.

Mason plodded over with him and handed his keys to Deputy Montgomery. "I'll be in touch, Doug. Have the drone take one final survey around the property and relay anything you see on the satellite phone."

Doug nodded and took the keys back to his car with him. Moments later a country song began to play as he settled in to wait.

Mason climbed onto the other machine. "Let's go."

Music to Jon's ears. He followed Mason up the steep incline. The thick vegetation made it slower going than he'd anticipated. He accelerated around Mason and motioned for him to stop a minute.

"What if we take the better road partway up? We can veer off when we are nearer to the cabin. We'll make better time."

"But we might have trouble getting back onto the minor trails Kade found," Mason pointed out. "I think we should stay the course."

Jon pressed his lips together and shook his head. "You go that way then. I'm getting up there."

He accelerated back the way he'd come to find the main road. From the sound of the engine behind him, Mason was continuing with his plan, but Jon couldn't do it. Too much time was passing, and he was frantic to get to Annie.

If she was even still alive.

He found the main fire road and raced up it as fast as he dared. Pausing several times to consult his map, he found the last turn before arriving at the cottage. He stopped and looked in both directions. A deer trail appeared to be to his right so he took it. It narrowed almost immediately and he got bogged down in trees so he reversed back out to the main road.

What if he walked up? It would be faster than meandering around in the brush. He could flit from tree to tree to maintain cover. Ten minutes and he'd be at the cabin. He pulled the ATV into the brush and pocketed the key, then set off for the summit. His breath came hard from hiking the steep slope, but he caught a glimpse of the cabin and ducked down into the grassy ditch beside the road.

There was no movement ahead so he half rose and hurried as fast as he could. He stayed bent over to provide a lower target.

He heard a voice as he reached the cabin's clearing.

"I know you're faking," Sean said. "You might as well open your eyes."

Jon peered over the branches of a small pine tree and spotted Sean putting Annie onto the ground. Why had he been carrying her?

Annie sat up and rubbed her ankle. "Sean, the only way to avoid the death penalty is to let me go. Premeditated murder isn't the same as accidental death. I'm sure you didn't mean to hurt those girls. It just happened, right? Don't make things worse on yourself."

"You don't know much, do you? The girls were quarry. Just like you."

Jon tensed, and he wished Mason had come with him. The sheriff had a gun, and all Jon had was his bare hands. His gaze fell on a large fallen limb. Maybe it would do.

/ / /

With lightning speed, Sean grabbed her arm and dragged her off to the north of the cabin. In only a few feet, the vegetation gave way to rocks and a sheer cliff. The cabin had been built practically atop the cliff's summit.

While it appeared she'd been massaging her ankle, she'd taken the opportunity to slip her switchblade up into her sleeve. From the glint in Sean's eye, she was going to need it very soon. Her breath caught in her throat as he pushed her closer to the edge.

She threw herself to the ground and rolled away from him.

When he aimed a kick at her, she rolled into a ball to protect her belly and worked to slide the knife into her palm. She didn't have much time.

"No!" A guttural cry came from behind Sean. Jon, his mouth in a grim, determined line, rushed toward them with a large branch held aloft.

Sean turned and raised the gun in his hand. Annie couldn't let him shoot Jon. She had the switchblade in her palm and opened it in an instant. Without thinking or planning, she buried it to the hilt in Sean's thigh.

The bigger man staggered and howled as he grabbed at the knife. The next instant Jon thwacked Sean in the side of the head.

Sean stumbled back and his arms pinwheeled as he lost his balance. His shoes slid in the thin shale, and he pitched over the side of the mountain without a sound.

Annie crawled on her hands and knees to peer over the edge. She could barely make out the outline of a body far below on the rocky slope. No one could have survived that fall. Knowing he'd stalked the girls like quarry made her shudder. Had he done this before? Were there more of his victims out there?

She exhaled and closed her eyes, and when she opened them, Jon was there with his arm around her. She leaned into his embrace and let tears of relief flow.

Somehow, against all odds, she'd survived. God was good. She'd go home to her baby girl after all. Kylie wouldn't be left orphaned.

No, not orphaned. No matter what it cost her, she had to tell Jon the truth. It was the right thing to do. She had to find the strength to be honest.

Annie turned her head at the *crunch* of tires in the dirt, and

Mason climbed off an ATV and ran toward them. "Annie, you're okay. Where's Sean?"

She gestured to the cliff's edge. "Down there. He intended to throw me off the cliff, but between Jon and me, we turned it around on him."

Jon told Mason what had happened, and the sheriff listened with a grave expression. "Annie kept her head. She took the right opportunity to use that knife she'd hidden."

She smiled and started to get up. "I don't think I could have readied it if you hadn't distracted him with your battle cry and the tree limb."

Mason held out a hand and pulled her the rest of the way to her feet. He did the same for Jon. "Let's get you guys home. Where's your ATV, Jon?"

"Parked down the hill a little ways. Just like you thought would happen, I ran into trouble once I veered off the main fire road, so I walked up as stealthily as possible. I didn't have a weapon so I grabbed a tree branch. When I got here, he was about to throw her off."

Now that the surge of adrenaline had passed, Annie was wilting, and she could barely put one foot in front of the other. Fatigue coated her thought processes and slowed her limbs.

Jon glanced at her. "You need some rest." He guided her to the porch and got her settled on a step. "I'll go get my ATV and come right back. We'll get you home with your daughter."

She glanced at Mason. "Could I use your satellite phone to call her?"

Mason nodded and handed it over. "I'll get my ATV too."

Annie called Bree who picked up immediately. "Bree, it's Annie."

Bree stared to cry. "I thought it would be too good to be true that you escaped death twice. God is so good. Here's Kylie."

"Mommy?" Kylie burst into tears. "Mommy, you got away from the bad man?"

"He'll never hurt us again, Bug. I'll be home in a couple of hours. I love you." She was so tired it was hard to even talk.

She was barely aware of Mason telling her he'd stay behind to process the scene while Jon took her down the mountain. Her eyes drifted shut as Jon loaded her onto the ATV and began the trek back to Mason's car.

At last, she could close her eyes and rest in the knowledge the danger was truly past.

FORTY

KYLIE WAS STILL SLEEPING WHEN ANNIE ROSE AT SIX, pulled on her bathrobe, and went to start coffee. She felt more rested and like herself this morning. When she entered the kitchen, the aroma of coffee already filled the room, and Jon sat at the kitchen table with a cup. He was staring blankly out the window into the backyard.

He looked up when he saw her in the doorway. "I slept on the sofa last night." Shadows rimmed his green eyes, and fatigue pulled at his mouth.

His concern touched her. "Why? Sean is dead. You should have gone home and had a real rest."

"I know you should be safe with Sean dead, but my anxiety wouldn't let me drive off. I'll rest later. It feels like we went through an earthquake or some kind of natural disaster. First the lake and then the mountain."

She came into the kitchen and put her hand on his shoulder. "We did. In more ways than one." Someone knocked on the door, and she turned toward the sound.

"I'll get it," he said. "Have some coffee. I'll fix breakfast in a few minutes."

She thanked him and went to pour a mug of coffee. She recognized Kade's and Mason's voices as they tromped their way from the front door, so she poured two more cups of the brew and carried them to the table.

"Hope we're not too early," Mason said.

She handed him a cup. "I'm up. You have news?" She gave Kade the other mug, then settled on a chair.

Mason took a sip of his coffee before he sat at the table. Coffee in hand, Kade leaned against the wall.

"We finished searching Sean's residence and business, as well as the cabin," Mason said. "You mentioned he called the girls 'quarry,' which would suggest he'd targeted them specifically. Did he mention anyone else being involved?"

Annie shook her head and set her coffee down. "He said he made sure Hussert didn't know because he would have gone straight to your office."

"Sean might have been who killed Chris Willis. We found some pictures of the Willis crime scene in his bedroom. And of one other besides that we've matched to another missing female over near the Soo."

"What about Poole? Eddie said there were two men who attacked him," Annie pointed out.

"True, but he wasn't killed like Willis so I'm inclined to believe it's a different sort of attack. At least Sean can't hurt any other people." Mason looked at her over the rim of his mug, then set it down. "There's more, Annie. There seems to be a tie-in with Sean and your sister."

She hugged herself. "Sarah? How could he be connected to her? She's been gone twenty-four years. Sean is only two years older than me. He would have been a kid when she went missing."

"I found some pictures of your family and some pictures of a girl who resembles Sarah a few years after she was taken. She's standing with a woman in front of a small cottage." He opened his phone and scrolled to his pictures, then handed the phone to her. "Have a look."

She swiped through the pictures. Some of the shots appeared to have been snapped from a distance, but there was no mistaking Sarah and her on the dock in front of the marina. Someone had been watching them. She came to the picture of the woman and girl. The little girl's face was circled by a black marker with Sarah's name and a question mark under it.

She enlarged the picture and stared at the girl's face. She appeared to be about eight in the picture, and she *did* look a lot like Sarah. But Annie had always heard everyone had a doppelgänger out there.

She couldn't bring herself to allow hope to creep in yet. "Are you saying she might still be alive?"

"It's possible. We've never found her remains."

Which meant nothing since so much of the U.P. was wilderness. But the faint stirrings of hope began to raise its head. "How can we find out more?"

"We'll keep digging into phone records and computer evidence. I wanted you to know before you heard it somewhere else."

"I appreciate it."

She couldn't see how Sean would have any knowledge of Sarah. Where would he have gotten pictures? "He made a strange comment yesterday. About it being perfect if my little sis was there. When I told him Sarah was dead, he grinned and said, 'Sure she is.' I thought he was trying to rattle me and didn't pay much attention, but it makes sense now, though I don't see why he'd be interested. Or even how he could know anything about her."

"He was a twisted human being, so it's hard to say what he

used as his excuse for anything. I'm going to keep searching though, and I'll figure it out."

Mason glanced out the back window where Taylor's cottage could be seen. "Is Taylor back there? She'll have valuable information about where she found that necklace."

"She hasn't come back yet. I tried texting her last night, but she didn't answer. I thought maybe she decided to vanish after lying about Jon, but her things are all still there."

Kade straightened. "I hope she hasn't gone missing."

Annie should have thought of that, and she put her hand to her mouth. "There's a connection between her and Sean. We need to find out what it is."

"When is she supposed to be back to work?"

"Today."

"I already have a BOLO out for her. We'll find her."

Jon held out a picture. "When I was searching Taylor's cabin for Kylie, I found this."

Annie stared at the familiar picture. "That's Sarah and me. Why would Taylor have it?"

"Where'd you see it last?"

"In my parents' room. Wait here." She ran down the hallway and into the bedroom. The frame was there, but the picture was missing.

With the empty frame in her hand, she returned to the living room. "She took it. She must have been who has been searching the house, leaving things in disarray."

Taylor had seemed to long for family, for a safe and stable place. Annie felt a pang of regret when she thought of Taylor's sad brown eyes. Kylie loved her, but Annie couldn't trust her any longer.

"We'll know more when we locate her." Mason gulped down the rest of his coffee and rose. "I'll let you enjoy your morning."

She went to the front door with the men and shut it behind them. Jon was behind her, and she shook her head. "I can't believe Sarah might be alive. Do you think it's really possible?"

"Anything is possible. I'll see if Mason will give us a copy of the investigator's report. There might be something helpful in it."

She nodded and headed for the kitchen as Kylie came down the hall rubbing the sleep from her eyes. Her eyes narrowed when she saw Jon. "What are you doing here so early?"

The belligerence in her voice broke Annie's heart. Even if Jon believed the news she had to tell him, they still had to get past Kylie's animosity, and Annie had no idea how to even begin that process.

Kylie would never accept another father in Nate's place, so where did that leave them?

/ / /

Jon had gone out to mow the yard when Kylie got all out of sorts, and Annie had taken her daughter to Bree's to pick up Milo. They planned to spend the day out and about until dinnertime, and he promised to grill steak and sweet corn for dinner. Kylie had glowered the whole time, but he'd done his best to be pleasant and ignore her attitude.

After mowing, he went into the living room, which smelled of stale popcorn and sour milk from before the abductions. He picked up the popcorn bowls and partially empty cups of milk and water. He'd made his share of the mess, too, with the plastic remains of his cherry Popsicles and the sticky ice cream bowls.

The least he could do was clean it all up so she came home to a clean house. He rinsed the dishes and put them in the dishwasher, then wiped down the countertops before he moved to the high bar to clear away bowls left from breakfast.

A paper lay faceup atop an envelope on the breakfast bar. He picked it up to stuff it back in the envelope, then noticed the letterhead was a paternity lab. *Paternity lab? What was this?* Assuming it was part of an investigation, he started to fold it, but his gaze fell on the child's name: *Kylie Pederson*. Annie had checked Kylie's paternity? Jon found Nate's name in the father's column.

None of this made sense. She had to know when Kylie was conceived. He ran through the columns of incomprehensible numbers, which was gobbledygook to him. At the bottom were the results, and he scanned them.

The alleged father is excluded as the biological father of the tested child. The conclusion is based on the nonmatching alleles observed in the STI loci listed above with a DI equal to 0. The probability of paternity is 0%.

He read it again until the truth sank in. Nate wasn't Kylie's father.

His knees went weak, and he sank onto a chair at the kitchen table while he tried to ponder the meaning of this. His thoughts raced back to the multiple times Annie had suggested he question what he was told about having children.

Was this the reason? She'd known all along Kylie wasn't Nate's? That the little girl was *his*? It wasn't possible, but what other explanation could there be?

He couldn't wrap his head around such monumental news. It shook his whole world, and it would shatter that little girl's heart. A little girl who didn't even like him. Some men were naturals when it came to kids. They knew how to make them smile, what made them happy. Most of the time around Kylie, he felt inept and out of his league.

If she was truly his child, shouldn't there have been some kind of immediate, natural bond? And why a test now after all these years? None of it made sense. Was it so Kylie had a guardian if something happened to Annie? He wasn't who Kylie would choose.

"Jon?"

He looked up at the sound of Annie's voice. She stood in the doorway from the living room. Her stricken gaze went from his face to the letter in his hand. "I can explain."

"Nate isn't her father? Then who?" Afraid to hear the answer, he whispered the words.

Her eyes bore into him. "I was only with one other man in my life, Jon. Deep in your heart, you know."

He held up the paper. "Why now? I don't understand."

"You've always said you couldn't have children, so I never questioned her paternity until she was diagnosed with celiac disease, and you mentioned you had it. Then I began to remember how she was born a month early. The doctor said celiac disease was often hereditary, yet it isn't in Nate's family. I resisted considering it at first. I didn't want that kind of wrinkle in our lives. But in the end, I had to know. For Kylie's sake. For our sake. I had to know. So I sent in Nate's toothbrush to be tested. The results came back yesterday."

He stared down at the paper again. The answer was there in black and white. No possible chance Kylie was Nate's biological child. Everything he'd believed about himself, about his future. It had all been wrong.

"She hates me."

"We don't have to tell her about this. Not yet. We'll know when the time is right. You can make visits when you can. Get to know her. Who couldn't learn to love you?"

"I have a job interview in Houghton next week."

Her blue eyes brightened, and her smile lit her face. "You're staying? Really?"

"I can't leave again. Even before I saw this, I knew I couldn't. I don't know what the future holds for us, but I can't go anywhere until we know."

She hugged herself. "I'm scared, Jon. I don't want to be hurt again."

"We can take it day by day. Go slowly and see if we can find each other again. Let's promise to be honest about our feelings. We're bound to have fights again. I'm not saying we won't. But let's examine what is behind it when it happens. If we'd done that nine years ago, things would be different now."

She nodded and took a tentative step toward him. He opened his arms, and she stepped into them. He rested his chin on top of her head. It was too soon to kiss her like he wanted. Not until he could examine how he felt about this.

It had rocked his world.

Annie's phone rang, and she pulled out of his embrace to answer it. "It's Mason."

The color drained from her face as she listened. When she ended the call, her eyes were wide. "Mason has Taylor in custody. Jon, she claims to be Sarah."

"Sarah? Your sister, Sarah?"

Annie nodded. "I've got to get to the jail and talk to her. It's not possible, is it?"

He took her by the shoulders and stared into her face. "God brought me back to you and Kylie. We have a lot of wrinkles to figure out, but I'll be here for all of it with you." He pulled her into his arms again. "We'll get through everything together."

Even with this monumental news, he knew they would figure everything out. The road might be rough, but he'd keep her hand in his, and they'd walk the path together. Coming back here had been life-changing.

But no matter what they faced, they'd have each other. And Kylie.

GLUTEN-FREE RECOMMENDATIONS

I'VE BEEN GLUTEN FREE FOR TWENTY YEARS OR MORE. There are a lot more choices now, and I wanted to share some of my favorites with you.

Poorrock Abbey's Jampot up in Eagle River, MI, is very real. The monks make the very best gluten-free cookies I've ever had in my life! And the thimbleberry jam is to die for. Everything in the small, unassuming store is delicious. It's worth a trip up there just to stop in at the Jampot!

https://poorrockabbey.com/

Breads

Sami's millet gluten-free bread. Available only from their website: https://www.samisbakery.com/. This one is my very fave.

Rudi's gluten-free bread (available in the freezer section of most stores)

Canyon Bakehouse

Udi's

Pasta

Tinkyáda has all types of pasta. This brand is far and away the very best I've ever found. They make everything from macaroni to fettuccine and lasagna noodles. It's so good, I can't even recommend any other brand. You'll find it at most health-food stores as well as many online sites including Thrive Market and Vitacost.

Cookies

I like to make my own cookies, but when I don't have time, here are some I like.

Simple Mills: I particularly like the chocolate chip ones, but they make all different kinds.
Tate's Bake Shop
Glutino

Gluten-Free Flour Blends

King Arthur gluten-free blend
There are recipes to make your own blends online, but I usually don't bother and buy King Arthur instead.

Gluten-Free Flour Staples

Rice flour
Almond flour (blanched is best)
Buckwheat flour
Coconut flour
Arrowroot starch

Oats (There are some that are certified gluten free.)
Potato starch
Pamela's Pancake Mix (for when I want to throw it together quickly instead of using Jon's recipe)
Tigernut Flour (This is a tuber and a new flour for me that I absolutely love!)

ACKNOWLEDGMENTS

NINETEEN YEARS AND COUNTING! THAT'S HOW LONG I've been part of the amazing HarperCollins Christian Publishing team as of the summer of 2021! I have the best team in publishing (and I'm not a bit prejudiced), and I'm so grateful for all you've taught me and all you've done for me. My dear editor and publisher, Amanda Bostic, makes sure I'm taken care of in every way. My marketing and publicity team is fabulous. (Thank you Nekasha Pratt, Kerri Potts, and Margaret Kercher!) I'm truly blessed by all your hard work. My entire team works so hard, and I wish there were a way to reward you all for what you do for me.

Julee Schwarzburg is my freelance editor, and she has such fabulous expertise with suspense and story. She smooths out all my rough spots and makes me look better than I am. I learn something from you and Amanda with every book, so thank you!

My agent, Karen Solem, and I have been together for twenty-two years now. She has helped shape my career in many ways, and that includes kicking an idea to the curb when necessary.

My critique partner and dear friend of over twenty-two years, Denise Hunter, is the best sounding board ever. Together we've created so many works of fiction. She reads every line of my work, and I read every one of hers. It's truly been a blessed partnership.

I'm so grateful for my husband, Dave, who carts me around from city to city, washes towels, and chases down dinner without complaint. He finished up radiation treatments for recurrent prostate cancer in the spring, and we're praying for good results. But my Dave's even temper and good nature hasn't budged in spite of the trials of the past year.

My family is everything to me, and my three grandchildren make life wonderful. We try to split our time between Indiana and Arizona to be with them, but I'm constantly missing someone. ☹

Over the past year I've had COVID, a broken ankle, and knee-replacement surgery—as well as caring for our daughter, who nearly died of sepsis. Even though life has thrown some rocks in our path, God is good all the time! He's been carrying us through these challenges, and I'm grateful for his loving care each and every day.

And I'm grateful for you, dear readers!

DISCUSSION QUESTIONS

1. Do you know anyone who can't eat gluten? Do you have a favorite bread?
2. Did you suffer a broken heart as a teenager? How did you handle it?
3. Annie found it hard to forgive Jon for putting his career ahead of her. Have you ever had to deal with that in your life?
4. Jon was an only child and felt the weight of making his parents proud. Do you know someone like that?
5. Have you ever had to deal with a child who takes a dislike to a friend for no reason? How did you handle it?
6. Jon realized material things meant more to him than they should. How do we keep our focus as Christians?
7. Annie didn't want to find out the truth about Kylie's paternity but she forced herself to face the truth. Have you ever had to face an unpleasant truth and learn to deal with it?
8. Annie set up a code word with Kylie. Have you ever done that with your children and how did it work?

PLEASE ENJOY THIS EXCERPT FROM *A STRANGER'S GAME*

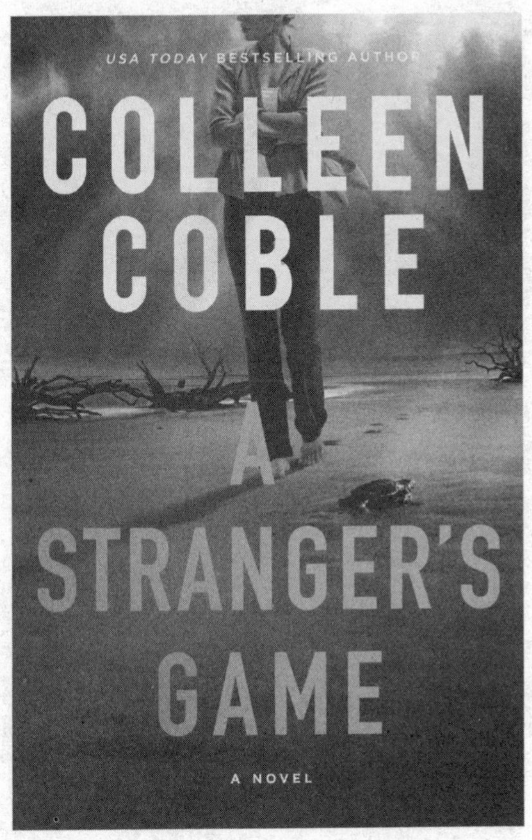

AVAILABLE IN PRINT, E-BOOK, AND AUDIO

ONE

VICTORIA BERGSTROM ALMOST FORGOT TO BREATHE AT the beauty of Georgia's Jekyll Island. Standing at the railing, she watched the sunset gild the undulating tidal grass with gold and orange and continue to paint its spectacular hues on sand and sea as the boat made its way along the Intracoastal Waterway to the wharf. The Golden Isles was an apt name this time of day especially. Her gaze landed on the hotel, and her chest compressed.

Then again, maybe dread stole her oxygen instead.

The garrulous captain gestured toward The Wharf restaurant, perched at the end of the wooden walkway. "There she is. It's a much prettier approach this direction instead of coming over the bridge. I still can't believe those people blocked the bridge."

Torie had planned to drive, but protesters advocating for the abolishment of the Federal Reserve had filled every inch of the bridge over the causeway to the island, and she hadn't wanted to be stuck in traffic for hours. She shook her head. Did the protesters really believe marching would accomplish their goal? And besides, the Fed helped to protect against bank runs and depressions. It seemed insane to protest about it.

The boat docked, and she grabbed her carry-on bag to disembark. The rest of her luggage would be delivered tomorrow once she knew where she was staying. "Thanks for the ride, Captain."

He tipped his hat. "You're welcome, Miss Torie."

Her heels clattered on the wooden planks past the restaurant and a storefront for boating excursions, and onto the sidewalk onshore. Time slipped past in a shimmering haze as she crossed Riverview Drive, avoiding the ever-constant bikers, and approached the Jekyll Island Club Resort hotel.

It had been eighteen years since she'd run and played along this water. Eighteen years since she'd smelled the river and listened to a bull alligator roar at Horton Pond. Eighteen years since she'd seen stiletto-tipped palmetto groves and moss-draped oak trees. The narrator on a passing tram droned on about the history of this place she'd once loved so much.

There it was.

The hotel that lived both in her dreams and her nightmares.

The tower in the left corner rose above the four-story structure, and the large wraparound porch beckoned visitors with thoughts of sweet tea and laughter with friends. She paused to tuck her white blouse into her navy skirt before she mounted the steps to the outdoor receptionist box guarding the doorway inside. It was unmanned at the moment, so she stepped into the hotel lobby. The scents of sandalwood and pine took her back to her childhood in an instant, and she swallowed past the constriction in her throat.

Audentes fortuna juvat. "Fortune favors the bold," the Roman poet Virgil had said, and though being here brought out all her insecurities, Torie had to find her courage.

Little had changed through the years other than fresh paint and attentive maintenance. The ornate Victorian moldings gleamed with a gentle glow of wax, and the wood floors were as beautiful as ever. She had never wanted to step foot in this lobby again, yet here she was.

Torie raised her head with a confidence she didn't feel and approached the resort's front desk. "Torie Berg. I'm your new IT specialist."

The alias flowed smoothly off her lips. She'd used it on her last assignment, and it was close enough to her real name to feel natural.

"Welcome to Jekyll Island Club Resort," the young woman said.

The blonde looked to be about Torie's age of twenty-eight and wore an engagement ring. Her open, friendly expression was perfect for the check-in desk.

"Marianne," a familiar voice said behind Torie.

Torie froze and didn't turn. While she didn't think the older woman would recognize her, she couldn't take the chance. The click of high heels went past her to the left, and she caught a glimpse of Genevieve Hallston's lavender blouse, her signature color.

"Come to my office, please," Genevieve said to the housekeeper she'd hailed.

The stricken look on the middle-aged woman's face said it all. Genevieve was on a tear about something, and it took all of Torie's resolve not to intervene. She'd been sliced by the older woman's razor-sharp tongue enough to know it wouldn't be a pleasant conversation.

But she had to remember her mission. If anyone recognized her, her cover would be blown and all of her plans would be in ruins.

Torie forced a smile and focused on the desk clerk again. "I was told there were rooms or cottages for employees?" The cottages had been added since she was a child, but she'd seen pictures.

The young woman nodded and handed over a key card. "You're in Stingray Cottage, Ms. Berg." She traced a path on the map in her hand and showed Torie the way to a cottage along Riverview Drive she could find with her eyes closed.

"Thank you. I believe I can find it. What's your name? I'm sure I'll be seeing you."

"It's Bella Hansen. I look forward to getting to know you." Her gaze went over Torie's shoulder, and she gave a reflexive smile to someone behind Torie.

Torie thanked her again and grabbed the handle of her suitcase. The wheels rolled smoothly over the floors, and she exited to follow the path around the pool and the entertainment area with its game tables and exercise room. Palm trees swayed in the breeze overhead, and the groundskeeper had done a great job with the banks of brightly blooming flowers and greenery lining the walk. She recognized Rozanne geraniums, hydrangeas, cosmos, baby's breath, and zinnias. There wasn't much she would change in the landscaping arrangements. It was perfect in every way.

She'd asked her dad to arrange for her to have the Stingray Cottage where Lisbeth had stayed. When she rounded the corner, she caught a whiff of artisan pizza baking in the wood-fired oven, and the aroma transported her back to her ten-year-old self. They'd had pizza every Friday night.

With a Herculean effort she moved past the temptation toward her cottage. Funny how things seemed smaller than she remembered. Perspective, she supposed.

She couldn't wait another minute to get her toes in the sea of her childhood, so she unlocked the door and put her bag inside. A bike had been left for her convenience, and she changed into shorts and a tee before she mounted it and set off for St. Andrews Beach, a four-mile trip. The ride would blow away the memories trying to surface.

/ / /

The cedar trees around St. Andrews Beach had been perfect for hide-and-seek when Torie was a little girl, and they'd grown in eighteen years. Dead trees that had once been part of the maritime forest lay toppled on the perfect beach just past the two-story viewing platform, and she caught a glimpse of sand and blue water melding into the twilight sky.

She kicked off her shoes and carried them as she walked along the wet sand. A thousand memories vied for space in her thoughts. The wind teased strands of hair from her coronet of braids, and she inhaled the aroma of salt and sea, a heady combination that made her feel as if she could actually accomplish the task before her.

"Hailey!"

She turned toward the frantic sound of the male voice. A man in his midthirties stood in front of a forest of oak and cedar trees. His light-brown hair fell across his forehead above clear green eyes. He was taller than most, even topping her six-foot height, and she estimated him to be six four.

There was no missing the sheer terror on his face. She dropped her shoes and ran toward him. "Can I help?"

"My daughter." He raked his hand through his hair. "She's missing. She's eight."

"How long?"

His gaze continued to scan the beach and water. "Couple minutes. I had a woman check the bathroom, and Hailey's not in there."

"Does she have a favorite place to go?"

His expression cleared and he nodded. "Of course. The turtle nest! She probably didn't wait for me."

He still seemed panicked even after such a reasonable

explanation, but she chalked it up to an overly protective father. "I'll be glad to help you find her."

He set off at a fast clip, and she followed across the soft sand. It was none of her business, really, but she had to make sure the little girl was all right. His long legs ate up the distance, but she had no trouble keeping up.

The Sea Islands of Georgia were known for loggerhead turtle nesting sites, and residents made huge efforts to protect them. The thought of seeing a nest after all these years made her pick up the pace. They went up a dune and down the other side near a clump of sea grass, and she spotted a young girl on her knees.

"There she is. Thank you, Lord." He stopped a few feet away. "Hailey, you scared me to death. You know better than to run off."

The girl didn't take her gaze from the turtle nest containing dozens of squirming black hatchlings. "They aren't getting out, Dad. I think we need to scoop some sand away."

"Yeah." The man squatted beside her and brushed the sand away.

The sea turtle "boil" was always mesmerizing to Torie. All those squirming black flippers held her in place. The hatchlings began to squirm out of the hole and their flippers scissored back and forth to propel them across the sand toward the sea.

The girl stood and walked beside the babies. "There are seagulls around. Pelicans too. I got here just in time to save the babies."

A lot of nests were logged and checked daily, but Torie found no glimpse of yellow rope or signs here, which wasn't too surprising. In good years Jekyll Island would have six hundred nests, and if the mother had come ashore just before a rain, her tracks would have been washed away.

Torie moved closer and shooed away a pelican. The last time she'd seen this sight she'd been with her best friend Lisbeth. Lisbeth had worn the same mesmerized expression as was on Hailey's face. It had been a perfect day of sun and sand, togetherness and giggling.

And it would never come again.

She bit her lip and exhaled. These trips back through memory lane weren't helping. She had to focus on the task at hand.

The man turned back to face her. "Thanks for your help. I'm sorry to bother you."

"I'm glad she's okay." She extended her hand. "Torie Berg."

His big hand closed around hers. "Joe Abbott. Vacationing?"

She shook her head. "Just moved here. I'll be working in IT at the Club Hotel."

"You'll like it here."

"Daddy trains sea lions to keep bad guys away," Hailey said.

Torie already liked the little girl. "How interesting. I've heard of the military using dolphins for defense, but I didn't know about sea lions." Hailey stepped close to Torie, close enough for Torie to smell the fresh scent of her shampoo.

"Simon is really cool," Hailey said. "He's Daddy's favorite, but he's not fully trained yet."

Joe fixed his daughter with a stern look. "It's a good thing I'm not a spy or something. Hailey would give away all the secrets."

What was bugging him? Torie moved away a few feet. A couple more minutes and she could mount her bike and get out of here.

ABOUT THE AUTHOR

Photo by Amber Zimmerman

COLLEEN COBLE IS A *USA TODAY* BESTSELLING AUTHOR best known for her coastal romantic suspense novels, including *The Inn at Ocean's Edge*, *Twilight at Blueberry Barrens*, and the Lavender Tides, Sunset Cove, Hope Beach, and Rock Harbor series.

Connect with Colleen online at colleencoble.com
Instagram: @colleencoble
Facebook: colleencoblebooks
Twitter: @colleencoble